TWEEN
LAT

01/27/22

Latimer, E.

Escape to Witch City

Escape to *Witch City*

Escape to Witch City

Witch City

City

E. Latimer

tundra

Copyright © 2021 by E. Latimer
Jacket art copyright © 2021 by Jo Rioux

Tundra Books, an imprint of Penguin Random House Canada Young Readers, a division of Penguin Random House of Canada Limited

Library and Archives Canada Cataloguing in Publication

Title: Escape to Witch City / E. Latimer.
Names: Latimer, E. (Erin), 1987- author.
Identifiers: Canadiana (print) 20200370804 | Canadiana (ebook) 20200370820 |
ISBN 9781101919316 (hardcover) | ISBN 9781101919323 (EPUB)
Subjects: LCGFT: Novels.
Classification: LCC PS8623.A783 E83 2021 | DDC jC813/.6—dc23

Published simultaneously in the United States of America by Tundra Books of Northern New York, an imprint of Penguin Random House Canada Young Readers, a division of Penguin Random House of Canada Limited

Library of Congress Control Number: 2020948788

Edited by Lynne Missen
Designed by John Martz
Printed in Canada

www.penguinrandomhouse.ca

1   2   3   4   5   25   24   23   22   21

Penguin
Random House
tundra | TUNDRA BOOKS

For the Word Nerds

Chapter One

"EMMALINE DORATHEA *BLACK*."

The shrieking voice echoed down the wide hallway leading up to the kitchen doors. It startled the kitchen's cat, a gnarled old tom who'd been investigating an interesting stain on the floor mat at the entrance, and it made Emmaline Black jump and fumble the tea tray from which she'd been stealing strawberry tarts.

There was a sharp crack as the tray hit the dessert cart, and one of the tarts she'd been squirreling away into her sash hit the carpet with a sad little *splat*.

There was no time to mourn the loss of the pastry though, because another harpy scream came shortly after the first, considerably closer this time.

Emma whirled around, abandoning the desserts, and ran full tilt down the wide hallway that led to the East Wing.

Her mother hated the East Wing for the same reason Emma loved it. It had been built after the rest of the castle by her uncle, Queen Alexandria's husband, now dead several years. The king may have been a little mad, Emma privately thought, but in the best possible way, because he had constructed a sort of warren, with a vast network of strange, crooked hallways and wildly looping staircases.

Most exciting of all, at the very top of the East Tower was the palace's largest library. There were so many places to hide from her mother, and more books than one could possibly read. The best sort of combination.

"Emmaline Black! I know you're here somewhere!"

The note of hysteria in her mother's voice gave Emma a tremendous burst of speed, and she took a reckless left at the next fork in the hallway, her flat shoes sliding on the tiles.

She knew exactly why her mother was trying to find her, and she wasn't the least bit interested in being found. Isolde Black had been trying to pin her down for ages in order to talk about the sentencings. Tonight, every member of the royal family would be in court.

Emma dreaded court sentencings, not just because the queen would be handing out punishments for witchcraft—though she found these increasingly unnerving, since it seemed *anyone* could be accused of magic—but because her mother seemed determined to wrestle her into a series of increasingly absurd outfits each time.

She had two outfits for this week, one for court and an even fancier one for Testing Day.

The thought made her feel a little nauseated. She'd seen tonight's dress, and it was bad, so she could only imagine The Testing Day ensemble. The high, starchy collar, the ridiculous puffed sleeves, the ruffled . . . well, everything.

No doubt another fight would ensue, with screaming and tears, and maybe someone would smash something this time. But there was no sense in having that fight until she absolutely had to.

Another left. A right. Two more lefts.

She was breathing hard now, but her mother's horrible shrieking did seem to be growing fainter. After another few seconds she let herself slow to a walk, which was necessary, because the hallway was becoming steeper and steeper. Eventually it turned into a staircase, but it was bizarrely constructed, as if the person building it had only remembered it was supposed to be a staircase at the last second.

At the top, the stairs smoothed out into another hallway. This one was even wider than the last, furnished with pale green wallpaper and glossy marble floors. The rest of the palace was decorated almost entirely in rich purples and golds, so this felt rather like a breath of fresh air.

The corridors here were just as laden with thistle as the rest of the palace—she could see the purple flowers lining the tops of all the wall sconces—but the East Wing was mostly ignored, and the plants had dried and crumbled. Queen Alexandria seemed content to simply pretend her husband, and by extension, the wing, had never existed.

If Emma stood on her toes and peered at the top of the nearest cabinet, she could see one sad bunch of flowers shriveled nearly to dust.

When she'd first discovered the newer wing several years ago, she'd noticed how different it felt. Here, the air seemed fresher. Within minutes, her head had felt clearer than it ever had, her limbs lighter. She'd wanted to skip down the halls singing at the top of her lungs. She'd felt somehow *vibrant*, positively bursting with energy.

Over the years she'd put two and two together: even being in the same room with thistle seemed to drain her. The fresher the plant, the worse it seemed.

Thistle was meant to affect witches. To drain their magic, to weaken them.

Of course, it was technically toxic to anyone if consumed in great quantities, so it could be that Emma was just sensitive. *Allergic* even.

At least that's what she told herself.

And now, if she could just find a spot to hide, she could sit and eat her pilfered jam tarts in safety. A nice distraction from everything.

From her mother's howling, from the court session tonight, and, most of all, from the fact that tomorrow was her thirteenth birthday.

Her birthday.

Inevitable. Dreadful. And worse than ever this year.

She'd always hated the parties her mother threw for her—huge and extravagant, filled with children she barely knew.

This year, there would be no party. No grand tea party. No mini masquerade. No ponies. Her mother wouldn't be able to turn this into some kind of show-off circus.

This year, Emma's birthday was the same day as The Testing.

She continued down the hallway, more slowly this time, fishing a jam tart out of her pocket. There were lanterns hanging from chains along the ceiling, and cabinets full of china plates and silver forks. Narrow windows were hung with dark green tasseled curtains. Decorative antique chairs sat along the hall at regular intervals, in case one became overcome with walking the full length and had to stop and rest.

Halfway down the hall, there came a dull, echoing *thump*. Emma froze.

The hairs on the back of her neck prickled, and she whirled around, sure she felt someone's eyes on her.

There was no one there, only one of the many royal posters fastened to the wall behind her—a black-and-white photograph of a young, solemn-looking Queen Alexandria.

Emma made a face at it, and then said, through a mouthful of tart, "*What?*"

Another thump. Closer this time.

Footsteps, heading her way fast.

She jerked around, heart beating hard. There was a set of long green curtains along the far wall, and Emma hurried over and slipped behind one. Pressing her back to the windowsill, she pushed the curtain forward, covering both of her shoes.

The footsteps grew louder, heavy and stomping, and Emma frowned, cocking her head to one side. The way the noise rang out on the wooden floor, the crashing and shuffling accompanying it . . .

That wasn't servants. The queen would never abide them stomping about that way.

Sure enough, a voice echoed from somewhere nearby.

"Couldn't we have met in the barracks? This place gives me the creeps."

"The captain said here. Something about privileged information. Don't think he cares about your creeps, McConnel."

There was a rough bout of laughter, which cut off abruptly as a voice, deep and stern, said, "At attention, men."

A beat of silence followed, and then the same voice said, "When we go in, keep your staffs at the ready. We don't know if she's with them, but if she is, don't underestimate her. Never forget that she's *very* dangerous."

For one ridiculous moment, Emma thought that her mother had finally snapped and sent the guards after her, but the phrase "very dangerous" cut that theory off at the knees fairly sharply.

Emma was hardly dangerous, save perhaps to her mother's blood pressure, and to the occasional jam tart.

The noises drew closer to her curtain, a shuffling of boots and a clearing of throats, and what sounded like someone rifling through papers.

"Beg your pardon, sir," a deep voice said, "but who is she?"

"You can see the name on the poster, soldier."

Emma was positively burning with curiosity. She leaned sideways the tiniest bit, peering around the edge of the curtain.

A troop of palace guards was standing in the middle of the hall. To her shock, they were not wearing the usual simple red-and-black uniform she was accustomed to seeing all guards in. Instead, these men were dressed entirely in black. They wore identical wide-brimmed black hats, and at each throat was a heavy-looking iron cross on a beaded rosary chain.

Witch hunters.

She gripped the curtain, biting at the inside of her cheek. If pressed to come up with something nearly as scary as a witch, that something would be a witch hunter. She hadn't seen them this close up in years—had hoped never to again—let alone this many.

They'd been out in full force for Testing Day last year, of course. They'd ridden through the crowd on their huge black horses, with the jingle of tack and the metallic clatter of their warding beads and iron. Each had brandished a thick thistle-wood staff.

At the time, she'd asked why they were there. "Just in case," Isolde had said darkly, and then refused to say anything more.

Emma bit the inside of her cheek again, harder this time. Usually there was only one reason witch hunters gathered in these numbers. And that was The Testing.

Tomorrow.

As soon as she tried not to think about it, that was all she could do. Last year had been bad enough, even just watching. Since they were royals, she and her mother had been allowed behind the fence to see the private Testing Pavilions for the court children.

There hadn't been many who'd turned thirteen last year, but it had nevertheless been horrible to watch. Emma had had nightmares about it for weeks.

Children filing into the white medical tents, being ushered out the other side by white-clad nurses. Passed off to palace guards who either waved them off or shunted them into closed carriages. One girl, the daughter of a noble, had to be pushed into a carriage screaming and thrashing. A year later, Emma *still* couldn't forget the look on the girl's face. The anger and terror in her expression.

The memory made her feel sick, and she pushed it hastily down, trying to concentrate on the witch hunters instead.

They couldn't be here for The Testing—not this far in advance—so why were there so *many* of them?

One or two usually lurked around the edges at court, keeping an eye on the crowd in case anyone were to show any sudden signs of witchery. And she often saw them in the streets when her mother dragged her out to the shops. They were always patrolling, monitoring the queen's subjects for signs of magic.

But this was a small army.

Watching them made all her muscles feel strangely tight, as if her body was unconsciously bracing itself for a blow.

The captain, a man with pale, sculpted features and very blond hair, was passing out slips of thick, cream-colored paper.

Official decree posters.

"Study that face, lads. You've got to know her on sight. We catch the rest of the coven, of course, but if she's there, she's the prize."

This caught Emma's attention, and she stood up a little straighter beneath her curtain. A *coven*, here in London? The idea seemed wildly improbable. Her history lessons said the last coven in London had been rooted out in 1807. They were the first to go in the witch hunts, as soon as the Black family came back into power.

Emma had been given a very child-friendly version of this story during her classes, but later she'd snuck into the East Wing library and read every bit of witch-hunt history she could find, fascinated and horrified all at once.

Between the shuffle of boots and the low murmur of the men came a faint, papery *shhhk* across the floor just beyond Emma's curtain. Glancing down, she saw that one of the men had dropped a poster. It lay a tantalizing few feet from her curtain, facedown on the floorboards so that she couldn't see anything but the faint black shadow of an illustration.

A wanted poster.

Suddenly there was nothing as important as getting her hands on that paper. Something in her needed to see it. To find out who exactly they were going after.

Emma had never seen a real witch before.

Her curiosity flared, so intense that her insides fairly itched with it.

She clenched her jaw, keeping her eyes fixed on the backs of the witch hunters. Only the captain was facing her, and he was too busy handing out the remaining posters to be looking at her curtain.

"... don't get overconfident—especially you, Laurence. I won't have you barging in before the rest of us ..."

Slowly, Emma inched her foot forward, toe pointed and homed in on the paper like a hunting dog after a duck. She held her breath, feeling the cold clamminess of her palms as she clung to the edge of the window frame. She had to move with the grace and precision of one of the court's ballet performers, and grace was hardly her strong suit, at least according to her mother.

Her leg shook slightly as she stretched out further. Her foot and ankle were now completely exposed, poking out beneath the curtain. Beads of sweat collected on her neck, and she froze as the captain shifted, clearing his throat. But he was only leveling his stern look at the man next to Laurence.

"The same goes for you. Stick together. No one moves without my say-so. Is that clear?"

The man said it was, and Emma relaxed a little, easing her foot out another inch. Another.

Finally, her toe touched down on the poster. *Triumph!*

Carefully, she began to drag it back, wincing at the quiet scrape of the paper on the wooden floor. But no one seemed to notice as the witch poster inched slowly under the edge of the curtain.

When she peeked around the side, the witch hunters were all facing away for the moment. The captain seemed engrossed in his lecture, which gave her time to lean sideways and dart a hand out to grasp the poster.

Emma's heart thumped painfully against her ribs as she ducked back behind the curtain and clutched the paper to her, trying to hold it as quietly as possible. *Does paper usually crinkle this loudly?*

"Alright, let's move."

She almost sagged onto the windowsill with relief as the sound of shuffling and thumping began again. The witch hunters were moving down the hall.

It took entirely too long, but at last, the sound of boots against the wooden floor receded enough that she felt she could turn the poster over and look at it properly.

She had to uncrumple it, smoothing out the wrinkles against the wall, but the picture was clear enough.

Her breath caught in her throat. The shock that hit her felt a little like someone had dumped a cupful of freezing water over her head.

For one wild, terrifying moment, she was sure the face staring up at her from the page was her own.

The brows, thick and black over dark eyes and long lashes; the face, short and heart-shaped with a pointed chin. Even the long, dark hair was similar, though when Emma stared a moment longer, she saw that hers was not nearly as wavy. Another moment went by, and her pulse began to slow a little as she realized quite a few of the woman's features did not match her own. This was not meant to be a drawing of her at all, but a much older woman. Someone nearly her mother's age, she would guess.

It was eerie though, and the longer she stared at it, the more she thought how much this woman looked like her mother.

Isolde Black was different in many ways, of course. She wore her hair pinned back in the fashion of the day, and she always powdered her face very white, so that even her dark brows were barely visible. And, of course, the illustration of the witch possessed the trademark wild black eyes and tangled hair, but ... there was no denying that this picture looked very much like her mother, and Isolde's sister too.

Queen Alexandria was even closer in appearance, actually, and Emma frowned down at the picture, wondering if Alexandria's hair would be curly like that if she wore it down.

Her pulse was thundering in her ears all over again, because now that the shock of the picture was wearing off, a realization had set in.

She'd always known her mother was one of three sisters. There had been Isolde and Alexandria and another—the youngest—who had died when the witches took the throne. They didn't talk about this sister for some reason; it seemed to make her mother too emotional. In fact, she'd forbidden all discussion on the matter.

Emma didn't even know what her name had been.

Three sisters.

She traced her finger over the lettering at the bottom of the poster, the witch hunter's question ringing in her ears: *"Beg your pardon, sir, but who is she?"*

The looping script below spelled out *LENORE*, and Emma could add the rest. She was almost sure of it.

Lenore Black. Her aunt.

Chapter Two

In the moments that followed, Emma was seized by a sudden certainty that her mother would appear from around the corner and ruin any attempt she might make to get to the bottom of this.

She ran, full tilt, straight for the library at the far end of the East Wing, skidding around corners, nearly barreling into china stands and ornamental vases. Twice, she almost fell down a staircase, and once she came very close to falling *up* one that seemed to have been built in a rather haphazard way.

It took forever to get there, and her journey was not made any faster by the fact that she had to pause before she rounded each corner, peering out to make sure the coast was clear. The witch hunters had gone, but she wasn't taking any chances.

At last, she arrived at the top of the wonky staircase and found the large, oak doors that led to the library. The archway above and around the entrance was hand-carved and decorated with dragons and lions and boats full of men fighting one another, images that seemed to have slipped right out of the pages of books.

Emma tugged on the heavy iron circlet set into the oak, and the door opened with a wheezy protest. She slipped inside and let it slam shut behind her, the noise echoing in the vast space beyond.

She'd found the library on her second day of exploring the East Wing. When she'd first walked through the impressive oak doors, she'd spent a full three minutes standing stock still, her mouth agape, staring at what seemed to be a kind of coliseum filled entirely with books. Shelves that took up three stories and featured an extended, wraparound balcony.

The king's old library was the perfect hiding place. Since the man hadn't had any actual royal blood, he'd been encouraged to "keep busy" in ways that kept him clear of any major decisions. Judging by its size, at least, the library seemed to have been his favorite project. It was absolutely massive. The main part of the library was a curious shape, like a cross between an octagon and a star. Each wall, jutting out at its own angle, was home to a well-organized section of books, and each section contained hundreds of subsections. Emma didn't think it would be possible to read every book in this library, even if one lived to a very old age.

The first time she'd visited, she'd wandered between the shelves, forging deeper and deeper, until she was completely lost.

It had delighted her. She'd pictured herself living there, constructing a makeshift shelter out of the thickest tomes, curling up on a mattress of old magazines and papers, and building fires with the queen's posters to stay warm at night. During the day she would wander among the shelves, surviving on scraps of stolen food and stories. She would become completely wild over the years, but have the finest of vocabularies.

And she'd never have to see her mother again, or go to the queen's court, or be tested for witchcraft . . .

She had no time for such fantasies now.

Emma made a beeline across the library, toward a section marked with hanging signs in the shape of a pointing finger. The first said *LAW* in boastful golden script, and the next, *HISTORY*.

The latter was the section she was heading for, and she put on a burst of speed, shoes clacking on the dusty floorboards. Once she was there, however, and staring up at the shelves—which stretched all the way up to the ceiling nearly eight feet above—she felt rather foolish. There must be hundreds, no, *thousands* of books here. Where exactly was she supposed to start looking for information about one woman?

Emma pushed the section's rolling ladder to one side in order to trail her fingers across the spines of the books. Since this was the royal library, the history section was only really concerned with England's history, which she normally would have found short-sighted and irritating. In this particular instance, however, it made her quest a little easier.

Still, there were too many titles to shift through properly, and she began to scan them as fast as possible, finger hovering over the shelves. *Battles Waged and Won*; *England's Triumphant History*; *A History of the Blackest of Magics*; *How the Great Battle Was Won*; *The Warrior Queen: London's Liberation*.

Emma paused for a moment on the book about magic, shivering slightly but still intrigued. She glanced over her shoulder. The feeling of being watched wasn't as bad in the library as elsewhere in the palace, probably because the royal posters weren't quite so enthusiastically plastered to every wall here.

Still, this volume was not typically the sort of thing she'd be allowed to read, and it certainly wouldn't be found in the main library in the Central Wing. But like everything else in the East Wing, this library was neglected—including in its adherence to the kingdom-wide purging of banned books. Over the past year, Emma had found and read many of these titles. Some were nothing more than romances deemed unsuitable for the castle, but others were closer to heresy.

Reluctantly, she dismissed the book and moved on. If she had just been hiding from her mother, she would have snatched it up in a heartbeat and tucked herself away in the darkest corner to read, but she was trying to find specific information.

A third Black sister. A royal witch.

She paused on a fat tome in the center of the bottom shelf— *The Royals: A Complete History*—and then drew it out. It slid from the shelf easily, and Emma nearly overbalanced with a startled grunt. She caught it with both hands and moved it carefully over to one of the long oak tables lining the center of the history section. The oil lamps were very rusty, and besides that, Emma had no flint to strike. Thankfully, there was a bar of sunlight sliding in from one of the narrow windows above the shelves, and if she tilted the book up on one of the bookstands, she was able to read.

She scanned as quickly as she could. A lot was familiar from her history lessons. The ruthless uprising of the witches; the cruel and merciless way they'd wiped out the Black family; Isolde and Alexandria smuggled out of the castle by their older cousin before they could be found . . . Emma had heard it all a thousand times. This was precisely why she never bothered with the history section. The blasted story had been drilled into her head so thoroughly she could recite it in her sleep.

Increasingly irritated, she kept flipping through. There was nothing here she didn't know already. Another page and another, and then she stopped, hand hovering over the open book, at a darkly drawn illustration. It was a pen-and-ink depiction of a woman sitting on the throne. She had wild curls of black hair and a thin, angular face half-covered by a smooth white mask. Pinned to one shoulder was a large black badge with a stark *W* slashed across the front in red ink.

The Witch Queen.

Emma's eyes went wide, and she leaned closer. She had learned only briefly about the rebel witches, since talking about them at all was generally discouraged. They were responsible for everything, a society of witches who believed non-magical humans should be slaves. They were the ones who had revolted, who had overthrown Emma's grandmother when Emma's mother was just a child. They'd pulled the queen and king from their thrones and slain them both. They'd found the youngest sister and murdered her as well, and then gone looking for Isolde and Alexandria.

Or at least that's what Emma had been taught.

It was becoming very clear that her lessons had been full of lies.

Shivering, she slammed the book shut with a loud *thump* that echoed off the history section's walls. As she picked it up to take it back to the shelf, she realized something odd. The cover felt strange. Initially, she'd been too distracted to notice, on account of the book's weight, but now ... She tipped the volume over, examining the edges of the closed pages, and lifted her brows. *Well now.* That was something different.

The width of the binding and the number of pages didn't seem to match up properly. And if that wasn't strange enough, there were odd gaps between the edges, as if there'd once been more pages.

Of course, it was feasible that some of them had fallen out over time, but *this* many?

She frowned, returning the book to the table. Letting it fall open to the first space that seemed too empty, she bent to examine it in the faint light and found she could make out the tiniest edge of yellowed paper. At least two pages, maybe three, had been cut from this section.

It was the same every few pages.

Someone had spent a *very* long time carefully cutting out certain pages from this book.

Pulse pounding in her ears, Emma pulled another book from the history section, and then another. She went through five, and then ten, tearing them from the shelf, slamming them down on the table, pawing through the pages without caring if they tore.

They were all the same.

"Why would someone do this?" Her voice was a breathy whisper in the silence.

She had several teetering stacks of books surrounding her, and it was because of this accidental book fortress that she didn't see the impending trouble until it was too late.

There came a sudden vicious "Ah hah!" and then the waspish, painted face of Isolde Black appeared over the top of *Great Wars of Northern England.*

Emma gave a startled squeak and jumped, nearly falling off her seat. She clutched the book she was holding to her chest without thinking, and immediately Isolde shot one pale, skinny arm out and ripped it from her hands.

"What's this?" she snapped, turning the book over to scowl at the cover. "What are you reading, holed up in this miserable place? *A Brief History of the Upper Class.*" Her upper lip curled, and she stomped around the table, slamming the book down in front of Emma.

"I've been trying to find you for simply *ages.* We've got the hearings tonight and The Testing tomorrow. We simply *must* have your dresses fitted today, and instead you're here!" She reached out and grasped Emma's arm, yanking her up out of the chair none too gently. "Care to explain why you're snooping around these old history books?"

Emma tore herself away, glaring up at her mother. "No. Why don't *you* tell *me* why half the pages in these books have been cut out?"

Isolde only blinked at her. Her eyes looked very wide and dark against the white paint of her face, and her lips, decorated blood-red, were very thin.

She looked from Emma to the books, and then back again. She cleared her throat and shook her head, pale brows drawing down. "Why on earth would I know, Emmaline? The king was half mad by the time he died. I expect he was paranoid or something."

Emma stared at her, eyes narrowed. She hadn't missed the look that had crossed her mother's face. Isolde Black was hiding something.

"I saw the witch hunters go out just now. They were looking for *her*." Emma thrust the poster toward her mother. It was even more crumpled after being shoved in Emma's pocket, and at first Isolde only frowned at it, until Emma sighed and grasped the other side of the poster, pulling it tight to reveal the illustration.

Isolde stumbled back, hands flying to her mouth.

She looked as though Emma had struck her. Despite the caked-on powder, two spots of color showed through high on her cheeks, and her eyes had gone wide and a little wild.

"I don't . . . put that away!" Isolde lunged for the poster, but Emma snatched it back.

"She didn't die in the Great War at all, did she? She's a *witch*."

It made a strange kind of sense. Emma's mother had always been incredibly closed off about her family. She didn't discuss the events of childhood—not the witches, and not the uprising that saw the Black family take back the throne. It was all taught so matter-of-factly in Emma's lessons, but if she mentioned any of it at home, Isolde would inevitably react badly.

Isolde said nothing, only stared at Emma with wide, dark eyes. It was hard to tell with all the makeup, but Emma thought her mother had gone pale now, because she swayed slightly on her feet, bracing herself on the table with one hand.

Was she going to pass out? Isolde had done it before, but never without anyone nearby to catch her.

"Mother?" Emma took a step forward, hesitant, and then squeaked with alarm when Isolde lunged forward and tore the poster out of her hands. Face twisted in rage, Isolde ripped the poster in half, and then proceeded to tear both halves to shreds so vigorously that Emma was hit by bits of flying paper.

When she was finished, Isolde bent to eye level and seized Emma's shoulders tightly, bringing her face inches away from Emma's own. "Don't you *dare* say anything about this to anyone. My worst fear in life is that you'll become like her. You're already close in so many ways. Stubborn, impossible. *Dangerously* reckless. I can only pray you don't have witch blood too."

Her voice was low and deadly, and Emma just stood there frozen. It was so out of character, so unlike her mother's normal, irritating banshee shriek. A chill dropped down her spine.

"Your father and uncle both died in the hunts when you were still in the womb. I won't have you dishonor them by speaking her name." Isolde straightened up abruptly, smoothing both hands down the front of her dress. She smiled stiffly and cleared her throat, glancing around the empty library. Her voice was full of forced lightness now.

"I'll expect you in our quarters in an hour for your fitting. Now please put those books away."

Isolde spun on her heel and left, her back ramrod straight, her skirts rustling noisily over the floors. It was so abrupt that Emma watched her go for a full moment, mouth hanging open. Then she moved slowly to the table, giving herself time to think as she picked up the books and reshelved them one at a time.

Her mother's reaction hadn't been her usual irritation; it had been something else. Isolde Black had looked *afraid*.

Emma swallowed hard as she slid the last book onto the shelf, sandwiching it between a thick blue book on the history of European artillery, and a smaller spine that seemed to be a volume about shipping and trading abroad.

This done, she turned to look at the scraps of paper littering the floor. Her mother had been thorough. No one would be able to piece the poster together, or tell what it had once been.

Still, she spent a few minutes picking up the pieces, stuffing them into the pocket of her dress before turning for the wide oak doors at the front of the library.

Emma would, she resolved, turn up to her dress fitting. She would even cooperate, for the most part, and wear whatever hideous thing her mother wanted her to. But as she made her way back down the crooked staircase, heading out of the winding labyrinth of the East Wing, she put her hand into her pocket and felt the rough edges of the torn poster.

She couldn't let this go. She needed to know more.

Her family was keeping secrets about Lenore Black, and Emma was going to find out what they were.

Chapter Three

"For heaven's sake, Emmaline, stand up straight or you'll get stabbed."

Emmaline pulled a face at her mother, but she obeyed, standing up straighter on the seamstress's box. Even that seemed like an effort. Her body always felt heavy and lethargic once she re-entered the rest of the castle. It was like the East Wing buoyed her up and she had to come back to earth once she left it.

The seamstress, a stout little woman with a waist-length braid of thick yellow hair, was hovering over by her left knee, pinning up one side of the cream-colored monstrosity. The woman had several pins shoved into her mouth, and she kept glancing down at the newspaper on the stool next to her, which boasted the blocky black headline "New Report: Witch Blood Down by 20 Percent. Are We Only Years Away from Total Purification?"

The seamstress completely ignored Isolde's chattering, a talent which Emma rather admired. She wished she could ignore Isolde too, but her mother was hovering over one shoulder, providing a constant trickle of waspish remarks. Emma's posture wasn't straight enough. She was slouching. Her hair was a terrible mess, and she had better not scowl like that at court!

Emma's reflection in the mirror across the room looked back at her miserably. The dress she was in was many-layered, puff-sleeved, and aggressively lacey, with tiny pearls sewn into the fabric.

She looked like a walking wedding cake.

The one benefit of the seamstress coming to their rooms was that she insisted on doing the fittings in the main parlor, as it had the best light. It was Emma's favorite room, with its wide balcony that looked out over the palace's gardens. The door was always kept open, even in the winter, and there was a cool, pine-scented breeze drifting in, stirring Emma's hair around her face.

From her position on the box, she could see the center of the rose garden. The rosebushes were bare, but the triple-layered, green-and-white marble fountain still filled the air with the cheerful trickle of water. It was quite pleasant, if you ignored the glowering stone statue of the queen that perched atop it.

"You're not listening. Stand up *straight*, Emmaline."

There came a demanding poke in the middle of her back. Emma jerked upright and immediately received a sharp stab in her left thigh that made her eyes water. The seamstress glanced up, eyes wide. She looked as if she were about to say something, but Emma shook her head hastily.

After giving her a long look, the woman sighed and returned to her work, head bent, and Emma relaxed.

"You must work on your posture." Isolde came over to stand next to her elbow, her gaze raking down Emma's form. She shook her head reprovingly. "You clearly need more lessons and less time running wild about the East Wing. I'll ask Mr. Davis to increase your finishing classes."

Emma scowled at her.

Of course her mother would restrict her access to the East Wing, and to the abandoned library within. This had nothing to do with Emma's posture. She would be kept in the dark, fed the same stories about her family history over and over again.

Her mother would never let her discover what had happened to Lenore.

Anger flared in the pit of her stomach and Emma tensed, fists clenched at her sides. The seamstress looked up from her newspaper, brow furrowed, and from somewhere in the back of Emma's mind came a dull, quiet sound.

Thump-thump. Thump-thump.

Her breath caught, a shiver of shock rippling through her.

Oh no, not here. She couldn't do this here.

It had been weeks since this last happened, and Emma had hoped against hope that she would make it to Testing Day without any sign of it, that perhaps she'd even grown out of it.

If it happened tomorrow, it might affect the outcome of The Testing. She couldn't let that happen.

Quickly, she shut her eyes and pushed the irritation down, taking a deep calming breath.

Sometimes, if she caught the Noise early, she could make it go away before anything really dreadful happened.

After a second it faded, and Emma let out a sigh, eyes fluttering open. She was startled to find Isolde's starkly painted face only inches from her own.

"Why have you got that look on your face?" Isolde said, suspicion clear in her voice.

Emma leaned back, dismayed.

Thankfully, at that moment a small commotion started up in the garden below: a high, annoyed-sounding shout.

Someone was sitting on the bench in front of the fountain. Emma couldn't make out who it was, but he was dressed in court fashion, a lord or duke perhaps. A member of the court waiting for the proceedings to start, most likely.

He was sitting up straight on the bench, waving his arms at a pair of black birds on the pavement before him.

The distant sound of his voice, high-pitched and shrill, drifted through the window. "Scat! Shoo, bloody birds!"

Emma watched, amused in spite of herself. Even from her position in the parlor, she could see he had some kind of biscuit or scone clutched in one hand, and the birds—crows, she thought, judging by their glossy black feathers—kept edging closer to his bench, hopping sideways over the paving stones.

"Get away!"

"Goodness. How undignified." Isolde's voice was so close to Emma's left ear that she jumped. Her mother was the picture of disapproval as she stared out the window.

"Maybe he's afraid of birds," Emma said.

As they watched—even the seamstress had sat up from her pinning, craning her neck to look out the window—the young noble finally lobbed his biscuit at the crows and ran. He would have made a clean getaway too, as the birds swooped down on the food, but one shoe caught the edge of the stone pathway, and he pitched forward, falling headlong into the nearest rosebush.

"Oh!" the seamstress said, and Isolde made a disapproving clucking sound.

"As I said, no dignity at all."

Emma groaned, cringing in sympathy as a pair of palace guards rushed to help the young man out of the bushes. Then she paused, eyes narrowed, as he struggled to sit upright. There was something familiar about him.

A moment later she realized what it was.

The tall, gangly frame; the shock of black hair.

Her cousin, Edgar. The prince.

Ugh. Maybe she didn't feel bad for him after all. His spill into the thorny bushes was well deserved, in her opinion.

Emma wanted to stay and watch the extraction of the young prince, but the seamstress finally stood up with a heavy sigh and announced that the pinning was done.

Isolde, who seemed not to notice that it was her nephew floundering in the distant rosebushes, was in a hurry almost immediately, demanding Emma slip out of the dress and accompany her to their chambers.

"We have simply *got* to do something about that hair. And are you still so adamantly against painting your face? The shadows under your eyes are so dark, it really would help, Emmaline."

Emma bit back a sigh, but she stepped off the box and stood still while the seamstress unbuttoned the back of the dress. While she waited, she kept an eye on the rose garden, but there seemed to be no further commotion. The guards untangled the prince, who brushed them off and hurried away down the path, straightening his jacket as he went.

Emma watched, sighing deeply as he vanished behind the hedges. Tomorrow was going to be dreadful, but at least she hadn't fallen face-first into a rosebush like an absolute idiot. Small mercies, she supposed.

But as she stood there staring at the empty garden, the sound of the fountain was drowned out by her mother, who had begun admonishing her for not holding her shoulders back, and Emma began to feel sorry for herself.

First she was forced into an atrocious wedding-cake dress. And now she was about to have her hair painfully yanked on for the next hour and a half. And on top of all that, her gaze kept straying to the wheel of the seasons on the wall beside the window, a small clay disc with a single wooden pointer that was turned to a new slot each day.

Another day gone, and now she had finally run out of time.

The sight of it sent a wash of cold through her and tied her stomach into uncomfortable knots.

On second thought, she'd take the rosebush.

Chapter Four

E mma scratched at her neck, miserable.

The Throne Room was so crowded there was barely an inch to move. People kept bumping into her, and the atrocious dress her mother had forced her into was unbearably itchy in the sweltering heat. There was a hearing day every month, and each time it seemed there were more and more nobles attempting to pack themselves into the echoing space, all of them dressed to the nines in cream-colored lace, purple silks, and the most ridiculous hats possible.

Emma made her way around the fountain at the front, avoiding the fine mist sent up from the rush of the purple-tinged waters, and headed toward a table heavily laden with food. She frowned as a gaggle of young women in high-necked gowns and peacock-feathered hats pushed past her, knocking her elbow. None of them seemed to notice they'd run into her; they were too busy staring up at the dais, raised above a set of five stone steps and sectioned off with heavy purple curtains. At the base was a life-sized statue depicting Queen Alexandria, her booted foot resting on one side of an upended, cracked cauldron. And looming over that was the queen's throne, empty now, waiting for Her Highness to arrive ...

Emma scratched again and looked over at the wheel of the seasons, this one a massive stone plaque that had been erected beside the dais. She shivered and looked away.

The Testing was what, twelve hours away?

When she turned back to the table, she nearly jumped.

A boy had appeared across from her. He was tall and pale, with messy dark hair. His posture was distinctly uncomfortable, and he stood with his arms dangling at his sides, as if he wasn't sure what he was meant to do with them.

Prince Edgar.

The mere sight of him was enough to put a sour taste in Emma's mouth. She turned away, crossing her arms over her chest.

He must have seen her too, but neither of them said anything to the other.

Emma had been expressly clear on the matter of her dislike for him, as she'd barely spoken a word to him in four years. She could remember down to the exact day—no, to the *moment*—when she'd decided never to speak to him again.

They'd been playing at Witch Hunter, a game that had consisted of Edgar playing the hunter and she the witch, both of them galloping down the stone corridors shrieking at the tops of their lungs until one of them "caught" the other.

It was a dangerous game, mainly because of the subject matter, but no one would have known if Edgar hadn't gone and ratted them out. He'd pushed her over during one round, and she'd shouted that she was going to curse him.

It had been nothing. An empty threat made in the spirit of the game.

But Edgar had run to his mother, and his mother had brought the witch hunters, and a terrified nine-year-old Emma had found herself in the middle of three large, stern men, being interviewed for nearly an hour, until her mother had come back to their suite and kicked the witch hunters out.

It was the one and only time Emma had seen Isolde stand up to her sister.

She would have remembered it with more admiration if her mother hadn't then spent the rest of the night yelling herself hoarse over Emma's foolishness.

She glanced at the prince from the corner of her eye. He was picking morosely at the strawberry tart on his plate, black curls flopping in front of his eyes. His cravat had been incorrectly tied and had come undone, and he appeared to have tucked a pen behind his ear and forgotten it, as it had stained his neck with a great deal of black ink. He had a thick leather book tucked under one arm, and there appeared to be a number of long, red scratches on his face and neck.

The boy was a *mess*.

Prince Edgar glanced up just then, as if sensing her glare.

Emma cleared her throat awkwardly, quickly shifting her gaze down to the food, as if she'd meant to scowl at a plate of deviled eggs rather than him.

The table was completely full.

There were platters of food piled high all the way down the long table: curls of thinly sliced peppered ham and white cheeses, poached grouse eggs arranged with salmon, and pastries with cherry and raspberry in the center.

She could hardly stand to look at any of it. Her stomach felt sour, a problem that seemed to occur every time her mother dragged her to court.

"I expect we'll hear about the coven."

Emma jerked upright, startled that he'd spoken. "What?"

Edgar didn't look at her; his gaze was fixed on the empty dais.

"You know, during the hearings. We'll hear about the coven, how the hunt went. I hear rumors it didn't go off as planned."

For a moment she stood still, pressing her lips together hard, caught between her moral outrage of four years ago and her current burning curiosity. The prince clearly knew something about the witch hunters she'd seen in the hallway the night before.

The pieces of the ripped-up poster were now safely squirreled away in one of her stocking drawers, but she could still picture the woman's face so clearly.

Had the witch hunters found her? What did Edgar mean when he said that things didn't go as planned?

She badly wanted to question him, but she also badly wanted to snatch up one of the tiny stuffed quiches and lob it at the side of his head.

She wasn't sure which impulse was stronger.

When she glanced back over at him, Edgar was staring at her expectantly, brows raised. He was waiting, she realized, for her to ask him about the coven.

Slowly and deliberately, she reached out and plucked a cheese square off the platter and shoved it into her mouth, chewing aggressively, sure to keep direct eye contact all the while.

That would show him she didn't need his stupid information.

Edgar blinked at her, clearly taken aback. "Uh," he said hurriedly, "I heard they got away, nearly all of them."

She stopped chewing, unable to hide her surprise. "Really? How?"

Prince Edgar grimaced, and Emma realized she'd spoken around a mouthful of cheese. "Er, well, I heard they set the place on fire while the captain was inside. Bad business all around."

The captain—the regal blond man who'd passed out the posters of Lenore. Emma remembered him saying how dangerous Lenore was. Had she been the one to set the house on fire? "I heard they may have been looking for one witch in particular. Do you know if they found her?"

Prince Edgar perked up a little. "Did you? I didn't hear that part. Who told you?"

Emma pressed her lips together. A familiar feeling had begun to steal over her, setting the hairs on the back of her neck prickling. She darted a look around the crowd to see if anyone was watching them.

She'd said too much.

Instead of answering, she said pointedly, "Fell into a rosebush, did you?"

Prince Edgar didn't reply, but his face went bright red and he looked away quickly, which was enough of an answer as far as she was concerned.

She snickered and let her gaze wander to the front of the room.

Beyond the statue, the wall was covered in a massive, painted mural. In it, Queen Alexandria was sitting very straight on the throne. Her neck was long, her chin thrust out, a half-smile on her full red lips. The painting was so detailed you could see the way her crown glittered under the light, and her black eyes shone as she gazed down at you.

At the base of the painting was the royal motto in scrolling script: *Semper Vigilo*. According to her tutor, it meant the queen was always watching over her people.

Emma, who found the whole thing rather unnerving, would rather she didn't.

Worse still were the figures just below the throne. Witches. Monstrous women with tangled hair and wild black eyes. A line of them stretched across the bottom of the mural. The first two had a hapless human between them in chains, demanding he demonstrate his magic, enslaving him when he failed. But by the end of the line the witches lay defeated, their black dresses in tatters as they crumpled in the dirt at the queen's feet.

Emma knew the painting was meant to celebrate the queen's defeat of the witches, and how she'd put a stop to their plans to enslave all of humanity. But the witches were still a nightmare, with black teeth and nails and eyes.

The painting had kept her awake for several nights the first time she'd seen it. She'd checked her face in the mirror for weeks afterward, looking for a darkening of her eyes or blackening of her teeth.

She turned her gaze downward, trying to shake off the chill.

Her mother was holding court just below the steps of the throne, no doubt a deliberate position.

Emma couldn't hear her, but she could see the familiar smile on her mother's face, the expression of benevolent superiority combined with a long-suffering air. She gestured regally at the people clustered around her and, at the same time, leaned heavily on the arm of the handsome young lord beside her, her fan clutched hard in one hand. By the way Isolde's companions were leaning close, Emma could tell her mother was speaking in that faint, whispery voice she so often used. Isolde Black would never be queen, but she was certainly good at capturing the attention of her admirers.

One of these admirers, a pretty young woman with thistle-shaped diamonds dangling from her necklace, reached out and clasped Isolde's hand, brows knit together in concern, and Isolde waved her off with a brave smile.

Emma rolled her eyes to the ceiling and then paused, noticing that the rafters had been draped with bows of greenery woven through with dried thistle flowers.

She missed the East Wing.

She turned her attention back to the cheese and was about to pluck another square off the platter when, behind her, one of the young ladies in purple silk pressed closer, jostling her arm. Emma tried to shove down the annoyance and bite her tongue.

The woman hadn't even noticed; she was too busy talking loudly to her companions.

"I hear Isabella wore an obsidian stone in her choker to the dance last night. Black as a witch's eye, I hear."

"Hush, Sophie!" One of the woman's companions darted a look at the empty throne, eyes round. "You say the most outrageous things."

"Well, you've got to wonder about a girl wearing black at all." Sophie flicked her blond ringlets over one poofy silk shoulder and wiggled her eyebrows. "If you ask me, it smells like a sympathizer."

"That's a serious accusation, Ms. Sophie," a tall, dark-haired man chimed in from behind them. The girls burst into nervous giggles and shot him flirtatious looks.

"Ugh, they're bringing the thistle wine out." Prince Edgar's voice jerked Emma's attention away from the conversation and back toward the table. He was looking at the front of the Throne Room, where a servant in the all-white livery of the queen's royal footmen had wheeled out a metal tea tray full of wine flutes, each glass filled with pale purple liquid.

Emma looked away quickly, her mouth twisted in distaste.

The prince didn't seem to notice her discomfort. "I hear it's even worse than the thistle juice mother makes me drink. Have you tried the juice?"

Had she *tried* it?

She whirled on him, fists clenched at her sides, hardly able to believe he could be so *stupid*. "Yes, I've tried it," she snapped. "The first thing they do when you're accused is make you drink it. I'm sure you must remember, Your Highness."

Edgar flinched, his face flushing.

Clearly, he remembered it now: the witch hunters showing up with a flask of the violet-colored liquid, one of them holding the back of Emma's neck as another forced the thistle juice between her lips.

She could still remember the bitter taste on her tongue, even now.

Anger swelled her chest and she turned her back on the prince, determined to ignore him for the rest of the evening. Just then, however, she heard something deep in the back of her mind—a distant, faint-sounding *thump-thump*.

Emma froze. Fear crawled up her spine and down her arms, making her fingers tingle, sending goosebumps rippling over her skin.

No. This couldn't happen again.

She bit the inside of her cheek hard enough to taste the bitter tang of copper, glancing sideways at her mother. Isolde was staring at her now, even though the handsome lord on her arm was leaning over, whispering in her ear. She stared past him, gaze locked on Emma, eyes narrow. Emma looked away quickly.

"I didn't mean that," Prince Edgar stammered. "That's not what I was saying."

The anger flared in her chest again, in spite of her efforts to shove it down, and to Emma's dismay, the Noise came a second time.

Thud-thud. Thud-thud.

It was a loud, steady beat now.

He was still blathering, clearly trying to pry his foot from his mouth. "I just meant, uh, I wasn't sure if you'd had it before, under other circumstances . . ."

This wasn't good. She had to calm herself.

Thud-thud. Thud-thud.

Now the Noise was drowning out Edgar's voice. It was getting too loud, too fast. She grappled in the back of her mind for the trick she usually relied on when it got out of hand: trying to picture herself locking the sound away, shutting it behind a door. But she couldn't seem to imagine the door in her mind, couldn't remember what it looked like or how she'd conjured it up before.

This wasn't working.

Emma turned, grasping for something, anything, to make the prince go away, to tell him he needed to leave her alone. But it was too late: his face had gone sheet white and, in the next moment, the Noise in the back of Emma's head cut off mid-beat.

The buzz of the crowd dropped into silence, leaving nothing but the echo of a hundred excited whispers behind.

Prince Edgar's mouth was open in a silent gasp, and one hand flew up to his chest, fingers splayed as he pressed his palm to his heart. He wheezed, and Emma stumbled back a step as cold panic raced over her.

No, no, no. This couldn't happen. Not here. Not to him.

She felt paralyzed, helpless to do anything other than stare, and then from somewhere behind her came a loud *crack*, and Emma jumped.

She whirled around, heart in her throat, to see several nobles clustered by one of the high, pointed windows set into the stone wall. A few of the women were staring up, wide-eyed, hands over their mouths. One enterprising gentleman had raised himself up on his toes to peer out.

"Bloody bird ran right into the window, poor daft thing."

There was a frantic thudding in her ears, but now it was only the sound of her own heart beating very hard. The Noise had gone.

Emma turned back around, thinking she'd find Edgar gone, run off to report her to the nearest witch hunter maybe, or cowering under the table. Instead, he stood with one hand braced against the table-top, staring hard at her. The color was slowly returning to his face.

"You . . . you're a wi—"

A second, louder crash from the front of the room cut him off.

Someone had flung both doors open at the entrance, and the doorman in his white livery jumped hastily to one side, cupping his hands to his mouth to call out, "Announcing Her Majesty, Queen Alexandria Black, High Empress of the Western Shores—"

Queen Alexandria swept forward, skirts rustling over the floor. Her pale face—painted white just like her sister's—was set in a terrible, stony determination as she marched toward the dais. The doorman's eyes widened imperceptibly, and he sped up his announcement.

"—Thistle Queen, Duchess of the Shadowed North, Slayer of Witches, and Savior of the People."

He ended his announcement just as the queen mounted the stone steps and settled onto her throne, one hand extended. Her foot servant had been waiting by the dais, and now he jumped forward, throat bobbing nervously, holding out a silver tray with a single flute of thistle wine. The queen took it delicately between finger and thumb and drank, tipping her head back, dark lashes fluttering.

All around the Throne Room the rest of the court was doing the same, tipping back the watery purple liquid. Some of the nobles gulped it back all at once, and more than a few lords and ladies hid their disgust poorly, attempting to conceal purple-lipped grimaces behind sleeves and fans. Emma chewed her lip, remembering the awful, bitter taste.

Queen Alexandria set her empty glass back on the tray. Her thin hands drifted like pale birds, trembling ever so slightly, before she folded them in her lap, shifting her attention back to the court.

The queen looked very much like her sister, though Emma's mother was a full head shorter. They had the same black eyes and hair, the same sharp edge to their expressions. Queen Alexandria seemed harder though. Even waif-thin as she was, she had a dark glitter in her eyes that made her seem a little dangerous. And that was on a good day.

Today was not a good day.

"Bring him in," the queen barked, and so the hearings began.

Chapter Five

The first man was deemed a possible witch. He had reportedly refused to drink the thistle wine his neighbor had gifted him, and was later overheard bad-mouthing the queen in a local pub. Both he and his wife were condemned to be Re-Tested. Emma winced as they were dragged away protesting.

What kind of fool would commit treason in the middle of a crowded bar? Everyone knew the queen would hear about it even if you so much as cursed her under your breath in your own living room.

The cases that followed were all similar, and they soon started to blend together. Had the last one been the woman who'd supposedly murdered her neighbors' cow with magic, or the one who'd been spotted cursing her neighbors' houseplants so they would shrivel up? Emma found her gaze drifting up to the wheel of the seasons next to the dais. She kept forgetting The Testing was tomorrow and then remembering with an unpleasant start—a pattern that seemed to repeat itself every few minutes.

By the time the tenth hearing was about to begin, the Throne Room was buzzing with fearful whispers—*"Did you see if his eyes were black?" "They were darkening, I'm almost sure of it!"*—but the noise cut off abruptly as the guards hauled the next subject through the door.

Emma looked up just as they dragged him past, and her breath caught in her throat.

The captain of the witch hunters looked nothing like he had that morning. His cool confidence had vanished. He was smudged with soot, and his wide-brimmed hat was crooked, his face twisted in fury. One of the soldiers walked behind him, carrying the thistlewood staff they'd confiscated, and as the procession passed, Emma caught a strong whiff of smoke. A few of the nobles around her stepped back, pressing handkerchiefs to their mouths.

The guards deposited the captain at the foot of the throne, and he stumbled and fell heavily to his knees.

For a moment there was dead silence in the court as the queen regarded him, her face thunderous.

When she finally spoke, her voice was like the lash of a whip. "You *lost* them."

A stirring from the court; people began to murmur.

"Captain Tobias McCraw, you are charged with criminal negligence in the line of duty." The queen's fist came crashing down on the arm of the throne with a dull, echoing *thunk*, and half the court jumped. "You failed your queen and your country. You were meant to find . . ." The queen paused, and for a moment her stony expression faltered. Then her face went cold and smooth once more. "You were meant to find the coven, and you failed."

You were meant to find HER. Emma was almost sure that's what Queen Alexandria had wanted to say. The captain was supposed to find Lenore and he hadn't.

"It wasn't my fault, Your Majesty." Captain McCraw's voice was a hoarse whisper. "We had the house surrounded. We were forcing them out." He wheezed and then gave a rasping cough, shaking his head. "I don't know what happened . . ." His brow furrowed and his gaze darted around the room. "I-I don't know what they did. The witches—"

"You were in the house." Queen Alexandria leaned forward on her throne, painted face twisted with fury. "They set the house on fire with you inside, and they escaped. It's a miracle you didn't burn. The entire coven, gone!"

The witch hunter's eyes were wide. "No, no, that's not possible. They were there, in the house. We had them."

"It was an illusion. You were enchanted, Captain. The witches are *gone*. They've disappeared."

"Impossible." His voice shook.

There was a buzz around the throne room, and Emma heard the same phrase passed from one spectator to the next.

Witch City. They've gone to Witch City.

The fabled town filled entirely with witches.

Emma had been fascinated when she'd first heard about it. She'd collected as many rumors as she could, combing through the library for any hint or mention. She'd even listened around corners for gossip.

She'd discovered that the more you looked into the rumors, the more outrageous they became. Blue gaslight that burned intruders; shifting streets that left you forever lost; fountains that pulled you in and drowned you.

Finally, she'd plucked up enough courage to ask her tutor about it. To her disappointment, he'd claimed the whole thing was nonsense, and Emma had finally resigned herself to the dreary fact that Witch City was nothing more than a wild fairy tale.

But lately, it seemed as if there was a lot she didn't know. A lot she hadn't been told, and a lot she couldn't learn from the history books, because pieces of those books seemed to have mysteriously *gone missing*.

All of this brought her back to the abandoned library in the East Wing. To her mother's revelation, and the words she'd said just after.

My worst fear in life is that you'll become like her. You're already close in so many ways.

If she was close to being like Lenore, did that mean she'd fail tomorrow's Testing?

Up on the dais, Queen Alexandria let out a heavy sigh and settled back into her throne. She waved a hand at the guards. "Get him out of my sight. A night in chains should remind him to keep his wits about him."

The crowd cleared out of the way as the guards dragged the witch hunter, who was staring in stunned silence, toward the doors. Captain McCraw kept trying to turn back, twisting and bucking against the guard's grip. "It's impossible! I had them!"

The doors slammed shut behind them, and Emma jumped as the noise echoed through the Throne Room. When she turned back, Queen Alexandria was standing up from the throne, composed once more. She nodded at her guard.

"We've found one of their children. Send out a task force for the others. They can't have gone far."

The guard vanished through the door, and after a beat of silence that followed the exit, a murmur began in the court. The palace's rumor mill never rested—at least not for long. Already the story would be traveling, passed on by servants and nobles, running through underground networks at lightning speed. Soon the entire city of London would know a coven had escaped capture. That a group of the most dangerous sort of people was roaming the streets.

Emma turned back to Edgar, swallowing hard.

His expression was dark, and he met her eyes for a second before turning his gaze up to the stone wheel on the wall. And even though they'd barely spoken to one another in years, she knew exactly what he was thinking, because she'd seen that expression on her own face. Every time she looked in a mirror. Every time she took stock of the date, and how many days were left in the season.

She knew that expression. It was dread.

Emma frowned at him. Why exactly was *he* dreading The Testing?

She stared at him, hesitating. She wanted to ask, but she couldn't. Not here in the middle of court.

"My friends." Queen Alexandria's voice was firm. "We will find them, and we will put an end to this. Magic will not rule us or steal our freedom *ever* again."

The crowd drew closer to the throne, a buzz of excitement swelling.

Even Emma could feel goosebumps spreading over her arms.

At times like this, she knew Isolde could never hope to take her sister's place. It was Alexandria who had the power to captivate, to lead the people, not her little sister.

There was a good reason she'd been the one to lead the uprising.

Emma had yet to be born when they'd risen up against the witches, but she'd heard the stories. Everyone had. She knew about the fighting in the streets, the clashing armies and the havoc the witches had wreaked on the city. The horrible things they'd done to the human rebels.

Until Alexandria had discovered their weakness, the key to their defeat.

On Yuletide Eve, she had risen up against them. She and her army had ousted the Witch Queen from the throne. They had taken the palace back, and hung the witches in the city square.

And that was why they celebrated every year, why the fires burned bright in the center of the city. Why they lit candles and hung bushels of thistle over every door. And why every child of thirteen would report to the city square on Yuletide Eve for The Testing. To make sure they weren't a witch.

"Tomorrow, we will have our Testing. Once it's over," the queen continued, "Yuletide day will come, and we will celebrate our freedom. We will sing, and we will *feast!*"

Now the buzz of the crowd grew louder. A few people even cheered.

Wordlessly, Emma looked over at Edgar. He gave her a wide-eyed stare in return, and they both turned to look at the stone plaque on the wall.

Tomorrow.

Chapter Six

The Testing began on Tuesday morning at 6 a.m. sharp, in the center of Piccadilly Square. The sun was rising, turning the peaks and towers of the London skyline into a show of dusky oranges and reds.

The gas lamps were still burning, casting stretched-out shadows onto the frosty cobblestones. As far as Emma was concerned, it was entirely too early, and no one had any business being out of bed.

She slumped on the velvet-cushioned seat, tugging the collar of her winter jacket up to her chin, pressing her face to the window as the carriage bumped and jostled her. She tried to ignore the heaviness in her stomach, and the fact that the stupid lace dress she had on made starchy crunching sounds every time she moved.

"*Stop* that."

A hand snatched at her wrist, and Emma found herself tugged sharply upright. Her mother scowled ferociously at her from over the top of the lace handkerchief pressed to her nose. "You're smudging the windowpane."

"I don't care." She glared right back. Not for the first time today, she felt irritation begin to swell in her chest. Here she was, completely dreading what was to come, and her mother was acting as if the whole thing was nothing more than a terrible inconvenience. As if she'd turned thirteen today out of sheer spite.

Isolde had moaned and complained the entire way to the square: Her constitution was too weak for a trip into the inner city. She was bound to catch some terrible plague from the common folk. She was too weak for the dirty air.

Emma had contemplated tucking and rolling out of the carriage and onto the street. Surely it would be less painful. Perhaps her ridiculous dress would cushion her fall. It certainly had enough layers.

"Just look at that. Barbarians, the lot of them."

Emma twisted in her seat to peer out the window. No doubt her mother meant the crowds on the street. Everyone was up early for The Testing, and the city was as bustling as it usually was at noontime. The shopkeepers were stringing garlands from the signs of their stores, and the vendors passing their carriage had carts loaded with fruits and grains.

There was an air of excited nervousness in the city, and the streets were full of traffic, all of which was heading in the direction of Piccadilly Square. The crowd, dressed in their best walking dresses and winter jackets, weaved through traffic and pushed past storefronts.

It was not a celebration yet, but even from behind the glass in the carriage, Emma could tell people were getting ready. Once The Testing was over, there would be time to let loose. To drink and sing and dance to the band in the square.

From the seat beside Emma, her mother made a series of disapproving tsking sounds.

Isolde disapproved of frivolity of any sort, especially if it was the poorer sort of people engaging in it. She sat back in her seat, red lips twisted in disgust, and crossed her arms. "Testing Day is hardly a party, but they use any excuse, don't they? I say we should ship the rabble-rousers off to Scotland with the witches. Get rid of them all in one go."

Emma grimaced at her mother and went back to staring out the window.

In the far distance, the clock tower rose above the rest of the city. It was a crooked, blackened spire against the light of dawn, still damaged from the Great War.

She shuddered, shifting her attention back to the street and to the bakery they were passing. Outside, a round man in a white smock was shaking a tray of bread rolls into a basket, his breath rising in silver clouds above his head. The shop was festive, decorated with thistle over the doorway. A cluster of holly berries was pinned to the mandatory *See a Witch, Say Something!* poster hanging in the window.

There was a second poster beside the first, this one larger, with tattered, sun-faded edges. In blocky letters it asked *HAVE YOU SEEN THIS WITCH?* Underneath was a drawing of a woman, though it was so faint Emma could hardly make out her face. Most of the wanted posters around town were very old. There were so few adult witches left in London.

She slouched in her seat as the carriage rumbled past, glancing away quickly. It was not a poster of Lenore, but it was still enough to make her stomach sour all over again.

If the magic in her blood was over 15 percent, she would fail The Testing. Would the witch hunters drag her away? Would they paralyze her with a thistle dart and put her straight onto the *Witch Express*?

"Oh my goodness."

Isolde's horrified voice made Emma turn, eyes narrow. But surprisingly, that tone wasn't directed at Emma. Instead, Isolde was staring out the window.

Emma twisted around in her seat to find the carriage passing a small, single-level cottage. Or at least, it had once been a cottage. Now it was more of a burnt husk. You could still see the outline of the house it had once been—four walls and a space for a door—but it was entirely blackened, hollowed out inside, and the roof was completely gone.

This time, when she pressed her face to the glass, her mother didn't say anything.

It wasn't just the charred stones of the cottage that sent a chill down Emma's spine, or even the fact that something on the inside of the ruined house was still smoking. No, it was the purple ribbon strung from the trees all around it, a bright red *W* pattern repeated over and over, encircling what was left of the building.

The symbol of the Witch Queen.

The sight sent a tremor of shock through her. Emma pressed herself back against the seat; across from her, Isolde gave a strangled cry.

Emma recalled the drawing of the Witch Queen she'd seen in the East Wing library, and the depiction of her army in the Throne Room mural. Somehow, those images hadn't prepared her to see the symbol in person. She felt instantly shaky, her heart crowding up into her throat.

Did it mean that the members of the coven had all been rebel witches? Were they still out there after all these years, plotting to enslave everyone again?

On the street, people crowded around, pressing up against the purple ribbon in an effort to get a better look at the scorched shell of the house. Several tall, black-hatted witch hunters circled the exterior of the cottage, and the crowd cleared out of the way as soon as they came into sight.

Emma's stomach suddenly churned with nerves. She imagined she could detect the faint scent of smoke.

"Oh, I'm beginning to feel faint." Her mother pressed the handkerchief more tightly against her face, blinking furiously, her eyes watering.

Emma turned her head toward the window, rolled her eyes, and craned her neck as she tried to get one last look at the ruins of the house.

"Oh." Isolde's voice was a soft gasp, and Emma felt her mother grip her arm tightly. She turned, alarmed to see Isolde's hand pressed over her chest, her face pale.

"Mother? Are you . . . ?"

Isolde drew in a long breath, and some of the color returned to her cheeks. She shut her eyes tightly, but didn't release her grip on Emma's arm. "Tell me when we've gone past."

Emma leaned against the seat, letting the carriage rock them back and forth.

She waited one beat, and then another just to make sure, before saying quietly, "Alright, we've gone by."

Isolde's eyes snapped open, and she stared at Emma. Abruptly, she twisted in her seat until her nose was inches away from Emma's own. The sharp tang of smelling salts assaulted Emma's senses and she wrinkled her nose. "Listen, Emmaline. Their witch child—the one who didn't get away—she might be at The Testing. Be sure you don't speak to *anyone* except your cousin, if you see him. Be sure to keep him company. Comfort him if he's scared."

And just like that, Emma's guilt was gone, replaced by a familiar, slow-burning anger expanding in her gut.

It was the first time her mother had shown any concern over someone being nervous about The Testing, but of course it was the prince she was worried about, and not her own daughter . . .

Emma made a noise of distaste and tugged her arm out of her mother's grasp. "No, thank you."

"Emmaline Black." Her mother sat up straight, clearly furious, and Emma braced herself for a lecture. But before her mother could explode, the carriage lurched to a halt, and from somewhere just outside came the high-pitched sound of a train whistle.

Both Emma and her mother leaned forward, and Emma shoved the velvet curtain out of her way. She had to lean to the side and mash her face against the glass, but she could see the sleek black side of the train as it snaked past in front of their carriage.

Her stomach clenched at the sight of the windows on the cars, each covered by a cage of thick iron. The noise the train made between whistles was audible even through the walls of the carriage, the heavy whoosh and pant of the engine like a giant set of lungs.

The *Witch Express* had been around for ages, since the end of the Great War, in fact. The queen allotted a tremendous amount of money for its upkeep every year, in order to keep the underground tunnels operating. It was miles and miles of track, all the way to the central city of Scotland, where witches were rehabilitated. These tracks, and the stations along them, were part of an entirely separate system from the one that regular folk used to get around. This was the first time Emma had seen the *Express* up close.

Immediately, she hated it. The noise of the heavy machinery pumping away; the wheeze and whistling of its engine; the steam hissing out from underneath. It was too loud, too large, too ominous. Too much of everything, really.

She watched it go past, trying not to picture it as an angry iron dragon on its way to devour witches. She breathed in deeply, forcing herself to relax as the train disappeared into a tunnel.

If she let herself get worked up, the Noise would start again.

The carriage jerked forward and they traveled in silence for the next few minutes, with Isolde still pressing the handkerchief to her nose, eyes fluttering shut.

For a moment, Emma let herself scan her mother's face. Whether Isolde had meant to or not, she'd had a lighter touch with the white face paint today, and Emma could see bluish circles beneath her eyes.

She really *didn't* look well, and Emma found herself wondering if her mother had increased her daily portion of thistle wine. At royal events, Isolde drank when the queen drank—the same as the rest of the court—but sometimes she would take it into her head that she must be better than the court, that she must follow in the footsteps of her sister, who consumed thistle at every meal.

She wondered when her mother's hands would start to shake all the time, like the queen's did.

No one, Emma thought darkly, would have the guts to say it out loud, but the thistle was undeniably poison in large quantities, even if you weren't a witch. She'd seen the effects, and she'd *felt* them after the witch hunter incident all those years ago. She'd been sick for a week. Isolde had confined her to her room, saying she was grounded for playing foolish games, but Emma knew it was to avoid suspicion.

The carriage jerked again and then slowed, and the driver called from up ahead, "The square, my lady."

They'd arrived.

Emma whipped around in her seat, one hand pressed to the window. Now her heart was thumping wildly in her chest. There was the square, with the massive stone pillar and the statue in the center. On the other side, she could just make out the top of a series of white tents.

Emma swallowed hard. Her mouth suddenly tasted horrible, as if she'd been sick and then immediately forgotten. She felt she might be sick now.

"Well, what are you waiting for?" Her mother's voice was sharp, and too close to her left ear. "We'll come to pick you up when you're done. The soldiers will escort you back here."

Emma didn't move. "The Test . . . d-did your sister take it? Lenore?"

Her mother didn't answer, and when Emma turned to look at her, the expression on her mother's face made her flinch. Isolde was glowering at her daughter, clearly thunderstruck. "H-how dare you—I t-told you never to—" she stuttered, and then cut herself off as the door swung open. The driver, in his neatly pressed black uniform, stood at attention beside the carriage steps.

Emma stood sharply and made her way out the door.

The entire massive space of the square stretched out before her, and it was filled, corner to corner. The lineups snaked out from a series of white tents and filtered through the square, roped off with red velvet cords. Purple thistle had been woven into the links, vivid and dark against the red ropes.

She felt a sharp poke in the small of her back, and heard the annoyed hiss of her mother's voice from behind her. "Go on. And you had better pray you *don't* take after Lenore."

Shocked, Emma stumbled down the carriage steps, flinching as the door slammed behind her. The carriage took off almost the moment her shiny black shoes hit the cobblestones. Fuming, Emma forced herself to turn around—toward the square, toward the lineups and the tents rising over the crowds of children.

Lenore. Isolde had actually said the name out loud.

It didn't seem like a good sign.

Chapter Seven

A number of solemn-faced guards stood at the entrance booths before the tents. Emma paused in front of the closest one, stomach churning. The guard jumped up when he spotted her, his eyes wide, and stammered that she should follow him.

He led her away from the crowds and around the back of the white tents, where a tall fence had been erected around a second, smaller cluster of canvas tents. The guard ushered her through the fence with a nod and a jerky bow, and then hurried away without a word.

Emma found herself in a strange little plaza. It was quieter here. There were only three tents—much bigger than the ones in the main square, but made of plain canvas. There were also fewer children: three lines, with no more than five or six children in each.

A few of them glanced over at her and then away, back toward the tents. All of them were visibly nervous. They were dressed in silks and satins, thick winter overcoats, fur hats, and shiny shoes. Their breath hung over their heads in silver puffs, and a few were stamping their feet against the frosted cobblestones, shivering. Emma recognized some of them, and she realized she'd seen them in court, though she couldn't put names to faces.

This must be the nobles section.

She hesitated, glancing back at the opening to the plaza. There was only one guard posted there. He was leaning against the fence beside the queen's poster, his expression bored. Emma was fairly sure she could walk past him if she wanted to.

But what then? Wander the streets and become a pickpocket? Hide in gutters and alleyways, hoping none of the soldiers would ever find her? None of that seemed realistic, so after a moment of hesitation, she joined the nearest line, behind a girl in a white lace dress and a violently pink winter jacket.

The line may have been only five children long, but it certainly wasn't moving. Emma shifted from one foot to the other, clutching the fabric of her dress in both fists, trying to ignore how tight her chest was.

At least there was plenty to look at through the gap in the fence. Vendors wove between the ropes of the lines, offering trays of sweets for sale, or jewelry made from dried thistle vines—the delicate blooms of the purple flowers trapped in clear stone pendants.

Several tall figures moved through the crowd, and Emma spotted the nearest one, his wide-brimmed black hat and the beaded cross at his neck.

He pushed his hat back as he passed, and Emma caught sight of wide blue eyes and blond stubble and felt a shock of recognition.

Captain Tobias McCraw looked very different than he had the night before. It was like all the fight had been drained out of him. His expression was bleak, and his entire posture had changed. His shoulders were slumped, and Emma noticed the top of his uniform was missing a button. His collar had been stripped of the shiny metal pins that signaled his status as a captain.

When McCraw paused, his blue eyes settling on her briefly, she felt frozen in place, as if her bones had turned to ice. He shifted his staff from one hand to the other, and her heart squeezed in her chest.

Did he recognize her somehow? Or worse . . . did he know about the Noise? Did he think she was a witch?

A moment later he turned and began to move through the crowd toward one of the tents. Her shoulders slumped in relief, and she let her gaze wander once more, this time toward the gate along the edge of the square. It was tall and laid with bricks, and there were witch hunters stationed at each entranceway.

Just beyond, the party was in full swing. Red and white circus tents rose above the crowd, and the brassy sound of the band echoed out into the surrounding streets. Even the blackened, half-crumbled structure of the clock tower looked festive from here, bathed in a rainbow of light from lanterns strung between lamp posts.

As soon as she made it through the tents, she could go beyond the gate. It would all be over once she passed the test.

If she passed the test.

All at once, reality set in. It felt as if someone had sucked all the air out of her lungs, leaving her dragging in short, shaky breaths, her head spinning.

The Testing was mere steps away. She was about to find out if she was a witch or not.

The line moved forward a few inches, and Emmaline shuffled after the girl in front of her. Her hands were shaking, and she curled them into fists at her sides. It was no good; every time she tried to shove the panic down it crawled right back up into her chest and throat, choking her. She'd barely taken two steps when the pulsing *whoosh, whoosh, whoosh* of someone's elevated heart rate echoed in the back of her mind.

No. Not here. It couldn't happen here. Not in front of every witch hunter in London.

Her panic spiked as the line moved again, bringing her closer to the tents. To The Test. She had to get this under control *now*.

Emma ground her teeth and pictured herself forcing the Noise back, slamming the door shut. There was still time to manage this, she told herself; the Noise wasn't nearly as loud as it had been at court the night before.

Emma could picture the door now: the thick oak wood; the silver knob. She pictured herself shoving a shoulder against the door, forcing it closed, sliding the deadbolt home with a metallic *click*.

The Noise cut off abruptly, and she let out a relieved breath.

Beyond the white fence, someone with a bullhorn had begun calling loudly over the noise of the crowd.

"Your Illustrious Majesty, Queen Alexandria, welcomes you! On this fine day, picture her in your head, the savior of our fair country, who swept in as the witches tried to crush us beneath their boots. Our Thistle Queen, brave and noble."

Grateful for the distraction, she stood on her tiptoes, trying to peer over the fence to see who was speaking. But a moment later a great murmur went up from the crowd, and someone in the distance cried out, "Stand aside, stand aside!"

Two of the girls in the line next to her seemed to have a better vantage point than Emma did, because they were giggling and nudging one another, leaning sideways to peer out the gate at something. The Coventry Twins. She'd run into them at court a few times, but they'd never talked to her. They looked identical, with their poofy crinoline dresses, blond ringlets, and faces painted in the court fashion, each wearing a white lace choker woven through with dried thistle flowers.

Emma glanced away quickly, hoping they didn't notice her.

Then she spotted the cause of the giggling and had to repress a groan. A pair of red-coated guards were escorting someone through the crowd toward them. A someone with messy black curls and a pale, pointed face. His hair was just as rumpled as ever, and he looked a little dazed as he was marched forward, but at least his neck was no longer covered in ink.

There was another loud giggle from the girls in the next line as he was escorted past them and straight into the nearest tent. Emma grimaced, first at them and then at him. Edgar kept his nose in the air, not looking at anyone, and only pausing long enough to chide one of the soldiers for making him drop his poetry book.

Behind Emma someone made an annoyed *hmm*. She turned to see a girl in a green-and-white lace dress, butterscotch-colored curls spilling over her shoulders.

Emma hadn't even heard her approach.

Emma squinted, trying to remember if she'd seen her before. She did look vaguely familiar. The daughter of some baron or another, she was fairly certain, though the family hadn't been at court in a while.

The girl didn't look at Emma. She was watching Prince Edgar go into the tent. Once he'd vanished inside, she began to jiggle up and down on the spot, muttering nervously to herself.

Emma understood how she felt. She couldn't stop thinking about her mother's words, just before Isolde had pushed her out of the carriage. Her gaze drifted back to the ruined clock tower in the distance.

How much had her mysterious aunt Lenore contributed to the burning of London? Had she been one of the witches who collapsed the clock tower and killed all those people? Had she cast horrible spells to mutate anyone who spoke out against the Witch Queen?

In the distance, the announcer was saying, "Step up, children, nothing to fear. Her Illustrious Majesty, the queen, has taken you under her wing, and you never have to be afraid again."

Nothing to fear. Just a possible blood connection to an actual witch and a strange power she couldn't get rid of. Her stomach turned.

"Illustrious Majesty, *honestly*."

Emma turned, mouth hanging open, to look at the girl with the butterscotch curls. She had a very freckly face and light-blue eyes.

"Do you think his lips get sore from kissing her bustle the way he does?" She snorted, arms folded over her chest.

Emma's eyes went wide, and she stepped back from the girl. "Y-you can't say that!" She darted a look over her shoulder, alarmed to see that the nearest witch hunter was only a few feet away. "You want to go straight onto the *Witch Express*?"

The girl smirked at Emma. "I'm not particularly worried."

"Not . . . worried," Emma repeated faintly.

They'd moved forward again. Emma glanced over at the girl, wondering if her family had been out of town for some time. Perhaps they'd forgotten what things were like in the city. That was the only explanation she could think of. She'd been to enough court sentencings to know that treasonous talk could get you a very long visit to the dungeons, or worse, Re-Tested.

The other girl was still talking. "I've heard Witch City has streets made of hot coals."

"I think that's hell, actually." Emma turned back to the tents, standing on her tiptoes to try to get a better view as the nurses guided a girl with curly red hair through the tent flap. "Besides, no one even knows if it's real."

"No, I'm fairly certain. I have a third cousin who's been there."

This brought Emma's attention back to the girl. She was so casual about it, as if her third cousin had simply been there on holiday.

"You're up next," was all the girl said, and Emma whipped around to see the tall girl in the white dress and pink jacket being guided past the tent flaps by a smiling nurse.

It felt a little like she'd swallowed a number of live eels. Emma pressed a hand to her chest, breathing in deeply. She was next.

"Are you nervous?" The freckled girl seemed determined to have a conversation. She was shifting from foot to foot, speaking very rapidly. "I'm not nervous, are you? I'm Madeline, by the way. Though I like to be called Maddie for short. What's your name? It's a good thing they've figured out how to test our blood, don't you think? Did you know, they used to just sort of guess at it, or wait until you accidentally blew someone up with magic or something?"

Emma was about to say that she *did* know, thank you very much. Everyone knew the history. Where had this girl come from?

Before she could reply with what would have been an admittedly snarky response, there came a loud *crack* and a shout from behind the fence. Both girls spun around.

A plume of black smoke was spiraling up into the air, sending a ripple of alarm through the crowd.

What on earth was that?

Witch hunters were running toward the fence from every direction now, and the sight was enough to make Emma's heart stop in her chest.

A moment later, the source of the smoke came into view, and Emma's mouth dropped open. Two of the soldiers were attempting to drag a girl between them, and a nurse in a white coat was hovering nearby, a long needle in one hand, as the girl bucked and kicked. The girl was struggling fiercely, and she appeared to be giving the soldiers far more trouble than someone her size should have been able to.

More astonishing still, she appeared to be *on fire*. Her arms flickered with orange flames. Seconds later, one of the witch hunters reached the odd little group. He snatched a blanket off a cart mid-sprint and threw it over the girl, smothering the fire.

"Hold her still! I need to get her percentage!" This shout was from the nurse, and a shriek of outrage could be heard from beneath the blanket as the woman in the white coat jumped forward, extracted the girl's arm, and plunged the needle in, drawing a measure of blood.

Emma felt ill just watching it. She continued to stare, mouth still gaping, as the soldiers dragged the girl past the gate. Then Emma couldn't see anything more, though she could still hear the outraged shrieks for another few seconds.

For a long moment, Emma and Maddie both stared at the gap in the fence. Finally, Maddie spoke. "Think she might be a witch?"

Emma nodded slowly, eyes still fixed on the fence.

Her pulse was racing, blood rushing in her ears. She'd just seen magic. The discovery of a witch.

And she was next.

Chapter Eight

In the moments after the burning witch had been dragged past, the buzz from the crowd outside the fence began to die down. As the noise settled, Emma could hear a steady *thump-thump, thump-thump*, disturbingly clear. It seemed to be growing louder with each step she took toward the white tent, with each trembling breath she dragged in. She clutched her fists at her sides, wishing her hands would stop shaking.

She didn't even know whose heart she was hearing. She rarely did. Each heart sounded slightly different, and this one had a quick double beat after every third pulse, so fast she would have missed it if it wasn't so loud in her ears.

Grinding her teeth, she concentrated once again on picturing herself slamming the door shut.

Be quiet!

"It's not as if I set myself on fire. And I really don't want to go to Scotland. I hear it's damp, and there's hardly any cities at all," Maddie was saying, and Emma realized she'd been talking this whole time. She hadn't heard a word. "Anyway, I just want to get this over with."

"Go ahead of me." The words seemed to burst out of her. For a moment Maddie only blinked at her, so Emma cleared her throat and continued. "If you want. Go ahead and you can get it over with."

She couldn't be tested right now, not when the Noise was like this. Maddie had to go first, to give her time to clear her head.

Thankfully, the other girl nodded. "Alright, if you're okay with it."

Maddie stepped hesitantly forward just as the flap was pushed aside and the nurse in the white coat poked her head out. Her hair was frazzled and her face flushed, but she still gave Emma a strained smile.

"Ready, Miss?"

Emma stiffened, but Maddie pushed forward before she could say anything. "She's agreed to let me go first."

The nurse nodded and waved her forward. Emma's shoulders slumped in relief as Maddie vanished into the tent without a backward glance.

She frowned, staying very still while she tried to force the Noise back. This time she shut her eyes and tried to picture the door as clearly as she possibly could—tall and thick, made of oak, locks all down the side. She pictured herself slamming it shut, hard, and sliding the locks into place with a *thud, thud, thud.*

Gradually the frantic thumping faded, and Emma let out a breath of relief.

She ought to thank Maddie for giving her the extra time. Maybe when she got out of the test she'd find the other girl in the crowd.

Curious, she edged forward, grasping the canvas tent flap and peeling it back an inch, revealing just a sliver of the space inside. If she concentrated, she could hear what was being said. One of the nurses had guided Maddie into a chair and was crouched in front of her, back facing Emma.

"Just a little pinch," she said, and Maddie stiffened, her eyes closed.

Emma chewed the inside of her cheek, suddenly nauseated.

The nurse turned, handing off the needle to a second nurse who was waiting at a long table in the far corner of the tent. Emma couldn't quite see what the second nurse was doing, but when she turned around she was holding a vial of murky liquid, which was rapidly turning a dark shade of purple.

What did that mean?

The nurse turned, holding up a piece of paper beside the vial. Emma could see it had swatches of various shades of purple on it. "Twenty percent," she said, surprise clear in her tone.

Emma's stomach dropped, but Maddie didn't move in the chair. Instead, she looked directly at the nurse with the vial and said in a loud, clear voice, "Five percent."

The nurse blinked at her. Emma expected the woman to call the soldiers in. But that's not what happened at all. The nurse just shook her head slowly and said, "Five . . . uh, five percent."

The nurse by the chair turned to her colleague, her face shocked. She started to say something, but Maddie tugged on her sleeve, and when the nurse turned back Maddie repeated firmly, "Five percent."

"Five percent," the second nurse murmured, her face slack. She shuffled to the back of the tent and pulled up the flap. "Off you go."

Emma watched, astonished, as Maddie got out of the chair and gave the nurse a cheeky wave before walking straight out. The nurse dropped the tent flap and turned back to the chair.

Maddie was gone.

And Maddie was a witch.

It took a moment to sink in. There had been no black eyes. No rotten teeth. No ghoulish, pale skin. Her hair hadn't even curled wildly about her face, like in the drawing of Lenore. Maddie had just looked like . . . a girl.

Emma didn't get much time to recover from the shock, because a moment later one of the nurses was walking straight toward her. Emma dropped the tent flap she'd been holding and stepped back, heart beating furiously against her rib cage.

By the time the nurse opened the tent flap, her face was composed again. She looked completely normal, and Emma realized she had absolutely no clue what had just happened. She might never realize she'd let Maddie walk straight out the back, even though she was unquestionably a witch.

For a split second, Emma wondered if she should tell her. Witches were dangerous. They enjoyed hurting people; they were toxic and evil.

But Maddie hadn't seemed evil, just nervous and a bit chatty.

"Come in," the nurse said. She gave Emma a reassuring smile, her blue eyes crinkling at the corners. "Nothing to worry about, just a little pinch and you're off to the races."

Emma found herself ushered straight into the tent before she could say anything.

The interior was very white and sterile looking. Someone had spread a large woven mat over the cobblestones, which muffled the sound of Emma's shoes as she moved farther inside. The space smelled of cleaning products, and there was a tiny hospital station set up on one side: two white cabinets and a long wooden table covered in glass vials and medical equipment, the sight of which sent a shudder of cold terror through her.

There was a pair of tall gas lamps set on poles on either side of the tent, with wide shades at the back—something Emma had never seen before. They cast light straight down into the middle of the space, toward a wooden chair and table in the center.

There a second nurse waited, a reassuring smile on her face as well.

Emma couldn't seem to take her eyes off the medical equipment, and as the nurse pressed one hand to the small of her back and ushered her forward, she felt a bit faint.

"You'll feel a little pinch." The nurse paused after this and squinted. Emma's stomach dropped.

Sure enough, a moment later the nurse's eyes went wide. "You're Lady Isolde's daughter, aren't you? I've seen you at court."

Emma nodded, and the nurse seemed to pick up on the fact that she had no desire to chat, because she smiled and patted her arm. "It's fast. Don't worry, dear. All ready?"

She wasn't, but she nodded again and clamped her lips shut tight, clenching her teeth as the nurse rolled back her sleeve. She shut her eyes and winced as she felt the cold pinch in her arm, staring determinedly at the table beside her, at the glass vials set on their metal stands, at the clear liquid glittering under the lamps.

"Just about done," the nurse said. "*There* we are."

Emma's eyes fluttered open. She watched as the nurse sunk the needle tip into a glass jar and transferred it over to her colleague. The second nurse tipped the slender jar over a wide-mouthed glass vial part-filled with water, which was set into a metal stand on the center of the table. A crimson drop of blood slipped below the surface of the water and spread out in a miniature cloud.

Next, the nurse swapped the glass tube of blood out for another, which was full of thick purple liquid, and repeated the process.

Thistle, Emma realized, as the nurse let a single thick drop of liquid out. In spite of the entire process being terrifying, it was all sorts of fascinating too. The books she'd read had talked about the discovery of thistle—the one thing that had turned the tides of war and returned the kingdom to the royals. Queen Alexandria had discovered that the plant weakened witches. But how exactly did they use it to detect your percentage?

The nurse took the vial and swirled it around until the water turned a light purple color. She then fitted the vial back onto the stand and turned a knob on the bottom. A flame flickered up at the base of the glass jar.

Emma's fingers curled tightly, nails biting into her palms as the liquid in the vial slowly changed. It went from light purple to violet rapidly, and then darkened slowly, a bit at a time.

The nurse's brows went up again, but this time her face was very pale, and she was silent as she reached into her pocket and held up the chart Emma had seen her use with Maddie. She rotated it, holding it up beside the jar, until the color on the paper matched the liquid in the glass vial almost exactly.

The nurses exchanged a frightened look, and the bottom dropped out of Emma's stomach as the one with the card turned back to her, eyes round.

"Oh dear. Forty percent."

Chapter Nine

Everything happened very quickly after that.

Emma was escorted out the back of the tent and into a waiting coach. It was a sleek black carriage with the royal emblem on the door—a flowering thistle winding up a tall oak staff. She took stock of this from far away, as if she were looking through her own eyes from a considerable distance. Someone else was walking forward, climbing the stairs of the carriage, sliding over the cushioned velvet seat.

She felt like someone had reached into her gut and hollowed her out.

The shock inside her echoed and rebounded back on itself, growing and expanding, until the only thing she felt was numb.

None of it seemed real.

The carriage door slammed shut behind her, making her start, and she found herself sitting across from none other than witch hunter and demoted captain Tobias McCraw himself. The sight of him seemed to jerk her momentarily back to reality.

Some of the shock dissolved as she edged back against the seat, eyes narrowed.

Neither of them said anything. Tobias McCraw turned to stare out the window, and Emma held her breath, hands gripping the seat very hard.

Again she was struck by how young he looked. Up close, she could see that his blue eyes were distant and a little glassy, almost haunted. And one was ringed with a faded bruise, as if someone had punched him in the eye.

He shifted on his seat, smoothing one hand over his chin, gaze flitting back to her as the carriage began to move. "I'll be your escort today, Ms. Black. I'm afraid I need to ask you a few questions."

She shifted her gaze quickly to the floor and nodded, trying to concentrate on breathing deeply and evenly. Some of the shock seemed to be settling in now: her ears were ringing, and she felt a little dizzy. She could feel sweat dampening the back of her dress.

"Have you had contact with any other witches?"

She looked up at him, startled. He was staring at her with narrow blue eyes.

"No. I don't know any. Why would I?" The dread curled and roiled in her stomach before settling like a brick, and she forced herself to meet his stare and hold it.

He frowned, clearing his throat. "Alright. What do you know about this so-called Witch City?"

Emma only blinked at him, mind racing. She wasn't sure what she'd expected him to ask, but it wasn't this. "I've heard it's not real. My tutor said it was all rumors. But then . . . maybe that's not true." She tilted her head, curiosity overcoming her fear for the moment. "Why else would you be asking?"

The witch hunter shifted on his seat. "I'll ask the questions, Miss."

But it appeared he was done, because through the window, she could see they were pulling into a station. As they began to slow, she caught a glimpse of a huge black train—the *Witch Express*—and just beyond it, tracks leading into a tunnel that disappeared under the ground. She looked away quickly, focusing instead on the plush carpet on the carriage floor, clutching herself with both arms to stop the trembling.

As they rolled to a stop, she looked up to see another black carriage leaving the station, curtains drawn. She caught a glimpse of the royal crest on the side.

Another witch for the train, no doubt.

McCraw sat still for a moment, eyes searching her face. It was as if he thought she'd been lying, that she *did* in fact know something about Witch City that she wasn't telling him. His jaw twitched slightly, and for a moment Emma thought she saw a flicker of emotion there. Frustration, maybe. It was gone as fast as it had come though, and he sighed and slid sideways on the seat, clumping heavily down the carriage steps to hold the door open for her. Emma was startled when he offered her his hand, and after a moment of hesitation she took it, allowing him to help her down the steps.

"Just this way, my lady."

Ah yes. *That* was why he was being so polite. She might be an accused witch, but she was still a royal, at least for now . . .

Emma tried not to look too hard at the train as they approached the tracks, feeling her stomach swoop wildly. She didn't want to see the heavy iron plates on the sides, or the thick bars on the windows.

But the *Witch Express* was hard to miss. The giant black steam engine sat alongside the platform, its engine rumbling and ticking, steam hissing from underneath. It seemed to crouch on the tracks, and the heavy *chug, chug, chug* of the engine reminded her of a pulse—the heart of some huge, ancient monster.

It filled her with the same dread the Noise did.

For one wild moment, she pictured running. Her chest swelled with the thought, sending a buzz of hot adrenaline through her body.

She could see herself turning around, making a desperate dash toward the edge of the platform.

And then what? Jump aboard the carriage and push the driver off? Run away into the city?

Before she could move, McCraw stepped forward, rapping sharply on the narrow door of the first compartment, which creaked open a moment later. He moved back and nodded to her, face solemn, and Emma just stared at him, frozen.

He was taller than she was, if it came down to speed. He also had a very heavy-looking staff she'd rather not get on the wrong end of.

After a deep breath, she straightened her shoulders and stepped onto the stairs, moving through the doorway into the *Witch Express*.

Inside the train, the carriage stretched out in a double row of wooden benches. The thin red carpet muffled the sound of her boots as she stepped forward. She tilted her head back to look at the luggage racks above the seats. The carriage ended in a red-paneled door, presumably leading into another compartment.

The door she'd walked through slammed shut behind her, and she jumped. There was the metallic rasp of a bolt sliding home, and Emma turned, noticing that even the narrow window in the door had a thick iron bar across it. She turned away, her mouth dry.

The other trains she'd been on had always been lavish. As royals, she and her mother had traveled first class. There'd been dining cars with fine china and crystal, and carriages with plush couches and ornate rugs.

But this was a prison on wheels.

Emma glanced around, dread sinking into her belly. There would be no way to get out. She was sure of that.

She wandered farther down the aisle. The carriage was dim and empty, but still . . . she felt the back of her neck prickle and then caught the reflection of a pair of burning eyes in the window before her.

Emma whirled around, heart in her throat.

It was nothing—just a scrap of paper attached to the carriage wall behind her. It looked like it had once been a poster of Queen Alexandria, but someone had torn both the top and bottom off so that only a sliver of the queen's face was left—her dark eyes and arched black brows. Emma froze, staring at the torn poster. It wasn't just the glimpse of the queen's eyes, dark and watchful, peering out of the wall at her, it was the fact that someone on this train had dared to rip down a poster.

She turned for the nearest wooden seat, palms sweating. She was about to attempt to squish herself into the corner as far as she could go, perhaps even hide underneath the bench, when she spotted the letter. It was posted beside the door she'd just come through. The stationery was cream-colored and very thick, and the royal seal was visible on the bottom. It was handwritten in tight cursive letters, and Emma took a step forward, squinting at it.

Welcome to the W *Express.*

If you are here, you have failed your Test. Remain calm. You will be taken to your new home in the countryside of Scotland. Please note: If you have any information on the location of the rumored "Witch City," please report this to the conductor. Reports yielding results will be handsomely rewarded.

Signed by Her Royal Highness, in the year of our Lord 1822
—Queen Alexandria

Underneath was a swooping black signature, and Emma stared at it with growing suspicion. If none of the rumors about Witch City were true, then why was the queen hanging signs inquiring after it? Why had McCraw been asking her questions about it?

The steady *chug, chug, chug* of the train's engine filled the compartment. For a moment, Emma lost herself in its rhythm—until the door between the compartments slid open with a loud *thwack*, startling her out of her thoughts.

There was a familiar figure in the doorway. He stood with both hands clutching the sides of the frame, his face slightly green. His silk shirt was unbuttoned at the top and his black hair stood on end, as if he'd been running his fingers through it. There was a smudge of ink on his nose and he was clutching a worn leather book.

His eyes were wild as he stared at Emma.

"You," he said.

She blinked at Edgar, and then finally managed to stammer out, "Y-*you're* a witch?"

His expression went dark. "*You're* a witch."

She gaped at him, trying to wrap her mind around this new development. Her cousin—His Royal Highness, Crown Prince of England, Earl of Chesterton, Duke of Cornwall, and Baron of Renfrew—was a *witch*.

Edgar drew himself up, glaring at her imperiously. "This is all your fault."

Anger flooded through her almost immediately. She took a step toward him, fists clenched. "*Excuse* me?"

Edgar didn't flinch, just puffed his chest out, his face growing red. "You did something to me in court. I felt it."

The Noise. Some of Emma's anger drained away—just a little bit. Because in a way he was right. She *had* done something to him, though she wasn't sure what.

Still, his accusation was ridiculous. "I didn't *make* you a witch, idiot. How would I even do that?"

Prince Edgar drew himself up even further. He looked as if he might be about to burst; his face had reached an alarmingly dark shade of cherry. "I don't know! You're a witch, aren't you?

You did something that made The Test say I was magic!" He threw his shoulders back, thrusting out his chest another inch. "Y-you hexed me or something!"

Emma could feel the anger burning in her stomach now. *Hexed him.* It was their childhood run-in all over again. He was going to accuse her of cursing him not once but twice.

"You are *unbelievable*. You're just as fanatical as your mother." It sort of burst out, and Emma clapped a hand to her mouth, darting a nervous look around the carriage. What on earth had possessed her to say that?

Edgar looked furious. "I am not!" he shouted. He too seemed to realize what he'd said, because he went silent, lips pinched together, and tilted his head back as if someone might be sitting on the roof listening to them.

Several seconds went by. Nothing happened.

Some of the color began to return to Edgar's face, and he darted another look around before stepping closer and hissing at Emma. "I *order* you to take your hex back!"

She stared at him in disbelief.

He really did think she'd cast a spell on him. In spite of the fact that he'd tested positive, he was going to blame her for it.

She narrowed her eyes at him. "I didn't do anything to you. We have witchcraft in our blood. Don't you know about Lenore?"

When Edgar only stared at her blankly, she rolled her eyes. She shouldn't have expected him to know about anything like that. He was always floating around like he was sleepwalking, or writing furiously in his little book.

"Take it back," he repeated. He took another step toward her, dark brows drawn down, and his tone only seemed to get more demanding. It irked her, and if she could have genuinely cast a hex on him in that moment, she absolutely would have.

"No."

Prince Edgar sputtered. "How dare you! Do you have any idea what my mother—"

"Oh, *move*, will you?"

The voice, very high and annoyed sounding, came from behind Edgar, who whirled around and stumbled backward, falling over onto one of the benches.

There was a girl standing in the doorway where he'd been a moment ago, looking back over her shoulder as she said, "There's two more."

When she turned and spotted Emma she paused, eyeing her warily. "Did you really put a hex on him?"

Emma stared at her, mouth wide open as she took in the girl's black curls, her soot-stained face, and the blackened bottom of her dress.

It was her—the witch who'd been on fire.

Chapter Ten

Emma and Edgar both took a step back, and Emma eyed the girl's burnt dress nervously, wondering if she was likely to burst into flames a second time.

There was a beat of silence in the carriage, filled only with the rumble and chug of the train's engine, and then Emma said, just loudly enough to be heard over the noise, "No."

Edgar gripped the back of the seat beside him. "You can't—I mean, they've put you on the wrong train! You can't be here. This is for nobles only!" He faltered when the girl looked over at him, her expression cool.

Up close the girl was very tall and skinny, with dark skin and tight curls that framed her face. Her clothing seemed to fit her rather awkwardly. Her sleeves stopped several inches above her skinny wrists, and the fabric of her dress bagged out around her waist.

"You're the prince," she said, and her voice was unmistakably accusatory. "I recognize you from the papers." She folded her arms in front of her chest. "Go on then, what were you saying? You were going to call your mother on us? Tell her we're witches?"

Edgar, who was at least smart enough not to answer, had edged behind one of the wooden benches. He continued to stare at the girl with wide eyes.

"Cat's out of the bag on that one, don't you think, Your Highness?"

When Edgar didn't answer, the girl turned to look at Emma, gaze dropping down to her clothing, brows raised.

Emma felt herself blushing and she glanced down at her black-and-purple lace dress. She did look very obviously royal, didn't she? Even down to the colors.

A second girl appeared behind the first, moving down the length of the carriage, a little unsteady on her feet as the train surged forward.

As the girl got closer, Emma's mouth dropped open. It was Maddie.

Her butterscotch curls were very messy, and she looked pale, her freckles standing out in sharp contrast.

"How are you here? I saw you get away."

Maddie rolled her eyes. "One of the soldiers stopped me to ask my percentage and lying didn't work. It only does about half the time."

"You just need training." The curly-haired girl shrugged when they all gaped at her. "What? It's true. I'm Eliza, by the way."

"Emma. And this is my cousin . . . uh, Edgar." She stopped herself from launching into his titles. She'd been about to go into a full introduction—the proper court etiquette her tutor had taught her. She could only imagine the other girls' reactions.

Emma bit her lip, forcing herself not to stare at them or back up into the corner like Edgar was doing. Everything she'd learned about witches was screaming at her to get as far away from them as possible. She could suddenly remember everything she'd ever read, all the ways they could torture you, all the horrible things they'd done to the people of London.

She stayed where she was though, because yes, these girls were witches, but so was she.

Edgar hissed at her from where he'd crammed himself into the farthest seat against the wall. He was holding the leather book in front of him, like it was going to ward the girls off somehow.

"Emma, get away from them!"

Eliza ignored him. "We're not going to Scotland, you know. The queen's a liar."

Emma's heart seemed to momentarily freeze in her chest, and behind her, she heard Edgar gasp. But Eliza only stood there, arms crossed over her chest, frowning around at all of them.

It was as if she didn't even realize what she'd said.

"You can't . . ." Edgar gasped out. He was now slumped over, leaning against the bench in front of him. He looked completely overcome. "You can't say things like that. She knows. She *always* knows."

"And what's she going to do about it?" Eliza asked. "Accuse me of witchcraft?"

Emma opened her mouth and then shut it again. Eliza was right. They were already in the worst possible predicament. It really didn't matter what they said. In fact, if she wanted to, she could probably jump up on one of the benches and scream to the world that Queen Alexandria was ugly and wore funny dresses, and nothing would happen to her.

Even the thought was enough to break her out in a cold sweat.

"You can't just say we're not going to Scotland," Edgar said. For a moment some of the haughtiness came back into his voice, and he straightened his shoulders, glowering at Eliza. "Everyone knows that's where witches go."

"It's not true," Eliza shot back. "Like I said, your mother is a liar, along with a bloodthirsty monster. The entire Black family is."

"Excuse me?" Edgar shot up off the seat. "I ought to have you arrested!"

He turned to Emma, as if expecting her to back him up, but Emma only flapped a hand at him. Excitement made it hard to get the words out. "What do you know about the Black family? Tell us everything."

Eliza frowned. "You've all been fed the same rubbish in your history lessons. You should know by now. She's called the Thistle Queen for a reason. Before she used thistle to test us, she used it to hang us. They'd make ropes out of it because it drains our power."

Emma frowned at her, exasperated. "Everyone knows that bit. She discovered thistle would stop them. She killed the witches and took back the country."

Saying it now, she found that the words rang a little hollow, like something she'd recited too many times. The cut-out parts of the history books kept swimming up in the back of her mind.

Maddie was nodding. "The Queen hanged the bad witches, but we're not bad."

Eliza made a rude noise. "Brainwashed, the lot of you. But we know better. We always have. And you'd better get used to it. She wants you dead now too." She glanced over at Edgar, her face hard. "Even you."

This seemed like a terribly dangerous conversation to be having, and Emma narrowed her eyes, darting a glance around the cabin. "How do you know all of this?"

Eliza shook her head, her expression scornful. "She's fooled so many of you."

Things were finally clicking into place. The other girl's confidence about the subject, the way she used "you" and "we" to set them apart. *We know better.* Her charred skirts, the soot on her face.

The cottage they'd driven past on the way to the square. The queen's complaint about only catching one . . .

Emma took a step backward, eyeing Eliza nervously. "Those witches they couldn't catch. You're one of them, aren't you?"

Eliza was quiet for a moment. Then, slowly, she nodded.

Emma sucked in a sharp breath, and beside her, Edgar paled slightly and leaned back in his seat. Maddie, by contrast, brightened considerably.

"Brilliant! I've always wanted to meet a real live witch."

Eliza rolled her eyes. "You *are* one."

"Oh yes. I'd forgotten."

"Y-you're part of a coven. You're one of the rebel witches." Edgar looked as though he were about to crawl under the seat, but Eliza was shaking her head.

"Of course not, idiot. There are none left anymore. None of the witches would take them in while they were being hunted, not after what they did." When Edgar gave her a sideways look, she folded her arms over her chest and rolled her eyes at him. "They were a fringe group. Fanatics. Most witches wanted nothing to do with them and their horrible policies."

There was a moment of silence, and then Emma worked up the courage to ask, "What happened? Why didn't you go with your coven when they escaped?"

Emma knew she shouldn't be talking to her. If she were smart, she'd run to the other side of the train and stay there. Eliza was a witch, and witches were bad. They had magic; they'd nearly destroyed London.

But again, she reminded herself . . . she, Emma, was technically a witch too.

"I was supposed to." Eliza hesitated. "But one of my coven was meant to stay and keep them in the house. Our leader, my gran. She's got the gift of visions."

When they stared at her blankly, Eliza explained: "She can make you see anything she wants. She made the witch hunters go inside the house and meant to keep them there. But they'd called the soldiers too. They were on their way." She bit her lip. "I told her to go, that I'd set the cottage on fire and trap them, and I'd catch up with them."

"But you didn't," Emma said softly. Again, the puzzle pieces were falling into place. The queen's words rang in her head: *It's a miracle you didn't burn.*

"They didn't burn because you didn't let them, did you?"

Eliza sat down heavily on a bench and sighed. "It was stupid. The witch hunters would hang me as soon as look at me. But yes, I couldn't let them burn. I stayed to keep the fire away until the soldiers got the captain out. Then I ran." There was bitterness in her voice as she added, "But not fast enough."

Emma frowned at her, puzzled. This didn't track with what she knew about witches. From the stories in the history books, witches seemed to enjoy burning people, or making them drown in their own saliva, or tricking them into believing there were bugs all over their skin until they went insane. Witches didn't s*ave* people. None of this made sense.

It was Edgar who broke the silence. "H-how do you know we're not going to Scotland? Have you been there?" He sprang up suddenly, startling them, and began to pace the aisle. "That can't be right. *Everyone* knows that witches are sent—"

"It's a lie." Eliza stuck an arm into his path, blocking him from storming past. "Think about it, Your Highness." She practically spat his title at him, and Edgar flinched. "Why would Scotland allow that? Where would all these witches go, and why isn't Scotland overflowing with them?"

Emma had never thought about that part. In fact, she'd never questioned any of it, but the more she thought about it now the less sense it all made. Perhaps nobody questioned it because nobody truly wanted to know the answers.

A week ago she would have brushed this all off, but something was different now. She kept remembering Lenore's face on the poster. She kept seeing the edges of the cut-out pages in the spines of the history books.

She'd been lied to. Maybe they all had.

"They keep it quiet, that's all," Edgar protested. "Would *you* want to admit you were stuffed full of witches if you were Scotland?"

Eliza scowled. "You need to *wake up* and realize everything she tells you is a lie. We need to get off this train *now*. Or we'll end up hanging."

"She wouldn't do that." Edgar was nearly shouting now, fists clenched at his sides, his face red. "She wouldn't do that to us . . . t-to me. She couldn't. She's my *mother*."

There was a beat of silence and, to Emma's surprise, Eliza's expression softened. She looked like she was about to say something when she was interrupted by a very loud, ear-piercing whistle from somewhere overhead. All four of them jumped, and Emma felt the carriage lurch. She grabbed at the seat nearest to her.

She glanced up, startled, as a soft glow came from overhead. There were iron lanterns along the roof, and they flared to life as the train began to glide forward. Emma turned back to the window, and her stomach plummeted as the scenery was abruptly cut off, plunging the cabin into a dimness punctuated only by the flickering orange light from overhead.

"We're in the tunnel!" Edgar shouted over the noise. Emma thought that was rather obvious, but before she could say as much, a metallic *clunk* sounded overhead.

She looked up just in time to see the compartments over the baggage racks spring open, their hatches dropping down. There was a cacophony of hissing from overhead, and a fine powder of green dust began to rain down on them.

Eliza gave a shout of dismay and brought the tattered sleeve of her dress up to her mouth, her voice muffled as she shouted, "It's thistle. Whatever you do, don't breathe it in!"

Chapter Eleven

It was too late. In her shock, Emma had already taken a deep breath, and now she felt something acidic sticking to the back of her throat. She gagged and coughed, eyes watering.

Instantly, the dim insides of the carriage seemed to blur, and she felt dizzy and sick. Beside her, Maddie let out a string of muffled curses, pulling the collar of her dress up over her mouth and nose.

The powdered thistle continued to shower down, and Emma felt a jolt of horror as she realized it was coating her skin and hair. If it drained her just by being around the palace, what would it do inside her lungs?

Eliza and Maddie were both sheltering their faces with sleeves and collars, and Edgar had retreated hastily between two benches, pulling his jacket up over his face.

At last the hissing cut off, and the compartments overhead snapped closed with a self-satisfied *thwap*.

There was only the rumble and chug of the train now, and Emma stumbled forward, muscles feeling strangely heavy, and leaned against the nearest bench.

The carriage seemed to be wavering around her, dissolving into blurred lines and then reforming. This was far worse than usual.

She gasped and coughed again, pressing her sleeve more firmly over her face. "What do we do?"

Eliza was already moving, staggering toward the window with her face pressed into the crook of her elbow. She reached her other hand through the bars and placed it on the glass, expression tight with concentration.

It looked for a moment as if Eliza's fingertips glowed orange in the darkness, though Emma couldn't be sure with the way her vision was blurring.

There was a sharp *crack* as the glass shattered, shards bursting outward.

Cold air rushed in through the window.

Emma's eyes were still watering, but the sensation of choking seemed to ease, and she was able to stand up straight, as if heavy weights had been stripped from her arms and legs. It felt like walking into the East Wing, times one hundred.

"That was meant to knock us out, so we can't fight when they lead us to the gallows."

Eliza whirled around and ripped the letter off the wall. She held it up, gripping it so tightly that it crumpled around the edges. She looked at Emma over the top of her sleeve, eyes glittering. "We need to get off this train and get to Witch City."

Maddie scoffed, though the noise was muffled by the collar of her dress. "Witch City is hidden. No one knows where it is."

"My coven is headed there. If we can get away, we can find it," Eliza said.

Emma nodded slowly.

Eliza was right. Whatever else they did, they needed to get off this train immediately. If the lies about Lenore hadn't convinced her, the thistle dust had.

Wherever they were going, it wasn't Scotland.

She tried to imagine the rumors of their escape circulating through the palace. Three royal witches and a coven member breaking out of the *Witch Express*. The scandal would be endless, which meant her mother would be utterly furious.

If Emma had lived by any kind of code in all her thirteen years of life, it was that if something made her mother furious, it was probably the best route.

"Let's do it." Her voice felt faint and weak, but she tried to put as much enthusiasm into it as she could muster.

She glanced over at Edgar, half expecting him to protest, but he was quiet, his shirt sleeve still pressed over his mouth.

It was Maddie who spoke next. "Well, hold on. Even if we tried to escape, the door is bolted." She waved toward the end of the carriage. "Besides, there's a conductor. Don't you think he'd notice us trying to jump off?"

"I can try to burn through the lock. Melt it off," Eliza offered.

Emma blinked at her, remembering the way she'd broken the window. She'd seen Eliza's hands grow hot enough to shatter glass. "Can you just . . . turn it on and off like that?"

Eliza looked startled. "Well, yes. Most witches can."

Now Edgar sat up straight, lowering his sleeve, an expression of horror on his face. "You can't just *use* it whenever you want. It's *magic*."

"Of course it's magic! My coven is teaching me how to use it." Eliza's face went dark. "Or they *were*."

Emma glanced over her shoulder at the shattered window. It was still only darkness outside.

"We're in a tunnel. If we jumped out, we'd be killed."

"Exactly what they're counting on, I'm sure," Eliza said. "What is it you do?"

When Emma only stared at her, she snorted. "You know, what landed you here? What does your power do?"

"Uh, nothing helpful." Emma felt her cheeks grow hot as Eliza stared at her. "I . . . hear people. Their heartbeats." It was the first time she'd ever said it out loud, and it sent a pang of nausea through her.

Eliza huffed and turned back to the door. "Bloody fantastic."

"It isn't as if I picked it out. I'd get rid of it if I could." When she glanced at Edgar, he was staring at her over the top of his collar, eyes narrow, and she turned away quickly.

Obviously, he knew her power was more than just *hearing* heartbeats. She braced herself, waiting for him to accuse her, but to her surprise he said nothing. He just stared silently out the window.

Eliza turned to face Edgar. "What about you, Your Highness? Do you do anything helpful?"

Edgar muttered something at the windowpane. Emma couldn't be sure, but it sounded like "not a witch."

Eliza laughed bitterly. "You're a bad liar, Your Highness." She threw up her hands and turned back to the others. "None of this is any good."

The steady chug of the train fell into the silence between them, and Eliza paced to the other end of the carriage, pausing in front of the door and frowning at it as if she could knock it down with the force of her scowl. Maddie followed, and Emma trailed behind her.

"We could blow it up," Maddie offered. "You know, set the boiler on fire or something."

Edgar looked dismayed, but before he could protest, Eliza said, "That won't work. My gran said it's fire-less. Specially to transport explosive goods. Like chemicals."

"Or witches," Emma said sourly.

"Alright," Maddie said slowly. "What if we *stop* the train?" Maddie's voice was hushed, and she darted a look at the door.

"How would we stop the train?" Eliza kept her voice low. "Explain."

Maddie hesitated. "Maybe you can . . . I dunno, mess up the engine somehow. Make it quit so we just coast to a stop. Then you can burn the door and we'll get out."

"That's . . . actually a good idea." Eliza sounded so surprised that Emma thought she would have been rather insulted, but Maddie just grinned.

Eliza turned to the door, pressing a hand to the knob, her face grim. "This could take a while, and you may want to stand back."

"Wait, hold on." Maddie ducked down, fishing around in her boot. "I know I've got one somewhere. Here." She straightened up, triumphant, a thin silver wire in her hand.

"You keep lock-picking things in your stockings?" Emma raised a brow at her, and Maddie smiled.

"It's a hatpin. I filed it down a bit so it wouldn't skewer me in the foot, but I always keep one on hand." She faltered a little at this, her smile fading. "Uh, anyway, let me see the lock."

Emma watched as Maddie crouched by the door and slid the thin silver pin into the lock. She wiggled it back and forth for a long minute, tongue poking out between her teeth.

Emma kept an eye on the crack in the door, heart beating hard in her throat, half expecting the conductor to hear them and come bursting through. But there was nothing; probably the train was too noisy for him to hear anything.

At last, something must have clicked, because Maddie straightened up, beaming at them. "Got it."

Emma grinned. Funny how the train was packed with thistle in case they tried to use their powers, but apparently not one of the adults had considered what a single hatpin could do . . .

Now that the door was unlocked, Edgar rose from his seat, alarmed. "What on earth are you doing? Shut that immediately—"

"Here, let me go in first." Eliza crept forward, pushing the door open an inch at a time.

In the faint orange light from the lanterns, Emma caught a glimpse of the compartment beyond. There was a wall of machinery at the front, brass tubes and pulleys and pipes emitting strange clanking sounds. Perched on a wooden chair overseeing it all was the conductor, his hat pulled low over his eyes.

Thankfully, the engine was so noisy that they didn't have to worry about him hearing them.

Eliza leaned back to whisper in Emma's ear. "If I can burn some pieces of the engine it might stop working, but he's going to know what's going on pretty quickly."

Emma nodded, taking a deep breath. "Do it."

Maddie and Eliza exchanged a look, and Maddie's eyes were round in her pale face. Emma was fairly sure she was thinking about the first time they'd seen Eliza, flames flickering up her arms. Behind her, Edgar kept moving, shifting from foot to foot and wringing his hands, whispering anxiously that this was a terrible idea, and that his mother was going to be furious.

He didn't cease this until Emma turned and hissed at him to shut up.

It took an agonizingly long time. They watched Eliza focus on the palm of one hand, eyes narrowed in concentration. Finally, something began to happen: a spark at first, and then a flicker of flame at the tips of her fingers. Eliza grinned.

At the start, there were several uncertain moments when the flame looked like it was going to flicker out, and Eliza glared down at it, mumbling angrily under her breath, brows knit together. Then, without warning, the fire flared. Eliza yelped and pulled back, bumping into Emma's left shoulder. The train lurched just then, and Emma gasped as her boots slid on the floorboards and she pitched over sideways, her shoulder crashing into the chair across the aisle. Eliza gave a shout, which was followed by a shriek from Maddie. Emma scrambled up in time to see a huge orange fireball burst through the compartment, bathing the cabin in stark, blazing light and enveloping the startled conductor.

A great deal of noise and chaos followed.

The conductor gave a series of high, panicked screeches as he stumbled forward, beating at his coveralls. This was punctuated by Edgar wailing at Eliza, "He's on fire!"

Emma was forced to jump back as the conductor charged toward them, crashing into Eliza, who fell over onto Maddie and Edgar. The conductor plowed past into the adjoining carriage, howling and beating at his jacket, before running straight into the door at the other end with a resounding thud.

Emma watched in shock as he fell, landing flat on his back in the middle of the aisle with all the grace of a felled tree. The flames on his coveralls were extinguished as soon as he hit the ground, eyes rolling into the back of his head.

There was a stretch of heavy silence, during which Eliza let out a shaky breath and said, "I think he's knocked himself out," and Emma, staring at the unconscious form of the conductor, realized that although the driver was no longer with them, the train was still moving.

They were all in a great deal of trouble.

Edgar seemed to be thinking the same thing, because his face drained of color. "Don't . . . don't we need him?"

"Where's the brake on this thing?" Eliza leapt forward, casting a frantic look over the machinery, and Maddie and Emma joined her, spreading out to look around the cabin. There was the conductor's chair in front of the valves and gears, and the front of the train seemed to be completely covered in metal tubes.

A pang of fear went through her. It was no good; she couldn't tell what any of it did. How were they supposed to pull the brakes if they couldn't find them?

"I can't tell what's what." Eliza's hands were in her hair, her eyes wild. Emma herself could feel sweat collecting under the collar of her lacy dress.

"It's got to be somewhere near his chair, doesn't it?" She kept looking. There were a number of knobs with red tops, and a large gauge with a ticking needle in the center, and metal tubing that snaked up the side of the cabin. None of it looked like a brake.

There had to be some kind of pulley or lever, a long metal stick jutting from the floor. Something you could yank on.

There was nothing.

"This was a terrible plan." Edgar was yelling over the sound of the engine, his face furious. "You've completely botched this up, I can't believe—"

"You shut up," Eliza snapped back at him. "If your horrible mother hadn't—"

"Hush, both of you!" Emma yelled over them. "Keep looking for the brake."

"I have no idea what it looks like." Eliza's voice was strained as she leaned over the chair, searching all around it. "This is bad!"

"I think it just got worse."

They turned to look at Maddie, who was peering out the window. "Look."

Outside the window the quality of darkness had changed. The tunnel seemed wider now, and streetlamps went by rapidly, sending patterns of light and darkness flashing through the train.

The thing Maddie was referring to was clearly visible through the front window, where, just ahead, the track curled up and up and then ended in a solid brick wall with a large black-and-white sign lit up in the darkness.

END OF TRACK.

Chapter Twelve

There was little time to brace themselves.

Emma yanked Eliza back and out of the engine carriage, screaming at her to run, and they bolted down the aisle and over the prone form of the conductor.

Edgar was attempting to wedge himself under one of the benches, and Emma followed suit, grabbing Maddie and Eliza and pulling them under the nearest bench. She wrapped her arm tightly around the iron leg closest to her.

"Hang on!"

It started with an earth-shattering impact, a crash that reverberated and multiplied, repeating until it reminded Emma of a chaotic heartbeat. The floor beneath her shook so hard she felt her bones might rattle out of her skin, and she bit her tongue hard. She clung to Eliza and Maddie as the world crumpled and twisted, the sound of shrieking, grating iron all around them.

Something slammed into her left shoulder and hip. The pain was sudden and shocking, but she was too intent on holding tightly to Maddie and Eliza to really notice. Somehow, they had to stay together.

Another impact followed, lurching them forward and then back again, slamming her shoulder and sending a second shockwave of pain through her body. She screamed, and the floor trembled beneath her.

And then . . . there was silence, and stillness, and only the quiet, troubling sound of something hissing off to their right.

Slowly, she opened her eyes.

At first, she thought it was strangely dim. In her confusion she wondered if the sun had set. And then her eyes adjusted, and she realized that the reason it was dark was because the lanterns had gone out and the light filtering in from the window above was thick with the remaining thistle dust.

Feeling sick, she threw her arm over her mouth and nose and then frowned, blinking upward.

Wait, *the window above*? She looked blearily at the ceiling, and then realized with a stab of alarm that they appeared to have *flipped over*. The windows were above her, sending a stream of faint yellow light into the carriage, shadowed by the iron bars.

She felt someone shift beside her then, and realized something was gripping her arm very tightly.

"Emma? Are you okay?" a voice said. Emma blinked hard in the dim light, barely able to make out Eliza's face.

"I'm fine." Her voice was shaky. "You?"

"Fine." Eliza shifted, and then froze when the floor beneath them creaked. "Where are the others?"

There was a low groan, and then Edgar's voice came from somewhere off to the left. "I'm here. I think I'm bleeding." A horrified gasp followed this, and he said, "Blast! I've lost my book."

"Ouch," said a voice from the dark patch over Emma's left shoulder. She felt a flood of relief, hearing Maddie. "That hurt."

Slowly, Emma raised herself up to her hands and knees. There was a clatter and thump of something falling overhead, and she froze as the train let out a shuddering creak.

"Hold on," Eliza whispered. There was a small flicker of light coming from the same direction as her voice. All at once, the crumpled train car was bathed in the orange glow of a tiny flame in the palm of Eliza's hand.

Emma gaped around at the wreckage. The back of the carriage they were in had somehow survived almost unscathed on one side. The other sides, though, had been crushed. The compartments overhead had separated from the wall and were dangling down into the carriage. The front was even worse. It was almost entirely crumpled in on itself. Emma couldn't even tell where the engine had been; only fragments of the pipes and controls were left, glittering darkly under the flickering light.

Eliza's face was tight with fear, her eyes wide and white in the darkness. A little behind her, Edgar was also on his hands and knees. He was squinting against the light, his face pale and shell-shocked. His black curls were flat on one side, and there was a streak of blood on one temple.

A little off to the left, Maddie was sitting up straight, peering around at them. Her butterscotch curls had turned into tangles. She'd ripped the front of her dress, and she had a nasty-looking scratch on one cheek. "What now?"

Emma winced, glancing around the train car. Most of the wooden benches had been smashed to bits, and they were now on the wall to her left, instead of on the floor where they were supposed to be.

"We've flipped." Saying it out loud made it seem real, even though her ears were still ringing and everything seemed a bit distant.

As if in response, another loud creaking sound came from somewhere overhead, and the floor beneath them trembled.

Emma felt the palms of her hands begin to sweat, and her chest slowly constricted as panic crept in. If the train collapsed on them, they might all end up buried.

Eliza must have been thinking the same thing; her fire flickered and then jumped in her palm, suddenly shooting almost to the roof. She hissed in alarm and clapped her other hand over top, nearly extinguishing the flame and allowing the darkness to rush back in.

"Careful," Emma whispered, thinking that the engine might be rather combustible at this point.

"Sorry." Eliza's voice was shaky, her dark brows knitted together. "It gets all . . . jumpy when I get nervous."

Emma knew all about that.

As if on cue, or perhaps because she was now thinking of it, she suddenly became aware of a faint whooshing sound—the steady rush of blood pumping. She tried to wrestle the panicked thoughts down, to tell herself to take deep, even breaths.

There came a rattling *thud* from the side of the train car, and the floor beneath them vibrated. Emma sat back into a crouch, nearly hitting her head on one of the shattered benches beside her.

"It's shifting." Eliza thrust her little flame up toward the roof. "Come on, we've got to find a way off this thing."

"How do we get out?" Emma asked.

Together, the four of them turned toward the door—or at least to the spot where the door should have been.

"This means the door is . . ." Edgar let his words trail off as he tipped his head back to stare at the ceiling.

Eliza and Emma exchanged a look, and Maddie's face went paler still. Slowly, all three girls looked up.

There was the door, cracked open and showing the barest sliver of daylight, on what was now the roof.

Chapter Thirteen

"Well," Maddie said weakly, "at least it's open."

"You have *got* to be kidding me," Eliza said.

A loud thump sounded from somewhere above, and Emma stiffened. It was different from the train settling—more like something heavy had dropped onto the roof.

"Eliza, can you light up the door? We have to see if we can get it further open before we try to get up there."

Eliza answered by lifting her hand. The flame on her palm flared brighter suddenly, jumping higher, and she flinched but held steady. Emma was willing to bet she was thinking about accidentally setting the conductor on fire. They couldn't afford to blow anything else up.

"There's just enough space," Edgar said, sounding relieved. "I can fit through that, no problem."

"Little problem, actually." Maddie had her head tilted back, staring up at the roof. "How are we meant to get up there?"

Knowing they didn't have long, Emma looked around frantically. Most of the benches near the door were ruined, but the one that had been directly in front of it was still mostly intact.

"If I stand on the bench, I should be able to give you a boost up to the door," Eliza offered.

Emma jerked upright as another thump rattled the length of the train. Whatever that was, it couldn't be good.

"Let's try this." Eliza was the first one to climb onto the bench. "I'm the tallest; I'll boost you up. Maddie, you first, you've got to be the lightest out of us."

Emma frowned. Eliza was already so precariously balanced on the half-shattered bench that it was hard to imagine her boosting anyone, but there also didn't seem to be any other way. She wrapped her hands around Eliza's ankles, steadying her. Eliza laced her fingers together and nodded at Maddie, who took a breath and placed her foot into Eliza's hands.

"Try to be quiet once you're out," Eliza hissed at her. In spite of the annoyed look Maddie shot back at Eliza, Emma couldn't help but agree.

Someone had to be looking for them by now, maybe even digging through the wreckage for their bodies.

Maddie pushed the splintered door open just enough to fit her upper body through, and Emma watched, wide-eyed, as she inched her way out. Finally, her feet disappeared, and the door shut behind her with a gentle thump.

For several long seconds nothing happened, and Emma had the terrible thought that Maddie had jumped off and run, leaving them behind. Edgar seemed to be thinking the same thing, because he shifted and muttered, "Where is she?" A second later, though, the door swung slowly open with a ponderous shriek of metal on metal, and they all squinted, shielding their eyes as yellow light flooded the carriage.

Maddie stared down at them, face pale, hair tangled and disheveled, and Emma felt a surge of relief—along with a healthy dose of guilt for ever doubting her.

"Half the tunnel's collapsed on the back of the train," Maddie whispered. "Hurry and come up."

Eliza spun around, locking her fingers together. She lifted Edgar next, who seemed to have recovered his book from the floor, and insisted on stuffing it inside his jacket before climbing up. Maddie reached down and caught his wrists, hauling him onto the roof, and then it was Emma's turn.

When Emma hesitated, Eliza whispered fiercely, "Get on with it. You'll pull me up once you're on the roof."

Emma obeyed, placing her foot carefully in the cradle of Eliza's hands, gasping as the other girl lifted her upward. She wobbled slightly, and then Maddie and Edgar leaned in through the open door and grabbed her arms.

Emma tried not to make any sound as they hauled her up through the door, though her arms were scraped terribly on the frame and her stomach definitely felt bruised.

At last she found herself on the roof of the carriage—or what was once the side, she supposed—on her hands and knees, relieved to find everything much brighter outside. She rose to a crouch, and immediately she could feel the difference getting out of the train made. She dragged in a deep, revitalizing breath, blinking at her surroundings and feeling a little as though she'd just woken up.

While most of the thistle dust had blown out when Eliza broke the window, it had obviously still been affecting her.

Maddie grasped her arm to steady her, pressing a finger to her lips. Edgar was very still where he stood, looking wide-eyed at their surroundings.

Emma glanced around. They were in a set of large, cavernous rooms—an underground station made of stone, with vaulted ceilings hundreds of feet above them. Everything was lit by gas lanterns in ugly iron brackets along the walls.

So this was where the tunnel led.

"Look at this," Maddie breathed. "We've got to get her out before any more of it collapses."

Maddie was right. The tunnel leading into the station was in a bad state. The train had crashed into the barrier and derailed, and the mouth of the tunnel had collapsed onto the back of it. There was a scattering of rocks along the top of the train—pieces of the tunnel had been tumbling down onto it every time it shifted.

So *that* explained the thumping noises they'd been hearing.

The train was a crumpled wreck. The car they were standing on was bad, but the cars behind it were completely compacted. Emma winced. Thank goodness they'd been in the first car when the train crashed; otherwise, they wouldn't be standing here right now. The conductor was probably alright too, she told herself. He'd been in the first compartment with them, although she hadn't seen him amongst the splintered benches.

For a moment, all three of them just stood there, looking out over the wreckage. The entire thing looked like a toy train some giant child had kicked off the track during a temper tantrum. It didn't seem real.

Before any of them could move, a shout came from somewhere down the length of the train, and yellow light began to pour through the crumbled mouth of the tunnel. The sound of muffled voices reached them.

Someone was on the other side, trying to dig through.

They had to get Eliza out now.

Emma turned back to the door, shuffling closer to the frame, and Maddie and Edgar did the same on the other side. When she looked down though, she felt a sinking sensation in her stomach. Even standing on the bench the way she was, Eliza wasn't tall enough to reach the door. Getting her out was going to be incredibly difficult.

The crash of more rocks falling onto the train made them all jump, and Emma realized with a burst of panic that the people trying to dig through were only going to ensure that more of the tunnel collapsed on the train.

Maddie seemed to realize this too, because she whispered, "We've got to be quick. Give us your hands."

Eliza's face was strangely resigned as she balanced on the bench and reached her hands toward them. "You're not going to be able to pull me up. I'm too heavy."

"Shush up and put your hands higher." Emma edged forward, wiggling closer so her belly was pressed into the edge of the doorframe. When she reached down, she was able to grasp Eliza's wrist, but the angle was terrible. She couldn't seem to get a solid grip.

"It's no good, you'll have to leave me." Eliza's voice broke, and Emma shook her head fiercely.

"Shut up and grab my hand." She turned back, about to tell Edgar that he might try actually *helping*, when she realized he was no longer there.

Her mouth fell open when she spotted him. He was moving away from them, walking the length of the train, carefully picking his way around shattered glass and over the bars on the windows.

"He's leaving," Maddie hissed. "The coward!"

Before Emma could reply there was a shout from behind them, followed by another crashing rumble. A huge chunk of the wall bounced down the rockslide at the mouth of the tunnel and slammed into the train. The carriage shuddered beneath her. There was now a space at the top of the tunnel where light filtered through, and the muffled voices of the men—soldiers, likely—became clearer.

"Almost through. Keep digging!"

Emma turned back to the door, pulse galloping.

She and Maddie leaned down again, tugging frantically at Eliza's arms, and Maddie squeaked in alarm as she slid forward on her belly.

"Don't fall back in, you ninny," Eliza growled, "or I'll murder you myself!"

Emma stood back, despair jolting through her. "The angle is wrong, we can't—"

Emma stopped speaking and wiggled backward as someone came barreling up the length of the train. It was Edgar, red-faced and panting, dragging a thin wooden plank behind him. "Out of the way!"

For once she obeyed, jumping back as he slid the board into the doorway, calling down to Eliza, "Move!"

Eliza jumped back with a cry of surprise as the end of the plank hit the floor several inches from the edge of the bench. Edgar made a face as he struggled to push it forward. "If I can just get the angle right . . ."

Emma realized what he was doing almost at the same time Eliza and Maddie did. "Brilliant," Maddie said enthusiastically, and Eliza called up to him, "Yes! Just a little forward, you've nearly got it. Hold it there, I'm going to—"

She was cut off by another crash of rocks tumbling to the floor. This time, the hole at the top of the rockpile was wide enough to allow a thick wooden staff to poke through. Whoever was holding it knocked rocks back and away from the makeshift entrance. Emma's stomach clenched. She knew what was coming.

Even still, when the witch hunter leaned into the tunnel, she felt a shock. McCraw's hat was gone, and his hair was standing up wildly and covered in gray rock dust.

He stared right at the front of the train, and Emma ducked out of sight.

He'd seen her.

"Up!" Emma hissed, frantic. "Climb! Climb!" But Eliza was practically vaulting up the board already, face set in grim determination, skirts gathered in both hands.

She'd made it nearly two-thirds of the way up the board when it began to splinter.

Emma heard the wood crack before it happened, and saw Edgar, still holding the top of the board steady, reel back with the shock of the shifting weight. She lunged forward, hooking her arms under Eliza's armpits, her stomach and hips pressing painfully into the doorframe.

She wanted to scream as she slid forward, but she was too winded; all she could manage was a great wheeze of shock as she began to tip under Eliza's weight. A second later someone gripped her around the waist. Maddie and Edgar hauled her back, and Emma hit the roof of the train hard, panting, Eliza sprawling out beside her.

There was no time to rest. They could hear shouting, and the sound of heavy rocks falling. The bar of light coming from the hole atop the rockpile grew suddenly wider, and a shout of triumph echoed through the station.

McCraw was through.

Maddie practically hauled Emma up by the back of her dress.

"Get up! Get up and run!"

Chapter Fourteen

They ran, pelting down the length of the carriage, dodging crumpled metal and shards of glass, heading straight for the ruined engine car. They could hear someone yelling at them to halt, to stop in the name of the Crown.

They ran faster.

"We've got to jump down," Emma yelled over their thumping footsteps. "Get off the side and make a run for it."

None of the others looked happy about this, but they didn't argue. They didn't have time. Emma was already swerving to the left. "Jump and keep on running," she called, and then she jumped.

It didn't take any bravery, not really. It wasn't much of a jump, and the only other option was to run off the front of the smashed engine car.

She heard Eliza and Maddie jump behind her, and then Edgar a second later. They spread out, running for the opposite side of the cavernous terminal. Emma didn't look back; she could hear the shouting getting closer.

If they didn't find somewhere to hide, their escape would be over before it began.

The room seemed to be divided along the train tracks into large, spacious platforms, just like an ordinary train station, with the rock walls of the cavern sectioning off each individual platform. The vaulted ceilings made their pounding footsteps echo through the station, though the sound of the train shrieking and grinding as it settled on the tracks behind them was far louder. The air smelled like spilled petrol and something burning, but at least there were plenty of places to hide.

Emma darted around a corner and into the nearest section.

They found themselves in a wide-open space. A series of steps led up to a wooden platform in the middle illuminated by a line of flickering oil lanterns bolted to the walls.

This part of the station was odd. The platform wasn't a proper train platform at all; it was far too narrow and high, and looked more like a wooden stage than anything else. It was set against the length of the wall, with a crude wooden arch constructed in the center.

Then Emma saw them, tied at regular intervals along the length of the wooden beam that formed the top of the arch. Four twisted cords of black rope, the thick fibers woven with bits of green.

A shuffle from somewhere behind them, and then voices barking at one another. McCraw and his men were just around the corner.

"We've got to find a way out," Eliza hissed, eyes wide.

"There, behind the platform." Maddie's voice was sharp with excitement. "It looks like a door."

Maddie was right. There was a thick oak door set into the wall, banded with iron and locked with a heavy deadbolt from the inside.

Emma followed the others, pulse spiking as the pounding of footsteps grew closer behind them. If McCraw rounded the corner now they were caught.

Maddie was the first to get to the door in the wall, and she tugged frantically at the lock. "It's rusted shut," she whispered, eyes wide.

Emma leapt forward, fitting her fingertips into the rusted metal bolt beside Maddie's, forcing the stiff lock back as metal bit into her skin.

They shot through the door one after the other. Emma was last, and she held her breath, trying to close the door behind her as quietly and quickly as possible. If they got lucky, McCraw would run right past the platform without realizing they'd gone through the door.

There were stairs just beyond the door, leading up into the darkness. Eliza was already running up them, with Maddie and Edgar close behind. Emma followed. There was a stitch in her side, but she ignored it and pressed on.

The staircase was lit by more lanterns set into the stone walls, and the light made the shadows flicker and jump. Emma's heart raced every time she glanced back over her shoulder, expecting the witch hunters to appear. After a few minutes of rapid climbing, she didn't think she'd be able to get away if someone *did* show up to give chase, she was breathing so hard.

Eliza was still in the lead. "Come on, hurry. They're going to realize we unbolted the door any minute now. We've got to get a head start."

Emma wanted to point out that they *did* in fact have a head start, but she was far too winded. At last the stairs came to an end, and the door at the top led them into a bright, open hallway with checkered floors and a high glass ceiling that looked out at the clouds.

She staggered to a halt, surprised to find herself so suddenly surrounded by luxury. There were potted ferns draped over black iron stands on both sides of the hallway, and thick wax candles in gold wall sconces. There was even a stone fountain set into the wall across from them, where water trickled out of the open jaw of a roaring lion.

Along the walls a variety of gold and velvet furniture was arranged, chaise lounges and chairs with poufy, tasseled cushions, and just beyond that, a pair of open doors led out onto a small balcony.

Just under the tall windows that lined the corridor, a silver tea set was arranged on a cherrywood cart, and on it was a single fine china teacup, steam still curling from the lip, and a spread of sandwiches and scones.

Emma looked around, startled. "Where on earth *are* we?"

"Well, that's lovely," Eliza said waspishly. "Hang the witches and then walk straight up for lunch."

Maddie snorted at this, but Emma noticed Edgar had gone sheet white and seemed to be frozen. His eyes were the only things moving, and they were huge, darting this way and that as he took in the hallway.

"What?" She felt a sense of creeping alarm at his shocked expression. "What is it? What's the matter?"

"This is the palace," Edgar whispered.

"What?" Her stomach dropped, and she pressed a hand to her chest, trying to stop the frantic fluttering of her nerves.

"We're in the palace. In my mother's quarters." Edgar's voice was shaky. "This is where her rooms are." As he was speaking, he finally began to move, turning quickly on his heel. "We have to get out of here."

Emma hurried after him, and the others followed. The thought of running into her aunt was enough to light a fire under her. All those times her aunt had boasted about taking her kingdom back. She remembered the queen's sneering face, the glitter in her eyes when she'd talked about ending the reign of the witches.

Hanging the witches.

The black rope hanging from the platform. Had those been . . . ?

But no, she couldn't think about that, not right now.

They hurried down the lavish hallway, which only seemed to get wider. The candle sconces were soon replaced by a number of oil portraits, all stern-faced royals in collars and ruffles. Most of them looked as though they'd been sucking lemons.

They passed a noticeable gap in the portraits, a blank space on the wall, and Emma knew without thinking that it was the stretch of years that the witches had been in power, when the royal family had nearly been wiped out, the Black family legacy almost obliterated.

They had reached the end of the hallway now, and a closed door with a series of iron locks.

Edgar seemed to know the way, and after they had drawn back all the deadbolts, he led them down another, narrower hallway.

They were no longer in the queen's quarters. This was evidenced by the fact that the lights on either side of the hallway were now glass hurricane lamps, and the wallpaper was a smooth olive color, completely devoid of any flowers whatsoever. The portraits on the walls had changed too. There were a few bursts of angry-looking generals here and there, and several grave older women with squashed faces in tall collars, but no royalty.

She knew this place. It was the quarters for visiting nobles, a place where diplomats and distant relations of the royals stayed when they came to visit.

Her mother occasionally dropped by this wing, if she thought whomever was visiting was someone worth sucking up to, and Emma often found herself dragged along on these trips. She knew where they were now. Just down the way was a staircase that led to a number of long, winding passages, and the servant's quarters beyond.

If they could get there, they might be able to slip out the back entrance before anyone saw them.

"Keep going." Emma quickened her pace. The hurricane lamps flickered as they hurried past, sending shadows scurrying across the walls.

All of them were antsy, heads whipping this way and that at every noise. There was a strange, quick moment where they passed a dessert cart that someone had pushed to one side of the hallway, and Emma found herself whisking a handful of almond scones into her sash, operating completely on muscle memory, until Edgar hissed at her and swatted her arm.

"What are you doing? Keep going!"

They had paused at a branch in the hallway, and in the second of silence after Edgar's admonishment they all heard the muffled thump of footsteps up ahead. Emma froze, heart stopping in her chest, but Eliza beckoned to her, snatching at the front of her dress, yanking her around to face a large cupboard, one cleverly painted to blend in with the wall.

"Quick, get inside!"

The four of them jammed in and shut the door behind them. Emma found herself squished between Eliza and Maddie, with Edgar right behind her, his bony knees poking into her back. She was sitting on a pile of very soft, perfumed cloth.

They were, Emma realized, currently in the royal linen closet, sitting on some of the most expensive towels in all of England.

Her mother would be completely horrified.

The thought was strangely amusing, and she had to stuff her fist into her mouth to keep from laughing. She tried to imagine Lady Isolde Black yanking open the door and spotting her daughter curled up on the linen.

Of course, if that happened, her mother might turn her in.

The urge to laugh dissolved as quickly as it had come.

In that moment of quiet in the linen closet, the image she'd been carrying with her since the train platform began to truly sink in. Four black nooses. That's what had been hanging from the wooden archway downstairs. Four thistle nooses—for Emma and the others—hidden underneath the palace.

Had they been there all this time? Had Emma lived her entire life, walking these halls, stealing scones from carts and books from the library, never knowing that witches had been hanging just a few hundred feet beneath the floor?

And what about Isolde? Had her mother known?

She couldn't have. She wouldn't have sent Emma off to be tested if she had known.

Her jaw ached, she was clenching it so hard, and her pulse picked up, jack-hammering in her ears. She felt ill.

The others were similarly silent, and nobody moved, though they were wedged uncomfortably against one another. Emma wondered if they were all thinking about the same things.

Footsteps thumped past their cupboard, and they all stiffened. The sound faded after a moment, and when she was sure whoever had been walking past was gone, Eliza hissed at Edgar under her breath.

"Get your elbow out of my ear."

"Well, I don't want it in there either. There's no room!"

"Shut up, the both of you." Maddie shifted beside Emma, poking her painfully in the side. "What's that smell?"

Emma could smell it almost as soon as Maddie mentioned it, a faint smoky scent. "Is something . . . Eliza, are you *smoking*?"

"Don't you dare catch fire right now." Edgar's voice was threatening. "I mean it."

"I really don't like small spaces," Eliza whispered. "I can't help it."

There was a moment of silence, and then Edgar whispered, "'Of writing many books there is no end; / And I who have written much in prose and verse / For others' uses, will write now for mine—'"

"What the devil are you doing?" Eliza croaked, and Edgar shifted again, making Emma grunt as something dug into her back.

"I'm distracting you."

"Well *stop*. It's dreadful."

"It's Elizabeth Barrett Browning." Edgar sounded affronted. "How dare you—"

He broke off suddenly as another shuffle of footsteps reached them. A voice drifted through the door, hushed but still loud enough for Emma to make out the words. ". . . felt the whole palace tremble? Her Majesty just flew out of her suites."

Another voice replied, lower this time, and Emma only caught the last few words. ". . . going to do?"

"The Throne Room, I expect," the other woman said. "She's going to be on the war path now. Heavens, do you realize there are witches on the loose in the palace? It's a bit thrilling, isn't it? We should get to the Great Hall in case we miss something."

"How silly you are, Abigail!" The second voice was louder now. "You ought to be terrified, not pleased. Look, I'm shaking."

Abigail and her friend must have walked away down the hall, because their voices grew more and more distant. Emma was about to say they should get out and make a break for it when she heard it—the steady thumping of a heartbeat, distant enough to make her realize it didn't belong to any of her companions.

There was no anger to shove down this time, like she normally did, and she couldn't simply do the same thing with the fear clutching at her chest. It wasn't the same.

The noise continued, the steady *thump, thump, thump* of someone larger than them, someone coming this way very fast.

The sound of footsteps echoed outside in the hall.

The heartbeat in her ears was thunderous now. The person, whoever it was, was close.

She knew she shouldn't use her power. All magic was evil. But for once, it might also be *helpful*, and if she gave some beefy soldier a bit of a heart palpitation, he'd probably be fine, right? And far less inclined to chase after them.

She was still thinking this over when she heard the swishing of heavy skirts over stone. There was a slight pause, and then someone on the other side of the door said firmly, "That's a *very* noisy linen closet, children. You're hardly fooling anyone. Now, come out at once."

Chapter Fifteen

E mma stiffened, unsure of what to do. On either side, she could feel the others were frozen as well. No one moved.

A moment later, the door was yanked open, and she found herself staring up at a tall, severe-looking woman. She had dark skin, which contrasted with the frilly cream-colored dress she wore, and her black curls were a cloud around her slender face.

She frowned at the girls, the cameo pin at her throat glittering in the lamplight.

"Of course, that idiot girl just dropped you off here on your own." Her voice was slightly haughty and richly accented, and she seemed to be half talking to herself in her annoyance. "Everything's gone completely belly-up, hasn't it? Come along quickly. It's only a matter of time before the soldiers search this place. They're only waiting to clear it with the queen because I threw a fit and whacked one of them with my parasol. Come out from there."

Emma was the first to obey, perhaps because she was used to this type of attitude. The woman reminded her a little of her mother, with her haughty way of speaking and her sour expression.

Edgar had been staring up at the woman in astonishment, but he finally seemed to collect himself enough to speak. "Y-you're the ambassador to Irvingland . . ."

Instantly, Emma remembered a few verses of a little rhyme the tutor had taught her to remember the countries.

Irvingland. Compliant neighbor to the south, good for oranges, not much else.

It seemed rather rude, in retrospect.

"Yes, yes, your compliant little neighbor to the south. That's what she thinks, anyways. More importantly, I am your way out. Follow me." The woman waved a hand at them. "I'll take you to my quarters and we'll get you out from there."

Before any of them could move, the woman turned and began to stride purposefully down the hallway. Emma just stood there staring in shock, and Eliza and Edgar did the same. Only Maddie had followed her immediately, and now she turned around and waved a hand at them, brows raised.

"Well, come on. She's going to help us!"

Emma wasn't entirely sure why the ambassador would do that, or that she trusted her, but she hurried after Maddie all the same. Even over the rushing of blood in her ears, she could hear the thud of footsteps from overhead. Soldiers, like the ambassador had said. They were getting closer.

The Noise was impossibly loud now, filling the space between her own heartbeats, making her feel breathless. The more nervous she became, the louder the sound of the older woman's heart.

Alarmed, she shoved the Noise back behind the door, picturing the locks clicking into place as she banished the power. She wasn't sure if she could trust the ambassador, but that didn't mean she wanted to do something horrible to the woman.

At last the sound of the pulse faded, and Emma let out a relieved breath.

The woman stopped at a door in the center of the hall. She fished a silver key out of her glove, still ignoring the children as she slipped it into the lock.

Beside the door hung another large, glossy poster, and Emma suddenly had a sour taste in her mouth.

The queen looked like she did in every picture, her red mouth curled slightly up at the corners. But the picture felt different now. That *knowing* in her eyes—the one Emma had always thought made her look like she had a secret—now had a horrifying new meaning. All she could think about when she looked at the picture was the huge underground cavern beneath their feet. The black nooses waiting for them.

She forced herself to ignore the poster. When the key clicked in the lock, the woman held the door open and waited as they stepped inside. "I've already called up the doorway," she said. "It's all ready to go."

Emma was about to ask what she was talking about, but the sight of the room stopped the words before they could leave her mouth.

The ceiling, far over their heads, was made entirely of glass, and through it, they could see the towers and peaks of the palace against a blue sky. It was humid inside, and smelled faintly of flowers and damp soil. There were plants covering every inch of the space, ivy trailing tendrils around wooden lattices, and rows of ferns lining the stone walls. Bursts of color decorated the greenery here and there, flowers in vibrant reds and pinks.

The air inside was distinctly different than in the rest of the palace—cleaner, Emma thought—and the whole place was filled with the sound of trickling water coming from a large, multi-level stone fountain in the center of the room.

"Chop-chop. Quickly, children." The ambassador clapped her hands, startling them. "I trust your contact has prepped you for this, though clearly something went dreadfully wrong straight afterward, what with the remodeling of the palace and all."

"Contact?" Emma stared at her, frowning, her mind working frantically. None of this made any sense. What on earth was this woman talking about? And why were they all crowded around a fountain in the middle of a bunch of plants? "I'm sorry, but . . . what's going on here?"

The woman threw up her hands, exasperated. "For heaven's sake! You mean to tell me she wasn't actually with you? What happened?" When they stared at her blankly she grumbled under her breath, darting a look at the door before turning back to them. "The train was supposed to make one stop, at which one of our allies would sneak on. To brief you on the escape plan."

"There were no stops," Eliza said darkly. "Just the one we made happen when we crashed the train. So yes, safe to say this escape plan didn't go off as planned."

"Escape plan?" Edgar stood up straighter, his face lighting up. "Does that mean we're getting out of here?"

"If nothing else goes wrong, yes," the ambassador said peevishly.

Eliza was staring around the room, eyes wide. "I didn't know there was another coven in London besides mine. How many do you have?"

"We're not a coven," the ambassador said primly. "At least, not exactly."

"Who's organized this, then?" Eliza said. "Who's rescuing us?"

For one mad, ridiculous moment, Emma hoped the ambassador might say it was her mother, but the woman only shook her head and glanced over them, still frowning. "I would think that should be obvious, child. The same woman those blasted witch hunters have been searching for: Lenore Black."

Emma snapped upright.

A hundred questions crowded the tip of her tongue, but before she could ask any of them, a heavy thump came from overhead, making all of them jump.

The ambassador's gaze flicked up at the ceiling and then back to Emma and the others, and now her face was white and pinched. "Oh bollocks, you were supposed to have all this explained to you on the train ride over. We haven't got time." She stared at them intently. "Listen to me carefully. I can't go with you; I can only send you on your way. You've got to get to Witch City."

"So it's real!" Hope was starting to unravel the knot in Emma's chest.

"Of course it's real," the ambassador snapped. "Why else do you think the queen is so bent out of shape about it? Now, as I said, I can only get you started; you have to get through yourself."

"Through what?" Eliza said, clearly suspicious all over again. "My coven never said anything about *through*."

"Of course they didn't. Not many people know about the In-Between."

"What's the In-Between?" Emma frowned. She was about to demand a clear answer when the door behind them burst open, making all of them whirl around.

It was not the queen in the doorway but a woman in a white-and-blue servant's uniform. There was hair escaping from under her bonnet, and she looked very frazzled.

When the ambassador saw her she sighed, pressing a hand to her chest.

"Blast it all, Georgie! You nearly gave me a conniption."

Georgie ignored this, rushing over to the prince and enveloping him in a hug. Her voice was muffled as she pressed her face into his shoulder. "Oh, Edgar darling, I'll miss you so very much."

Edgar Darling, for his part, looked taken aback. He squirmed slightly in her grip, but let her continue to squeeze him. "I'll miss you too."

In spite of his blushing, there was an obvious note of affection in his voice, which left Emma feeling rather startled. She'd expected him to take on his familiar, imperious tone with someone in his mother's employ.

The woman released him and stepped back, smiling at each of them in turn. "Nice to meet you, girls. I'm Georgie, his nursemaid."

Even with everything that was going on, Emma saw Eliza and Maddie exchange a look, and Maddie tittered behind her hand.

Emma glanced away. She'd had nursemaids in the past, but her mother had a tendency to drive them away. Her last one, a short, cheerful woman named Judith, had left a year ago, after her mother had accused the woman of stealing. Emma had been furious, but there was nothing she could have done; her mother's mind was made up. It was only when Isolde had accused Emma of liking the nursemaid more than her own mother that Emma realized why poor Judith had been fired.

She still felt a little guilty about what she'd shot back at Isolde: *Of course I liked her better. It's not a high bar, Mother.*

Maddie was still grinning. "Aren't you a bit old for a nursemaid, Your Highness?"

Edgar shifted from foot to foot, his face glowing. "Ex-nursemaid," he mumbled.

"Alright, enough goodbyes." The ambassador glanced toward the door again. "Let's get on with this."

"Wait, wait." Georgie bustled forward, pressing the strap of a leather bag into Edgar's hand. "Your poetry books, lad. I know how much you love them."

Edgar brightened, taking the bag and sliding the strap over one shoulder. He looked more at ease suddenly. "Thank you, Georgie."

The ambassador waved at them. "Up onto the edge of the fountain. Stand in a row here." She patted the stone lip of the fountain, and then groaned when they all stared at her in disbelief. "We haven't got time for this."

Surprisingly, Edgar was the first to obey. He hesitated for only a moment, and then put one shiny black boot up on the stone, and then the other. He placed his hands on his hips as he stared at the ambassador expectantly.

Nothing happened. She only looked over at Emma and the others, brows raised.

Emma hesitated, and then followed suit, and Maddie and Eliza did the same. It wasn't difficult to balance on the edge of the fountain, as the stone was quite wide. When she looked down into the water, she realized it couldn't be more than a foot or so deep.

What exactly were they supposed to do?

The ambassador nodded briskly and cleared her throat, surveying them. She raised a hand, and Emma saw she was holding a long, cloudy-looking quartz crystal set into a silver chain.

"What's that?" Emma said.

The ambassador glanced over at her, mildly annoyed. "It's a spell. Alright, we're going to—"

"A spell?" Edgar nearly fell into the fountain trying to back up a step. "What do you mean a spell? It's a *rock*."

"For heaven's sake," the ambassador snapped at them. "Hush up, all of you, and listen to me carefully. You were supposed to get all of this information on the train! There's far too much to cover now, so I'm going to try to give you a crash course in under a minute. Once you make it in, you'll have to pass through the In-Between. Get to the other side of—"

There was a loud crash, and the ambassador's face went white. She whirled around as soldiers poured into the room. At the front of the party was Tobias McCraw. His hair was still standing on end, and he had a smudge of rock dust on his cheek, but his face was determined. He clutched his thistlewood staff tightly in one hand.

For a moment, neither party moved. McCraw's blue-eyed gaze flicked from Emma's face down to the edge of the fountain and back, and he frowned, clearly taken aback.

Emma felt completely frozen, as if panic had turned her limbs to stone.

There was no way out. They were caught.

A second later, a high, angry voice shouted at them to stop, and the queen appeared in the doorway behind her soldiers, expression twisted in rage, a terrible, white-faced figure in a blood-red dress.

Emma saw Edgar stiffen. The queen didn't even look at him; instead, she snatched at the witch hunter's shoulder, jabbed a finger toward Emma and the others, and screamed in a high, furious voice, "Seize the witches!"

Two things happened at once. First, Tobias McCraw looked straight at Emma, and then hesitated. It was a bare second that he stood there just staring at her, but long enough for the queen to turn her head and fix her gaze on him, enraged. McCraw jumped forward as if he'd been shocked.

The second thing was that the ambassador to Irvingland—compliant neighbor to the south, good for oranges and not much else—whirled on the spot and swept both hands out, lunging toward the children.

Emma squeaked in shock as the woman's arm crashed into her, shoving her backward. She heard Maddie's scream beside her as she fell back too, and the high, imperious voice of the ambassador cry out, "*Aperi ianuam.*"

Chapter Sixteen

She fell.
And fell.

And continued to fall.

There was no impact, and she didn't break the surface of the water in the fountain. Emma's eyes flew open in shock.

Strange shapes and colors burst and bloomed in front of her. She was staring at the glass ceiling of the atrium above and the sky beyond, both rippling strangely, as if they were under water and not she. It was like a distant picture above her, shrinking quickly, first to the size of a table, then a painting, then a postcard. Alarmingly fast. She could hear shrieking in the distance, and the smell of smoke seared her nostrils.

She squeezed her eyes shut, feeling a stab of terror.

A second later there was a distant shout of alarm, and her eyes flew open in time to see a hand plunging toward her. She caught a glimpse of thick fingers with short nails, the cuffed uniform of the witch hunter, and the strange, unnaturally stretched arm attached to it.

There was one horrifying moment when the fingers closed around her ankle, and Emma felt the drag of something heavy on her leg. She screamed, soundless in the strange void, and kicked violently. And then something grabbed her entire body from behind and sucked her violently backward, yanking her out of the witch hunter's grasp.

She had only a second's warning before impact.

One moment she was falling through a blur of shapeless color, and the next there was a flash of gray—a stone wall whizzing past.

Emma threw her arms out in surprise, body twisting as she tried to catch herself. Instead, she sprawled on her face on a surprisingly cushioned surface.

The wind had been knocked out of her on the landing, and Emma took a moment to regain her breath. Then she remembered the grasping hand. She scrambled upright, looking around in panic.

There was no one.

She'd landed in a stone fountain. Unlike the one back in the atrium though, this one was empty, and a great crack ran through the center, out of which sprouted a number of fluffy ferns. The cushioned surface she'd fallen on was a thick layer of moss blanketing the bottom.

Beyond the fountain, the doorway was empty. Tobias McCraw hadn't made it through.

Emma's shoulders slumped in relief. She let out another breath and then collected herself enough to take stock of her surroundings.

The elegant glass atrium had changed. The windows were still there, but half of them seemed to be cracked or broken, and the wind whistled in past the jagged edges.

There were old pots everywhere, empty and piled in stacks in the corners, or tipped over on their sides, dirt scattered across the floor. None of the pots held plants, but the plants had grown here anyway—ferns and creeping ivy and bushes full of sprouting flowers, all bursting through the holes and cracks in the floor.

There was nobody here but her.

A trickle of panic began to sink in past the relief.

"Maddie? Eliza? Edgar?" She jumped as her voice echoed back at her, and then frowned. She stood up slowly, and carefully stepped over the lip of the fountain.

It was disconcerting, this place that both did and didn't look like the palace. It sent an uncomfortable sort of shiver down her spine.

What had the ambassador called it? The *In-Between*?

Emma turned on the spot, hands clammy with sweat. Wherever this was, there was no denying she'd gotten here by way of magic.

And this place, as familiar as it looked, was not the room she had just left, so that had to mean it was magic too. On top of that it was damp and smelled of mildew, and it was dismally, eerily empty of any other human being.

None of her friends had landed here; in fact, judging by the thick layer of dust on the floor, no one had ever been here at all.

Emma wanted out.

She took a deep breath and then moved toward the double doors at the end of the room, the sound of her footsteps echoing off the glass ceilings. Her thoughts were in turmoil, and each step made the panic in her chest grow a little more. Maddie and Eliza and Edgar had been pushed into the fountain too. She'd seen it.

She couldn't be here alone.

Emma was breathing hard by the time she burst through the double doors with a shriek of rusted hinges. Staggering to a halt, she was shocked to find herself outside on a set of wide stone steps, and held on to the door to steady herself.

Nothing could have prepared her for the city spread out before her.

It was London. And yet, it was undeniably *not* London.

The city was laid out differently, to start—more sprawling, with wider spaces between the buildings. Or perhaps it was merely an illusion created by the greenery that seemed to have sprung up along the edges of the streets and between each building. Incredibly, there were *trees* growing throughout the city, a towering thick-trunked forest that seemed to be trying to take over entirely.

For a moment she just stood there, rooted to the spot, not understanding.

She hadn't known what to expect, but this . . . was impossible.

In London, the streets would be full of people at this hour, which Emma estimated must be around midday, and streams of smoke would be trickling from the rows of chimneys along the rooftops. But here nothing moved.

The streets were silent, the houses dark and empty, their cracked and broken windowpanes reflecting the orange of the sun. Displays at the front of the nearest shops showed rotten food and shriveled meat, and there were carriages strewn through the street, each of them rusted to a standstill.

A ghost town.

Dust motes hung in the air, illuminated by rays of light that slipped in through the cracks and spaces in the skyline, and Emma realized a moment later, a chill dropping down her back, that the sun was just now rising.

It didn't make sense. The sun had already risen, hours ago.

She clutched the door so hard her fingertips ached, struggling to wrap her mind around this new information. Not only was this a different London, but it seemed to be in a different time. Or at least the timing was off by a few hours.

It felt a little like something had reached in and clenched her heart in an iron grip. It was some kind of shadow London, a strange copy of the original. A ghost city swallowed up by a forest.

When she turned on the steps and looked across the city line, she could only see more enormous trees in the distance: thick branches twined around church steeples and burst through windows; towering trees dwarfing brick houses. Not only that, but some of the nearest trees had golden-brown and yellow leaves, and it wasn't nearly as cold as it had been this morning.

It had been winter in London.

She moved farther down the steps, unbuttoning her thick jacket a little as she went, trying to cram the panic back down. She had to find the others. They'd fallen into the fountain with her—

Emma stopped short, once again remembering the hand that had burst through the blur of color. If McCraw hadn't made it, who was to say the others had? What if he'd yanked them out?

She squinted up at the buildings around her, thinking hard. She'd felt them beside her up until . . . when? The second before she'd hit the ground?

Even if they had made it through, how was she supposed to find them? Slowly she turned and looked over the strange Forest-London spread beneath her—and spotted something that gave her another jolt of uneasy surprise.

The clock tower loomed in the distance, standing perfectly straight. In this London, it would seem, it had not been crashed into and burned up during a witch attack. Even from this distance, she could tell it was dilapidated in spots. The hour and minute hands seemed to have rusted into place, and one side was entirely covered in creeping ivy, but it was still standing, the tallest structure in the near vicinity.

Somehow, seeing the tower like this made everything sink in all over again. It felt like the earth had shifted beneath her. Her heart crowded up into her throat, choking off her oxygen. She felt dizzy, and forced herself to take a deep breath.

A moment later, the low sound of a pulse in the back of her mind surfaced unexpectedly, and she stood up straight. "Maddie?"

She turned on the spot, frantically searching the buildings nearby. "Eliza?"

There. Someone was emerging between the thick trunk of a tree and the side of a crumbling brick building, a rumpled-looking figure in a black silk jacket.

It was not Maddie or Eliza but Edgar. There was a smudge of soot on his left cheek, and the front of his silk jacket was torn. His black hair was disheveled and standing on end.

Emma leapt forward with a cry of relief, bounding down the steps to grab him in a fierce, desperate hug. Beneath her arms, Edgar made a surprised *oomf!* sound, and she pulled back a second later, realizing what she'd done.

Neither of them said anything for a moment, though Edgar looked just as relieved as she felt.

"I thought you'd all gone."

"Where are the others?" Emma demanded, and her stomach twisted when his face fell.

"I thought they were with you."

"No. No one came with me." Worry gnawed at Emma's insides. "They've got to be here somewhere. They can't have been left behind."

Edgar frowned. "Hopefully that witch hunter didn't pull them out."

"I think I shook him off just before I went through," she said. "I'm not sure though."

At this, Edgar glanced around, clearly nervous. "Well, you know, even if he didn't get through, I don't fancy staying here. It's creepy." He cleared his throat and threw his shoulders back, sniffing. "We should go."

Emma stared at him. The bossy prince act seemed to be back, and she found herself struck by the way he spoke. It was very like his mother, she realized: the haughty accent and the way he stated things as a fact, as if he was simply waiting to be obeyed.

She opened her mouth, about to say something rude, and then stopped.

Very distantly she could hear a frantic *whoosh, whoosh, whoosh*. At the end of every third beat came a quick double beat and then silence, before the whole thing started over.

She'd heard that heartbeat before, in the square the day of The Testing. That had to mean it was either Maddie or Eliza, didn't it?

"Wait, I can hear—"

A low rumble interrupted her, and Emma found herself rocked suddenly backward, nearly losing her balance.

An earthquake? Pulling Edgar by the arm, she dashed back up the steps and braced herself against the door. She heard Edgar give a squeak of dismay as he grabbed the frame beside her.

The city shook, the leaves on the nearest trees fluttering as if in a strong breeze, and as she watched in astonishment, Forest-London *shifted*.

It happened before her eyes. The clock tower blurred, as if it were shaking so hard it was merely a smear of color in front of her, and then it was suddenly gone.

Emma gaped as the buildings around it shifted, disappearing and reappearing in rapid succession, as if the city were indecisive in its shuffling. The roads too were moving, rearranging themselves with a great scraping sound of stone against stone.

At last, the rumbling tapered off and the ground went still under her feet. When Emma turned to say something to Edgar, she realized with a jolt that the door she was clutching was one of the only things that appeared to have stayed the same. They now stood on the steps of a great stone building with a pair of boarded-up windows in front. There were a number of iron smokestacks up top and, just above the door, a sign that read *Tuttle and Williams Cannery*.

For a brief moment neither of them said anything; they just stared at one another, wide-eyed, until Edgar finally murmured, "What . . . just happened?"

Chapter Seventeen

"It moves," Emma breathed, still staring out over the city. "Good God, this entire place moves. How are we supposed to find them?"

Cold horror was curling in her stomach, though she wasn't sure if it was due to the blatant display of magic by the empty city or the realization that this would make it nearly impossible to find their friends.

A second later though, mingled with the sound of her own frenzied pulse in her ears, she heard a faint *thump-thump, thump-thump.*

Emma jerked upright, pulling away from the door. She couldn't waste a minute, not this time. "I can hear one of them. Quick, this way."

She plunged down the steps and made it halfway across the road when Edgar finally caught up. "You shouldn't use your magic!" he said breathlessly from just behind her. "It's dangerous. It will turn your eyes black and rot your tongue in your mouth. Emma, wait. Slow down!"

She frowned, still hurrying forward, trying to concentrate as hard as she could on where the Noise was coming from. Up ahead was a long, winding street, hedged in on both sides by shops and hotels.

Maddie and Eliza had to be up there somewhere, but if the streets shifted again before they could get there . . .

Edgar was still protesting. "You can't use witchcraft, it's evil—"

She finally spun on him. "*Who* is evil exactly? It's *your* mother who was going to hang us."

Edgar fell silent, his face miserable, and she hesitated. "I-I'm sorry. I shouldn't have said that. I mean . . . my mother, I don't know if she . . ." She let her words trail off, unable to say it out loud.

Isolde couldn't have known.

Before Edgar could reply, there came another loud rumble, and the cobblestones beneath them shook violently. Edgar gave a cry of dismay, and Emma darted forward without thinking, grabbing him by the arms.

They couldn't be separated. She wouldn't let them.

The buildings overhead were shaking so violently, the trees around them quivering and blurring so much that Emma had to squeeze her eyes shut for fear of being sick.

The shaking was shorter this time, thankfully. When it finally tapered off, she opened her eyes, blinking around.

They were now standing in the middle of an open square, much larger than the last one.

It was vaguely familiar, and as she turned, looking around at the buildings, she began to think she'd been here before. There was a huge, L-shaped mansion in the distance, with siding that had once been white, though it had turned gray over the years. She could picture it in her mind now, with white walls and a pristine tiled roof.

Yes, she'd been here before, though it had not been empty like this. And the fountain in the middle wasn't quite right—here, it had a statue of a woman with a raven perched on her shoulder, which Emma was certain she'd never seen before.

But she knew where they were now.

This was Parliament Square—at least, she was fairly certain it was. It looked very different with trees looming over it, and the sides of the buildings covered in moss and ivy.

The square was also completely empty. There was no sign of Eliza or Maddie.

Her stomach sank, but she forced herself to walk farther into the square, to scan the surrounding buildings carefully. There was a startling moment when something gave a loud shriek from just in front of them, and then came the beating and flutter of wings as the raven on the statue launched itself into the air. Emma screamed and jumped back, and then gave a strangled laugh as she realized what had happened. She'd thought the bird was a part of the statue.

Beside her, Edgar tilted his head back, shuddering. The offended raven was circling above them now, soon joined by another.

Emma's adrenaline was still high after the latest earthquake, the blood still rushing in her ears, so it took her a moment to hear the faint thumping of another heartbeat. She snapped to attention as the sound became clearer.

There.

Behind her, Edgar gave a squawk of protest as she shot off toward one of the nearest buildings.

"Come *on*, before it moves!"

This seemed to light a fire under him, because he barreled after her, following her across the square and up the stairs of a building, the washed-out boards creaking under their feet. It was an old barber shop, complete with a faded red-and-blue pole outside, though it was lying flat, as if someone had come along and yanked it down. Emma couldn't see inside, since there were tattered yellow shades pulled over both windows. When she made her way to the weed-covered stoop and pushed the door open, she was startled to hear a bell above her jangle.

The shop was small. There were three chairs set up in front of a trio of dusty mirrors. There were even capes laid out, and jars full of rusted combs and scissors at each station. Bottles of shaving tonic stood beside them, covered in dust and cobwebs. At the back was a couch, and a coffee table that held several moldering books and magazines. Just beyond that was another door, a back room maybe.

Emma's footsteps echoed on the floorboards, which creaked loudly as she moved inside. The shop smelled musty, and she wrinkled her nose before cupping one hand to her mouth.

"Eliza? Maddie?" Her voice sounded small in the stillness. At first there was no answer, and then she heard a muffled *thud* from the back. She froze, eyes on the door. Whoever was behind there, it couldn't be Eliza or Maddie; they would have answered.

She almost jumped out of her boots when she heard shuffling footsteps behind her. She whirled around to glare at Edgar, who stood waiting in the doorway. He blinked at her when she shoved a finger to her lips, eyes wide, and then turned to point at the door to the back room.

Slowly he nodded, and held the front door open wider.

Thanking her lucky stars that he had at least some common sense, she crept forward, toward the prince and the exit. Whatever was thumping behind the other door, it probably wasn't anything they wanted to meet. Wild animals, maybe? A cougar or a bear wouldn't seem so out of place in this nightmare city, and she didn't fancy meeting either.

She was almost out, edging slowly past Edgar, when another thud came from the back room, followed by a sharp yelp. Emma stopped, the hairs on the back of her neck prickling.

That had sounded like Maddie.

She exchanged a quick look with Edgar, who was shaking his head frantically, and then turned back into the shop, inwardly groaning. What if it was Maddie and Eliza, and they were in some kind of trouble that didn't allow them to answer?

She moved quickly for the door at the back. If she had to open it, it might be better to take whatever was in there by surprise.

Emma yanked open the door, and then reeled back in shock.

Eliza stood in the center of a small, dimly lit room, her expression twisted with fear and rage. There were shelves of dusty boxes on either side of her, illuminated by the flames encasing both of her arms, all the way up to her shoulders. Standing at a safe distance behind her was Maddie, who spotted Emma a second later and flapped her hands, eyes wide.

"Eliza! It's her, she's back again!"

Eliza whirled to face Emma, throwing her hands up. Emma opened her mouth, about to tell them not to worry, when a huge, orange fireball blossomed from Eliza's hands, hurtling straight toward her.

Chapter Eighteen

E mma shrieked, darting behind one of the barber chairs as the flames shot past, inches away. The fire flickered wildly in the side of her vision and reflected back at her a thousand times in the mirrors, as searing heat flashed across her cheeks. "Eliza, it's me!"

"It's us!" Edgar shrieked from the doorway.

"It was you before." Sparks showered off the tips of Eliza's fingers, sizzling on the floor at her feet. "And then it wasn't."

"What are you talking about?" Emma peered out from behind the chair, gripping the moldering leather, fear making her throat tight.

She rose from her crouch, still holding on to the back of the chair in case she needed a shield again. "I'm me," she said urgently. "I have no idea what you're on about, but you need to calm down so you can put that fire out." It was only a matter of time before the sparks from Eliza's hands struck a dry spot in the ruined shop and started an inferno.

"We don't know it's her," Maddie said. She was looking hard at Emma, and then at Edgar. "But she *has* got the prince with her."

"She could be tricking us."

"What are you *talking* about?" Emma looked helplessly from Eliza to Maddie. They were acting as if she were the enemy. After everything they'd been through together . . .

"Ask her something only she would know," Maddie said, but Eliza only raised a hand higher, eyes wide and wild. The flames were licking at her throat now. Her fire seemed to be completely out of control.

"Alright, alright." Maddie turned to Emma. Her hands were trembling, and she curled them into fists at her sides. "Emma, do you remember when we first met, and I let you go in front of me?"

Emma blinked at her, feeling a trickle of panic run down her spine. First, they were treating her like the enemy, and now Maddie was talking nonsense. "I . . . what?"

Behind her she heard Edgar groan, and Maddie flinched and stepped back.

"Wait, hold on," she said quickly. "That's a lie. I let you go in front of *me*, because you wanted to get it over with. The Testing, I mean."

Maddie's shoulders slumped and her face relaxed into an expression of relief. "It's really her."

Eliza slowly lowered her hands, brows raised. A long moment passed while she continued to stare at Emma, and Emma held her breath, her entire body tense in case she had to duck. Then Eliza's shoulders relaxed, and her flames extinguished all at once, flickering away as if they'd been reabsorbed into her skin. She straightened her shoulders and shook her hands out. "Alright, maybe it is her."

"What on earth was that about?"

All three girls turned to look at the doorway, where Edgar was still standing, looking absolutely horrified.

"There's something out there, that's what." Eliza looked grim. "And it could come back at any moment."

"We should leave." Maddie glanced over at the door. "I don't like this place at all."

"What was it?" Emma said. "What did you see?"

"There was someone—or something—here," Eliza said. She was already heading for the door, and the others followed. "Something that looked like you, but it behaved . . . not like you. It tried to get us to follow it, and when we wouldn't, it chased us into the shop. I burst into flames and it ran."

Emma's skin was crawling. "It *looked* like me?"

"At first," Maddie said, her expression uneasy. "And then when it realized it wasn't fooling us, it looked like me, and then Eliza."

Emma caught a glimpse of herself in a pock-marked, dusty mirror and shivered. It could only be magic. Which meant there was a real live witch somewhere in Forest-London.

"That sounds horrible." Edgar shuddered. "You're right—let's get out of here."

Emma glanced through the doorframe to the strange city beyond. "Wherever *here* is."

"The In-Between," Edgar said. "That's what she called it."

"It's London," Emma said. "Or . . . something like London."

But eerily silent and half-swallowed by forest, not to mention constantly moving.

"We should go." Eliza glanced at the door to the shop, and then back over her shoulder. "We should keep moving, in case that thing comes back. The ambassador said to get to the other side of . . . something."

"London, it's got to be London." Edgar stood up straighter and cleared his throat, as if he hadn't just been ready to bolt out the door a moment ago. "We should get on with it."

"But it's completely ridiculous," Maddie said. "Getting across London could take days."

They crowded onto the doorstep, looking out at the crumbling buildings covered in moss, at the crooked stone street ahead of them, shadowed by trees stretching up into the sky. Even as they stood there a faint rumble could be heard, and Emma felt the ground tremble beneath her. They watched as the tops of buildings in the distance disappeared and reappeared.

"Or maybe longer." Maddie's voice was shaky. "I suppose you two have already discovered it does that."

"Yes," Edgar said darkly.

"Whatever you do"—Emma kept her eyes fixed on the shifting buildings—"stay very close together."

They made their way back onto the street, moving over the uneven cobblestones in a tight cluster, with Emma and Eliza in front and Maddie and Edgar just behind, nearly walking on their heels. She felt more like the leader of a jungle expedition than someone walking through a city.

Emma looked up at the brick buildings as they passed—shops with broken windowpanes, greenery bursting through blinds and rotten curtains, saplings growing up through porches and walkways. Hundreds of dark, empty windows peered down at them, creating the sensation of hundreds of dark eyes following their progress. It made Emma's skin crawl.

Maybe trusting the ambassador had been a terrible mistake. Maybe the witches were simply trying to finish off two more members of the Black family. If this had been a trap, they'd walked straight into it.

She kept watching the dark windows, half expecting to see herself peering out from behind the smudged glass.

They took a left down another narrow street, almost an alley, with rusted bins on either side and a fence that had nearly rotted away. The sight of it seemed to trigger something in her brain.

The picture was off. She'd been down roads like this back home, but this one was different, aside from obviously being overgrown.

No fog. That's what was missing. There was no fog here, no curling mist rolling along the streets and up off the water. London was nearly always covered in smog or enveloped in fog, but here the air was completely clear, revealing every crumbling building in stark detail.

It was also, as she had noticed earlier, warmer, and Emma unbuttoned her jacket fully as they went. As disturbing as this place was, it also made her feel like the East Wing always did. Lighter on her feet, more awake than usual. The telltale signs of a lack of thistle.

Beside her, Eliza had slowed to nearly a stop. Emma was just turning to tell her they needed to stay together when she caught sight of what the other girl was staring at. She started, cold panic jolting through her.

A moment later she relaxed, feeling sheepish.

What she'd mistaken for a person standing at the base of the nearest building was a statue carved in dark, glimmering stone. A woman in long, flowing robes. Her head was tilted back to the sky, and a smile was on her lips. She wore a tall, pointed hat, and in one hand was a wicker broom.

Eliza stepped closer to the base of the statue, and Emma and the others followed.

It was quite remarkable. Emma had never seen one carved in such fine detail. And the surface was so smooth and glassy that when she edged forward, she could see her own blurred and stretched reflection.

"A witch," Maddie said in wonder. She was right behind Emma, peering over her shoulder. She looked both transfixed and wary, as if she wasn't sure if she should get too close.

The stone woman's face was broad and handsome, and she had a full figure and wide shoulders. She looked fierce and rather stern, but all the same, the statue was nothing like Queen Alexandria's. There was no malice or poisonous secrets in this woman's stare.

Eliza frowned, moving around the back of the statue. "Who's she supposed to be? There's no plaque."

Emma's mind was working furiously now, trying to remember the first statue she'd seen. Parts of the face had been worn away, and she hadn't paid close attention to the other details.

Were all the statues in this Forest-London of witches?

Edgar was fidgeting behind her, and when Emma glanced back she found him clearly distraught.

"What's the matter?"

He looked at her, eyes wide. "What if we're already here? What if this is Witch City?"

The was silence for a moment as this statement sunk in.

It was almost as if Edgar had struck her. Emma felt dizzy at the idea, off balance, and she reached out a hand to brace herself on the base of the statue. The stone was cold and smooth under her fingers.

The strange copy of London, the shifting streets . . . it made a horrible kind of sense.

"That can't be true." Eliza was shaking her head furiously, fists curled at her sides.

"But just *look* at this." Edgar glared around at them. "It's a witch statue. It makes sense."

"But there's no one here." Maddie glanced up at the building in front of them, where row upon row of empty windows peered down.

"Why would the ambassador send us here?" Emma said.

Edgar looked at her, expression dark. "She's a witch. When have witches ever helped the Black family?"

"You can hardly speak." Eliza growled the words. A faint trickle of smoke rose from her closed fingers. "The Blacks *kill* witches."

"We were only returning the favor." Edgar's expression was sour. "You lot started it by killing the queen, my *grandmother*."

"You've been fed a bunch of lies." Eliza's voice was low and tense. "We never killed her, she was *one of us*."

Edgar instantly bristled. "What? Don't be preposterous. Witches wiped out my entire family. They're evil, murderous—"

There was a sudden *woof* sound, and fire sprang up from Eliza's hands, the flames licking up her arms.

Edgar jumped back, jabbing a finger at her. "See? Murderous!"

"And I suppose your mother was perfectly happy to hang her own son, because she's all about *justice*."

Edgar looked stricken at this, and he stammered his outrage. "That's not . . . that isn't—"

Emma'd had enough of this. "Shut it, both of you!"

They both turned to stare at her, shocked, and Emma scowled back at them. Her head was still spinning from Eliza's revelation about her grandmother, but they couldn't afford to fall apart now.

She had goosebumps running up both arms, and she kept wanting to jerk around and look over her shoulder. They were too exposed standing in the middle of the street arguing like this, too vulnerable to anyone, or anything, that might be watching.

"This isn't helping anything. We've got to keep walking. We keep going, and we find Lenore. Like the ambassador said."

A beat of silence followed this. Eliza and Edgar both looked deflated.

Maddie's voice was quiet. "But how?"

Emma's thoughts were turning rapidly.

"Alright, look. I don't think it's true that this is Witch City—or at least, it's not the whole truth. The forest here has obviously been growing for years. If Witch City was destroyed years ago, the queen would have told her people." She glanced over at Edgar. "You know she loves her speeches. But that poster on the train said she was still looking for information. The ambassador said we had to get through the In-Between first, so this can't be Witch City, right?"

Slowly, Eliza and Maddie nodded. Eliza sniffed and shook out her arms, her glower fading slightly. For a second she stared down at the flames, blinking, and shook her arms again. At last the fire died out.

Edgar still didn't look convinced.

"We're going to go to the edge of the city, on the other side, because that's what the ambassador said to do," Emma said firmly.

She had no idea if that was right, or if it was even possible with the way the city was moving, but they had to do something. Nothing good was going to come of standing there shouting at one another.

"Right," Maddie said eagerly, and a little desperately, Emma thought. Eliza only nodded, though she looked less panicked. Edgar said nothing; he just shuffled his boots over the cobblestones, pressing his lips together tightly.

He was clearly trying to keep himself from giving orders or lecturing them about something, and Emma turned away quickly, before he could get started.

Truth was, the sight of the witch statue had sent a dagger of cold fear through her stomach, and she felt about as sick as Edgar looked. If he was right, and this was Witch City, they really were in trouble.

She'd hadn't been sure what to expect, but it certainly hadn't been to find Witch City abandoned and overgrown . . .

But there was no sense getting the others worked up all over again.

"Let's go." She began to move away from the statue, but they'd hardly taken two steps when the shaking began.

This time it was more violent, and Emma pitched forward, nearly falling. Eliza grabbed the sleeve of her dress to steady her and Emma found herself clinging to the others, arm wrapped around Maddie, hand clutching Edgar's wrist, desperately yelling "STAY TOGETHER" over the roar of noise as the earth bucked and surged below them.

She could see buildings rushing past, and her mouth dropped open a second later when she realized why they were moving so fast. The buildings *weren't* moving—it was the street they were on. It was whipping forward like the head of a cobra about to strike, so fast their surroundings were a blur. Emma had to squeeze her eyes shut as they sliced *through* the bases of buildings, which melted out of the way as if made of smoke.

It was the type of thing that might drive you mad if you watched for too long.

At last the street lurched to a halt, and the four of them staggered, collapsing in a heap on the cobblestones.

Emma cracked her eyes open and uncurled slightly. She groaned as someone shifted and an elbow dug sharply into her ribcage.

"Sorry," Maddie whispered in her left ear.

Slowly they untangled themselves and looked around.

They appeared to be in quite a different part of town. The buildings here were bigger, for one, and the streets less crammed together. There were bright striped awnings, windowpanes of frosted glass, and colorful displays in the windows of tea shops. It was all just as faded and crumbling as the last part of town they'd seen, but there had obviously been wealth here at one time.

They had landed directly across from a hat shop. The center window in the storefront had been shattered, and ivy had grown up into the display of hats. The hats were all rather moldy looking, and it appeared that a family of mice may have sampled the wares, because a number of them had holes nibbled in the brims.

For a moment, nobody said anything. Then Maddie shrugged, still in the midst of dusting off the hem of her dress, and said, "Anyone fancy a hat?"

It was ludicrous, but Emma couldn't stifle the laughter that burst out of her. Even Edgar looked faintly amused, and Eliza shook her head, one corner of her mouth inching upward.

Emma was still staring at the display, nose wrinkled as she imagined trying on one of the moldy lumps on the hat stands, when she saw it—a flicker of movement in the window, a flash of black between two towers of faded pink hatboxes.

She backed up a step, heart cramming into her throat.

"Uh, I think I saw—" Her voice cut off as another darting flash of movement could be seen through the window. And then the door to the shop began to creak slowly open.

Chapter Nineteen

All four of them froze as something appeared in the doorway in front of them. It was a *face*, one with glittering dark eyes. Framed by long, wild black hair.

Emma's breath stopped.

It was *her* face, but not a version she'd ever seen before—one that looked as if she'd gone completely wild.

Almost immediately, the low *thump-thump-thump* started up. It brought her straight back to the court hearings, and the look on the prince's face that day. It was Edgar's heart. She darted a panicked look at her cousin. He was standing closest to her, still staring wide-eyed at the monstrous creature in the doorway.

In spite of the fear, Emma ground her teeth and slammed the door on the Noise, jamming it back behind her defenses.

The pulse faded, and she had a moment of relief before the creature in the doorway suddenly lurched forward. It moved impossibly fast, darting through the door and then skittering to a halt a few feet away. It was very tall, much taller than any of them, and seemed to be put together out of a jumble of leftover parts, a series of crooked limbs.

A person who was not quite a person. Just like this London was not quite London.

As they watched, the creature's face began to slowly change, skin stretching over its bones, rippling and shifting, its features morphing. Emma stumbled back, nausea washing over her. She felt as though an ice-cold fist had plunged into her chest and seized her heart.

The creature's face was now freckled and pale and still horrifyingly familiar. Behind Emma, Maddie gave a strangled cry.

The thing that now wore Maddie's face crept closer. One step. Two. Emma felt Eliza grab her arm tightly. It felt as if her heart had stopped. She was frozen to the spot.

"Why does it look like that?" Maddie's voice was a whisper at first, but it climbed to a high screech of terror. "Stop that!"

"I think we should run." Edgar was tugging Maddie back. "Come on, *run!*"

Abruptly, the monster with Maddie's face launched itself forward. It ran straight at them, mouth dropping open in a screeching howl.

Emma whirled around and snatched at Eliza's hand. Edgar was already yanking Maddie around, pushing her out of harm's way, and the four of them sprinted for the nearest building. Fear sent a rush of hot adrenaline coursing into Emma's chest. As she sprinted forward, she could feel the Noise starting up again; the chaotic sound of four heartbeats echoed through her head.

She had time for one fleeting observation—she'd never heard more than one before—and then sheer terror took over.

The cobblestones were uneven beneath their feet as they dashed onwards. Worse still, she could hear a low, increasingly familiar rumble. Emma shrieked, seizing Maddie's hand on one side and keeping tight hold of Eliza's on the other.

Edgar almost fell before Maddie grabbed a fistful of his shirt, hauling him up and pulling him after her. This caused them to slow for a few seconds, but thankfully, a nearby sideroad shifted, and the shaking made the monster stagger and nearly lose its balance as well.

"Run!" Emma shouted, and then screamed in wordless frustration when the building they were making straight for—a squat, brown-tiled saloon with old-fashioned swinging doors—vanished without warning.

Before they could change direction, another low rumble sounded and a new building arrived—a tall white mansion with green shutters and thatched eves. The faded lettering on the sign in front said *Ashberg Hotel*.

It would have to do.

Emma put on a burst of speed, heading for the stairs leading up to the wraparound porch.

As they sprinted across the street, Emma and Eliza were in the lead, with Maddie and Edgar just behind. Flames had burst from Eliza's palms and were licking fiercely at her arms now, forcing Emma to let go.

The creaky staircase was very long and narrow, and they were forced to run up in a single file. The rotting wood nearly sent Eliza through the top step, but Emma managed to snag her arm, pulling her back before she fell and then shoving her forward onto the porch before she herself caught fire.

Thundering footsteps sounded just behind them, and Emma glanced back, horrified to see the creature reaching one spindly arm out for Edgar.

"Look out!"

Her shriek came a second too late. The creature managed to snatch the back of Edgar's silk jacket, and he was pulled up short. He screamed as his feet slid on the stairs, and then, to her astonishment, he twisted around and issued an order—in the loudest, most imperious voice she'd ever heard: "I command you to let me go *immediately.*"

This seemed to startle the monster into stillness, at least for a second, but it was enough to give Edgar time to shrug out of his jacket and vault the rest of the way up the steps. The howl of rage that followed only propelled them on faster, and they bolted across the narrow porch toward the hotel doors, skidding to a halt in front of them. There was a brass lion's head door-knocker on the front, and heavy, iron bands crossing the door. Emma tried to turn the knob on the left side. It wouldn't budge, and her stomach sank.

Angry groaning noises came from behind them. The creature was slashing at the silk jacket with jagged claws that appeared to be growing directly from its long white fingers. The silk coat fell away in strips.

All four of them backed up into the far corner of the porch as the creature's head snapped up, and it stared at them, eyes glittering. It dropped the coat and began to crawl up the steps.

The most horrifying thing about the monster's slow, jerky process was that its face changed every few seconds. First it was Maddie. Then the flesh of its face rippled and it was Edgar, and then Eliza. Another ripple and Emma was staring straight into her own face all over again. No matter whose face it wore, it kept darting wide-eyed glances at Eliza.

It was afraid of her fire, Emma realized. But not afraid enough to stop coming for them. Not quite.

"Through here," Maddie screeched. "This one's open!" She yanked on the other door, and it opened with a rusty shriek.

They shot through the entrance, first Emma and Eliza and then Edgar. Maddie came last, slamming the door shut behind her with an echoing crash. Then they were pelting down a long, dim hallway full of doors marked with faded numbers, their footsteps muffled by thick carpet that sent up plumes of dust as they went. They streaked past door after door. Emma didn't know where the hallway led, and she didn't particularly care, as long as the answer was *away*.

They had made it about halfway down the hall when a crash from behind them echoed off the walls. Emma put on a burst of speed, knowing the creature must have smashed its way through the front doors.

The hallway ended in a narrow, carpeted staircase, and she took the stairs two at a time, hearing the others thundering up behind her. A second corridor stretched out before them, wider than the last, with brass lamps along the walls. The wallpaper had peeled and was lying on the floor in drifts. Emma kicked it out of the way as they went.

"We should go into one of these rooms," Eliza suggested. "Lock ourselves in."

She paused in front of the nearest door—*Number Nine*, according to the stained golden plaque. Thankfully, it was unlocked.

As the others darted inside Emma hung back, glancing down the hallway. It was dim and silent; there was no sound of footsteps in the distance, or on the staircase. She followed the others into the room and closed the door as quietly as she could behind her. The lock was rusted open, and she couldn't budge it, so at last she turned away, pressing her back to the door. They'd have to hope the creature wouldn't be able to find them here.

It was quiet inside the hotel room, and dark, save for the sunlight that leaked in past the tangle of blinds on the window and the orange glow of Eliza's fire. In the silence, Emma realized she could still hear multiple heartbeats, including her own, and she turned away from the others, struggling to push the Noise back behind the door so she could think straight.

The hotel room was surprisingly spacious. The wallpaper, which had once been a pink-and-white floral pattern, was now water-damaged and stained green, and ivy had climbed up into the corners and cracks. The floorboards were carpeted with moss, and there were vibrant green ferns growing just under the window.

In the center of the room was a double bed, with a thick layer of moss growing over the mattress like a strange bedspread. Over the headboard hung a faded painting of a ship on the ocean. Everything was covered in a layer of dust, and sheets of cobwebs hung from the light fixtures and bedposts.

It was a strange sight, this once-luxurious hotel room being slowly devoured by nature.

On the other side of the room stood a dresser. The large, oval mirror attached to it reflected their pale, shocked faces back at them. Edgar kept glancing over his shoulder at the door, and Maddie stared around the room. Eliza's arms were still completely encased in fire, and she glared down at her hands, brow creased.

There was a flutter of black in the mirror, a reflection of the window. When Emma whirled around, heart in her throat, it was to see a large black raven peering in at them through a crack in the blinds. She could hear the muffled scratching of its talons on the sill.

Instinctively, her gaze drifted to Edgar, who had turned to look as well. His face was very white, his eyes wide as he stared out the window.

Something clicked then, and Emma was suddenly sure it wasn't as simple as her cousin being afraid of birds. He'd refused to tell them what his power was, and she was beginning to suspect that birds were somehow a part of it.

But now was hardly the time to discuss it.

Emma was about to whisper to them all to keep still and quiet, that they simply needed to wait out the monster, when she became aware of the muffled thumping of a heartbeat.

This one was slower than Edgar's had been, steadier, and Emma stared over at the others. She hadn't heard it before, had she?

Which meant it wasn't any of them.

She froze, her own pulse fluttering in her throat, and began to back up slowly toward the corner of the room. The others took note and followed her lead.

The corner held only a narrow dresser and a cracked porcelain wash basin in which some enterprising bird had constructed a nest. Emma edged in beside it, pressing herself flat against the wall.

The heartbeat had ceased. There was nothing but silence. That was almost worse though. Was it the monster just outside the door, trying to figure out how to get in?

They were all staring at the door when it happened—when the knob slowly, ever so slowly, began to turn. Emma sucked in a breath, Maddie snatched at her sleeve, and Edgar was inching toward the window, as if he were thinking of flinging himself out. Only Eliza stayed where she was as the door swung inward, the flames on her arms jumping higher.

The figure in the doorway didn't move at first, although it was immediately obvious that this wasn't the crooked creature who had been chasing them through the streets. The man's hat was missing, and his hair stood up every which way, but Emma recognized him instantly.

The words tumbled out before she could stop them: "Witch hunter!"

Chapter Twenty

Tobias McCraw stared at her, blue eyes wide and a little wild. "Witch," he said, and before she could move he lunged forward. Emma shrieked as he seized her arms, yanking her close against his chest. His arm slid around her shoulders, trapping her.

Eliza shouted, starting toward them. The flames on her arms flared higher as she growled out through clenched teeth, "*You.*"

Emma couldn't see the witch hunter, but she could feel him go still against her back, and his arm tightened around her ever so slightly. It wasn't painful, but she definitely couldn't move.

So it had been his heart she'd heard outside the door, not the monster's.

"You stay back," he said. "I recognize you."

Surprisingly, it was Edgar who stepped forward now, leveling a stern gaze at the witch hunter. "You let her go. It's me you want."

The witch hunter snorted. "Hardly. What I want is for you to lead me to Witch City. Then nobody gets hurt."

Emma froze in his grip, startled. She would have thought he'd take them straight back to the queen. "We . . . we don't know the way."

"That's where we're trying to go, idiot," Eliza snarled. "Would we be hiding in some hotel if we knew how to get there?"

Edgar seemed to have wilted slightly. "You don't have orders to bring us back?"

Eliza crossed her arms, which were still flaming, and continued to glower at McCraw as she spoke to Edgar. "Hate to break it to you, but we don't matter in the big picture. Finding Witch City has always been the hunters' top priority. That and Lenore Black. That's why they were formed in the first place."

McCraw frowned very sternly at this, and Eliza smirked. "Why do you think adult witches go to the dungeons and not straight to the noose when they're accused? They drill them for information about the city."

"That's classified information." McCraw's voice was a low growl from above Emma's head.

"I'm a witch." Eliza rolled her eyes. "We've known for ages."

A moment passed while they all stared at one another, and Emma briefly considered breaking out of his arms and running for it. Then the silence was interrupted by a shuffle and thump from overhead, and they all looked up at the ceiling.

Before any of them could move McCraw released Emma, shoving her forward. She stumbled, nearly falling on her face before Maddie caught her. "Stay there and don't move," he said tersely.

The witch hunter leapt back and slammed the door shut, struggling with the rusted lock, before it finally turned with a sharp *snap*.

"That thing's been following me for hours. I thought I'd lost it."

"It chased us in here." Emma rubbed her arms, glaring up at him.

"What is it?" McCraw's expression was dark as he looked at each of them in turn. "What does it want?"

"Something awful," Maddie said. "We should push the furniture against the door. Block it out."

"With you on the outside," Eliza suggested, with a pointed glance at Tobias McCraw.

The witch hunter ignored her. He was still staring up at the ceiling. "Another witch?"

"We don't know. Maybe." Emma shuddered. "It wears other people's faces. It changes. It's been following us on and off."

And stalking the witch hunter in the "off" moments, obviously.

A witch hunting a witch hunter. It would have been almost funny if that thing out there wasn't so terrifying.

"Maybe it's on the next floor up?" Maddie whispered, and Emma nodded slowly. That was a good thing. If it had gone straight past them and continued to the next floor, it obviously didn't know where they were.

Maybe now was the time to sneak out of the hotel and run for the edge of the city—that is, if the witch hunter would let them.

As if one murderous problem wasn't enough.

The Noise had retreated slightly ever since the witch hunter burst into the room, so when another heartbeat started up again, more distant than the others, Emma froze, head tilted to listen. This one was . . . different, she realized, and a shiver dropped down her back.

There was something very off about the rhythm.

The sound of a human heartbeat was so familiar to Emma, so natural. In contrast, this one was utterly strange. In fact, there was something terrifying in its sheer *wrongness*.

A second later she knew what it was, and the realization sent a sliver of cold horror through her.

It was far too slow. There was a long pause between each deep thudding beat, so long that it seemed impossible the creature was alive at all.

Which meant it was *not* human. Maybe it wasn't even properly *alive*.

"It's here somewhere. I can hear it," she whispered, half to herself. "It's trying to get in."

The witch hunter didn't ask how she knew this. Instead, he set his back to the door. "This is oak. It shouldn't be able to break it down."

"You've met this thing," Maddie said, her voice trembling. "You should know it's determined."

It had gone quiet out in the hall, and no new noises could be heard from the ceiling above, but Emma could still hear the awful pulse of the heartbeat. The creature was still there, but . . . what was it doing?

A second later, a loud crash answered her. The door jumped violently in its frame, and the witch hunter gave a cry of surprise, his back still braced against it. The base of the rusted lock had shattered, sending splinters of wood skittering across the floor.

Emma lunged forward without thinking, jamming her shoulder into the door on one side of the witch hunter. Another earth-shattering crash, and the wood shuddered violently against her. Edgar had braced himself on the other side, his face grim. "It's too strong!"

Maddie looked at the witch hunter, eyes wide. "Can't you . . . hit it with your staff or something?"

"Tried that earlier. It shook it off like nothing." The witch hunter grunted as another shuddering blow pushed him forward. "You two, open the window. We'll get out that way. Wait on the roof for me."

Maddie grimaced at him before running over to the hotel window. She jerked at the frame, trying to pull it up. It gave a rusty shriek and stuck fast a few inches up the track. "Eliza, help me!"

Eliza was still standing in the middle of the room, arms wreathed in flames, her face ashen. She shook her head. "It won't go out! It—my fire is stuck!" Her voice was climbing in pitch, laced with panic. "It seemed harder to put out the last few times, but I just thought it was because I was stressed. Something's wrong!"

There was another series of crashes from the door. They weren't as strong this time, and Emma was able to brace herself well enough. Above her, the witch hunter muttered, "It's not properly trying to get in."

From where she was leaning, Emma had a clear view of the doorknob as it began to turn. She shrieked, grasping the knob to stop it, but her palms were sweaty and her hands were shaking. Her fingers slipped.

Emma screamed, alarmed to feel her feet sliding on the carpet as she was pushed forward. The witch hunter growled under his breath, turning to shove his shoulder to the door, planting his boots more firmly onto the carpeted floor.

The creature was alarmingly strong. It somehow managed to push them forward another full inch, even with three of them shoving back with all their might.

There was an excited screech from the crack in the door, which sent shivers of horror down Emma's spine.

"How is it so strong?" Eliza shouted, and her flames jumped higher.

Emma groaned as she slid forward, and then yelped as several thin, spindly white fingers hooked around the edge of the door inches from her left shoulder.

Across the room, there was another crash. Maddie had managed to slide the window up at last. "Come on, let's go!" she yelled, beckoning frantically.

For a moment no one replied. They could all immediately see the ordeal they were in. If they let go of the door to run for it, the creature would get in. It was too fast. They wouldn't make it in time.

"Change of plans," the witch hunter grunted. "You four hide in the closet. I'm going to throw this blasted thing out the window instead."

Emma stared up at Tobias McCraw. She knew he was trying to get them to stay in his sight. If they slipped out the window while he fought the creature, his entire mission was blown. "How are you going to do that?"

"You let me deal with that." He scowled down at her. "You both let go on three."

Before either of them could argue, the creature behind the door gave an excited shriek and shoved them forward another inch. In that moment, Emma knew they had to do what Tobias said. At least if the witch hunter tried to fight it, they could make a dash for the window while he was distracted. She glanced past him and looked at Edgar, who nodded.

"On three," Emma shouted over the noise, "One, two—"

She didn't get to finish, because in the moment between *two* and *three*, something very strange happened.

One second the witch hunter was standing between her and Edgar, and the next, he was gone. There was only empty space between them, and Emma stared uncomprehendingly at Edgar, who looked just as shocked.

But there was no time to question it, because the door was shoved violently forward and this time, without the weight of the witch hunter, Emma felt herself slide nearly a full foot. An excited wail came from the doorway, and a thin, crooked arm shot through. Emma screamed as it hooked around her neck and shoulders, dragging her sideways.

"Emma!"

Eliza's scream mixed with Maddie's and Edgar's, and there was a great thunder of footsteps. Emma struggled to hold the door shut as she thrashed against the creature's bony arm. Its skin was horribly cold and clammy, and the only thing she could think about was how much she wanted it off of her.

A moment later, Maddie rammed her entire body against the center of the door, slamming into the space between Emma and

Edgar. Eliza crouched down next to Emma, curling one flaming hand around the monster's wrist. It gave another high-pitched scream, this one filled with pain, and yanked its arm away, slamming Emma's back into the door and striking her head on the wood.

Dazed, Emma heard Eliza give a cry of triumph as the door slammed shut, and then Maddie snatched at something near the base of the doorframe. There was the rattle of a chain, and the sound of a bolt sliding home. When Emma glanced down, blinking spots out of her eyes, she was relieved to see a chain across the door. She hadn't even seen the second lock at the base.

"Deadbolt," Maddie said, breathing hard. "They always have them at hotels."

No one asked how she knew that; they all just stood back and stared at the door. The chain was thick, and only a few inches long. The crackle and pop of flames and the heavy sound of their own panting breaths filled the silence.

When the door crashed again, they all jumped, and then Emma let out a shaky breath when it stopped short, caught against the chain. A screech of anger could be heard through the crack.

Maddie spoke over the noise. "Window's open."

They gathered themselves, staring around the hotel room. The window was indeed open wide now, letting in a steady, pine-scented breeze. Slivers of wood littered the floor in front of it, and a wide crack ran down the frame.

They could still hear the creature growling and muttering behind the door, rattling the chain as it pressed against it. For the moment, it seemed, they were safe, and as some of the adrenaline left Emma's body, her legs suddenly felt as if they were about to give out beneath her. She stumbled over to the bed and sat down on the mossy blanket. Her entire body seemed to have gone weak.

"What just happened?"

Chapter Twenty-One

None of them knew why the witch hunter had disappeared, or where he'd gone, but since the creature on the other side of the door didn't seem to be giving up, Emma knew they'd have to get out soon.

Slowly, Emma stood and moved over to the window, trying her best not to make any noise. She wasn't sure how intelligent the monster was, but she didn't want it to guess their plan. When she leaned out the window and peered down, the ground didn't look as far away as she'd thought. They were only on the second floor. A fall from this height wouldn't kill them, but it was still a long way down. They couldn't risk broken bones, not when that creature was following them.

She leaned out a little farther, holding tightly to the ledge, and scanned the rooftop to her right. It was steep, and the black tiles were almost fully covered in a thick layer of green moss. That would make things rather slippery.

The window next to theirs, the one she'd be aiming for, was only about ten feet away, and the ledge under the windows, though it was covered in dirt and rotten leaves, was wide enough to walk along. If they could climb out onto the ledge and walk to the next window as quietly as possible, they could simply slide into the room beside this one and escape while the monster was still hammering at their door.

From up here, Forest-London looked wild yet beautiful. The sun had risen fully now, its rays glittering off hundreds of cracked windowpanes, flooding the forest of fall leaves and towering pine trees with light that made everything green and gold.

She tiptoed back over to the others and told them the plan, keeping her voice as low as possible. Maddie and Edgar both looked grim. Eliza only seemed to be half paying attention; she was still preoccupied with the flames licking at her arms. Emma glanced at her, worried, and Eliza shook her head.

"They won't go out."

"Alright. Um . . . we'll sort it in a bit." It was a problem, but they had to deal with the immediate threat first. There was another round of rattling thumps as the monster tried to knock the door in. "Just . . . try not to set anything on fire for now, okay?" she said quickly.

Eliza glanced over at the door and nodded.

They crowded around the window, and there was a brief but silent squabble over who would be the first to go out. Finally, Emma simply swung one leg over the sill and slid out onto the ledge, being sure to grip the sill with both hands as she turned slowly and got a solid footing before facing the next window.

Outside, things seemed different. The ledge was thinner, for one. It only *appeared* to be a foot or two across. One wrong step and she would slide off the side of the building.

She felt dizzy suddenly, her head swimming. The ledge was slick under her feet, and she clung to the sill, her knuckles white, fingers aching. Then she forced herself to push off, placing her hands on the mossy roof slats, inching forward and then forward again. Just another step, and another. She was so close to the next window.

It seemed to take forever, but finally she could reach out and grasp the edge of the frame. A wave of relief rushed over her. Thankfully, this window was less sticky than the one she'd just come through, and she managed to slide it open enough to wiggle into the room, dropping as quietly as possible onto the floor. This hotel room was much the same as the last—overgrown, and filled with moss and peeling wallpaper, with a dust-covered mirror that reflected her white face back at her.

Maddie and Edgar came next, both clearly reluctant and terribly slow, but at last Emma was able to pull them in. When she looked up from helping Edgar in, Eliza was already halfway across the ledge, nearly about to let go of the first window frame, her face set in grim determination. Already a few small fires were starting, and Emma watched, holding her breath. A spark shriveled a patch of moss under Eliza's hand and then fizzled out, and a clump of damp leaves sent up a wisp of smoke. Thankfully, the thick layer of green moss that covered everything here didn't seem particularly susceptible to catching fire.

Emma's gaze drifted from Eliza to the open window, and then to the window just across from theirs. The sun was directly overhead now, a glare of yellow light reflecting from the pane, combined with the flickering glow of Eliza's flames. Emma squinted, frowning. She could see her reflection in the dusty glass. Her face, pale and wan, her black hair wild around her shoulders.

Emma froze.

She could feel Edgar's shoulder touching her own as he leaned past her, could hear Maddie breathing beside her, so how was it that only she was reflected ... ? The Emma in the windowpane twitched, her black eyes glittering, a smile snaking across her face.

Not a reflection, Emma realized with a jolt of horror. It was there. Somehow, the monster had gotten into the room across from theirs, and it was watching them.

"Eliza," she croaked out. Eliza paused and looked up at her, still just past the frame of the first window, and nearly out in the middle of the slender ledge.

"What? What's wrong?"

Emma's throat seemed to be closing up. It made her voice come out high and strangled. "Run."

Chapter Twenty-Two

Eliza turned, wobbling in the center of the ledge, bracing herself on the roof. The monster snaked one hand onto the edge of the windowpane. It was gibbering excitedly, tugging the window upward. Emma could hear the window creaking in its track. It was stuck, like the other had been, but the monster was strong.

Eliza seemed frozen, staring back over her shoulder.

"Run!" Emma hissed again, and even through the dusty glass she saw the monster twitch, turning wide lamp-like eyes on her. In the dim light those eyes seem to glow with a sickly yellow radiance.

"You have to run *now!*"

But Eliza didn't move.

"What are you doing? *Move*, Eliza." Edgar's upper body was hanging out of the window now. His voice was sharp and commanding, but Emma could hear the faint tremor in it. She half expected Eliza to whirl around and yell at Edgar to shut up, but she stayed where she was.

The creature had sunk down in front of the window now, its bony shoulders hunched, its horrible face tucked down low into the rest of its body. As they watched, it flattened itself against the sill and, horrifyingly slowly, it slunk through the crack in the window. Emma watched, mouth open wide. The creature's movements were boneless, almost snake-like.

She had time for one terrible thought—if this thing had ever actually been human, it hadn't been for a long time now—and then it was through, spilling out onto the ledge, unfolding its long, crooked frame.

Emma clutched the windowsill so hard her fingers ached. In the middle of the ledge, Eliza was as still as a statue. Why wasn't she moving?

"Eliza." Edgar's voice cracked. "*Come on.*"

The monster placed one foot on the ledge, tentatively, its face swirling and molding itself into strange new features, as if it were too distracted to settle on one.

Eliza still didn't move, but the flames on her arms flared higher.

Finally, the monster leapt forward. Emma screamed, hands over her mouth, as it hurtled across the gap and crashed onto the roof, digging its claws into the tiles, skidding to a halt a second before going over the edge and landing deftly on the window ledge. There was less than ten feet of distance between itself and Eliza now, and it was making an excited kind of screeching, its open mouth revealing a set of broken, yellow teeth.

Emma's throat was tight. "Eliza, move!"

The creature bounded forward, one hand outstretched, the other clinging to the ledge. Finally, Eliza moved. Her entire body had gone stiff, and her brow was creased with concentration, but she lifted her hands.

The flames on her arms shifted abruptly, flickering once before vanishing into her skin, as if they'd been sucked straight into her blood. A breath later, fire burst out of her hands, and two huge, roiling balls of flame bloomed in the air over the roof with a furious roar. They lit up the entire side of the hotel, illuminating the mossy roof, glittering off the cracked windowpanes. Clumps of smoldering moss and leaves rained down onto the streets below.

The creature screamed and reeled back, pale eyes huge in its gaunt face. It scrabbled for purchase on the ledge, claws screeching on the stone, and then it fell.

Emma leaned forward, hands over her mouth, and saw it plummet down, flipping end over end, skinny limbs flailing. It fell past the roof and out of sight, and the high-pitched keening cut off abruptly.

When Emma looked back up, it was to see Eliza picking her way carefully toward them. Her dress was singed in large black patches over her shoulders and collar, but there was no sign of flames anywhere.

The others watched, silent. When Eliza finally reached the window, they grasped her and drew her over the sill. Emma didn't let her go, instead hugging her tightly, full of relief. Edgar and Maddie clung to her too, and for one odd moment they stayed that way.

Eliza smelled like smoke, and her skin was still very warm, and Maddie's hair tickled Emma a little on one shoulder. On the other side, she could feel Edgar's elbow poking her. Still, it was strangely comforting after everything.

A moment later they broke apart. Maddie was beaming, and Edgar's face was bright red. Eliza cleared her throat and rubbed the back of her neck, glancing down at her shoes.

"I-I... sorry," Edgar stuttered. "I just ... we thought you were going to die."

"It's okay. I thought I was going to die too." Eliza brushed at her burnt dress and shrugged. "I knew that if I couldn't get my power under control, I would. It's hard to control when I'm scared." She took a breath and looked around at all of them, expression grave. "But . . . I realized you weren't about to leave me, and if that thing got past me, it would go for you next. I couldn't let that happen. It was like that thought gave me control over the fear."

A smile curved one corner of her mouth. "You know, I think I'm getting the hang of it—even without my coven around to teach me. I think you all just helped with that."

Emma nodded slowly. For the first time since she'd left the palace to be tested, something warm eased through her insides, taking over the fear.

So that was why Eliza had stood her ground. Emma had thought she was frozen with fear, but she'd actually been determined to protect them. Wordlessly, Emma reached out and touched Eliza's arm. Eliza smiled back before they turned to look out the window one last time.

The winding, grassy streets and ivy-covered tops of the buildings below were empty. There was no sign of the monster.

They made their way back down the stairs and through the hall to the entryway, all of them treading very quietly. Once outside, they jumped at every little squeak of the porch, and Maddie hushed Edgar furiously when he stumbled, his boot thumping on the wooden floorboards.

Emma held her breath the whole way, and then paused abruptly at the top of the stairs, her mouth falling open at the sight spread out below them.

There was still no sign of the monster. Instead, the streets laid out before them appeared to be entirely filled by birds.

Chapter Twenty-Three

They were everywhere: perched on the roofs of empty carriages, lining the windows and eves of buildings, filling the branches of the nearest trees—all of them huge, black birds with glossy feathers. As Emma and the others stood on the porch, they were greeted with a great rush of noise. Rustling wings and clicking beaks and soft croaking.

Behind her, Edgar gave a strangled cry and stumbled back, hands flying to his mouth. Emma turned to see him staring around, face filled with utter horror. She'd hoped he'd be comfortable enough to tell them soon, but this . . . well, he could hardly deny this was magic, could he?

"Is that your power, Ed? Birds follow you?" Emma finally said.

For a moment she thought he would deny it. He was shaking his head. His mouth worked soundlessly, as if trying to provide excuses but failing to come up with anything. Then, at last, he seemed to deflate, shoulders slumping.

"They come when I get scared."

"That's magic." Eliza looked out at the birds, brows raised. "That's what happens when you're untrained and you've got strong emotions."

"Just ignore them," Edgar muttered. "Eventually they go away."

Eliza looked like she wanted to argue, but Edgar began making his way down the stairs. They walked single file down the street, and surprisingly, the ravens cleared a path for them. It was like walking some strange, feathered gauntlet of watchful black birds.

The ravens followed their progress, beaks turning as the four of them went past, hundreds of black eyes following their every step. A shiver dropped down Emma's spine as she stared at them, but none of them seemed to notice her. They were all looking at Edgar. Watching him.

She swallowed hard. "What do they want, Ed? They must be here for a reason, right?"

Edgar did not answer this. Instead, he marched forward at full steam, his shoulders rigid. His posture said that he was ignoring the birds so thoroughly they might as well not be there. That he denounced their evil magic and would have nothing to do with it.

He didn't slow his pace until he was forced to—when the city gave another great rumble and the ground heaved beneath them. Emma squeaked in alarm, shooting an arm out to grab him by the back of his shirt.

A great white archway had risen up before them, and Emma immediately had a strange jolt of recognition. The weekly trips to the park; her mother's nagging insistence that she wear her best dress and the shiny shoes that pinched her feet. The time she'd nearly fallen off her horse and her mother hadn't even noticed, too busy soaking up all the attention as her procession rode down the wide lane.

Hyde Park had just appeared before them.

No one said anything, but it was obvious they would have to go through it, for the park stretched out on either side as far as the eye could see.

Emma felt a wave of despair as they made their way slowly to the thick stone archway. If Forest-London kept moving like this, how on earth were they supposed to get to the other side of it? They could be stuck wandering forever.

As they stepped under the archway, Maddie sucked in a breath, and Edgar and Eliza both paused. Edgar let out a groan of dismay. Emma stopped just behind them, trying to process what she was seeing.

Hyde Park had changed.

When they'd visited, Emma and her mother had mostly stuck to the riding path or the promenade along the river. The promenade had been her favorite. It had been almost peaceful, with slender, leafy trees growing on either side, forming a kind of open tunnel you could walk through.

But the trees she was looking at now were not at all like she remembered.

It was as if whatever spell had settled on this strange In-Between had mutated them. They were massive, towering over the promenade and the fences along the outside of the park, their roots snaking up through the pathway and upending stones.

The neatly trimmed lawns were gone too, replaced by wild, hip-high fields of grass that rippled in the wind. There were benches all along the pathway before them, though it was as if the earth was attempting to swallow them up. Vines and ferns and tiny saplings were growing around and through the slats of the seats.

It was a tangled thicket, like some kind of jungle, and Emma had a sudden, unwelcome thought: if there were wild animals here in this strange overgrown London, this was where they would be living.

No one spoke for a moment, and then Edgar, still staring up at the thick forest before them, said in an awed voice, "What do we do? Do we keep going?"

Emma wasn't sure what to say. She turned to the others, hoping that someone else might have an idea. She wasn't sure how she'd ended up in charge of what direction they went. She'd expected Eliza to have opinions, or for Edgar to order them to move this way or that. But they were all staring at her expectantly.

She cleared her throat. "We have to get to the other side of the city, right? We could try to go around, but that could take a lot longer. I guess . . . I guess we should just cross through. We'll stick to the path."

Or what was left of the path.

No one else seemed to have any suggestions, so they forged onward, entering the thick forest and keeping to the path as much as they could. The going was slow, as they had to dodge around cracks in the pavement and pieces of the path that bulged up, thanks to the roots beneath. It was eerie the way the trees towered over them, impossibly thick-trunked, the branches stretching up so high they cast the entire pathway into shadow.

They moved at a middling sort of pace. Edgar was the slowest of them, trailing along behind, and every few minutes, Emma checked back to make sure he was still there. No one seemed very happy, but she noticed that Edgar looked more miserable the deeper into the forest they went. She dropped back a little, reaching out to poke him in the side as they came over the next rise in the path.

"What's the matter?"

He blinked at her, and then glanced up ahead to where Eliza and Maddie were pushing through the underbrush, Maddie complaining loudly to Eliza that there was a rock in her shoe.

"I've always had a raven or two around." He kept his voice low. "But I never really thought about it, or even noticed it much, because the castle is so loaded with thistle. I think it pretty much kept it under control."

She nodded, waiting for him to continue.

"The first time it happened—I mean, truly happened—I was with her."

Emma's mouth dropped open. "Your mother?"

He nodded. "It was on a hunt through the forest. We were after pheasants that time, I think." He grimaced, and then shrugged. "Anyway, we'd broken away from the group, because I'd told her I didn't want to hunt witches when I was older. She was furious, lecturing me about what the witches had done to our family. She told me I was joining the witch hunters when I turned eighteen, that it didn't matter what I wanted, and I started panicking." He swallowed, looking up at the treetops like he was picturing it. "That's when they showed up."

Emma nearly walked into a tree branch, she was so fixated on his story. She brushed it away impatiently. "What happened? Did she see them?"

"No, that's the absolutely mad thing. She was so angry at me. She was jabbing at me with her finger, just red-faced and furious, lecturing about personal responsibility, and I look up and the trees are just *filled* with birds. Every branch in every tree. But it's like"— he hesitated—"it's like they knew to be quiet, or something. They didn't make a sound, and she just . . . never looked up. Not once."

He fell silent for a moment, and Emma shook her head in disbelief, stepping over a rock jutting up in her path.

"It seemed like something out of a dream, except that I always noticed them after that, and I *knew*. I knew I was going to fail The Testing." He shrugged, face mournful. "And I did. Twenty-five percent."

"I'm forty." Emma shrugged when his eyes went wide. "I think I knew too, though I didn't want to admit it."

Edgar only nodded in reply. His expression was strained, and she thought about suggesting they take a break for a few minutes so he could sit down. Before she could say anything though, she heard a distant sound—a quiet, faraway *thump-thump, thump-thump*.

It was familiar. She'd heard it in the hotel. Not the too-slow version of the monster's heart, but the steady, deep pulse she'd heard before that.

Witch hunter.

Fear blossomed in her chest, and she glanced around at the trees, at the shadowy spaces between them. There was no movement there, no dark figures flickering between them.

But she knew it was him. "Hold on, I hear him. I hear the witch hunter."

Edgar staggered to a halt, a look of dismay on his face. "But . . . he disappeared. We saw it."

"Maybe it was this place moving." Emma searched the trees again briefly, stomach fluttering. Still nothing. "Maybe he's found us again."

"What do we do?" Maddie, too, was darting sharp looks around at the trees, eyes wide. "Do we hide?"

Emma tried to gather her thoughts. He was following them, but his heartbeat sounded distant, too quiet for him to be close. She lowered her voice. "We keep going, but I think he's following us, hoping we lead him to Witch City. We'll have to lose him at some point. For now, we pretend we don't know he's there."

It wasn't a good plan, but it was a plan. They pressed on, and eventually the heartbeat faded away. But the deeper they went into the woods the more Emma felt like something or someone was watching them from the shadows between the trees. Now that they were walking again, she kept seeing little flickers of movement between the trunks. Was it just the mix of shadows and sun filtering through, or was something actually moving there?

She picked up her pace without even really meaning to, ignoring the brambles scraping at her face and clothing, scratching her cheeks.

The path was barely visible now, but they pressed on until a loud rustling sound from up ahead stopped them in their tracks. Emma shook her head in frustration. The sound of the blood rushing in her ears was so loud that it drowned out everything else.

"Is it the witch . . ." Maddie started to ask, but her words trailed off as something slid out of the bushes before them.

It was not the witch hunter, but a slender, inky-black cat.

Chapter Twenty-Four

E mma blinked, startled. She'd expected the witch hunter, or maybe the horrifying, face-shifting monster, but certainly not a house cat.

The animal sat back on its haunches and tilted its head, blinking right back at them.

A laugh slipped out before Emma could stop it. She'd been worried about the wild animals that might be lurking in this park, but it was this tiny black house cat that had come to stare her down. She supposed it made sense: if people had lived in this abandoned London at one time, they'd surely had pets. And now those pets were living in the wild.

The cat padded forward and then stopped, settling back on its haunches again, apparently content to sit and examine them as they examined it. It had very green eyes and a white-tipped tail with a crook in the center. The cat twitched its tail at them and blinked, and to Emma's surprise, it seemed to look directly at her.

A beat later, the cat stood up and turned around, looking back over its shoulder at them. It jerked its tail at Emma as if to say, *Well? Come on!* Then it trotted off, vanishing into the thick of the forest.

She turned to look at the others. "I think it wants us to follow."

Maddie blinked and Edgar frowned, shaking his head. "It's a cat. Cats don't *want* anything. They're just cats."

"Have you ever actually *met* a cat?" Maddie snorted, and Eliza was nodding.

"Cats aren't just cats when you're dealing with witches," was all Eliza said. She was the first to turn and begin moving in the direction the cat had gone.

Edgar pursed his lips. For a moment he looked as though he wanted to say something, but he just shook his head and followed.

It was hard to keep up with the cat, especially because its black coat blended with the dim forest surroundings, but Emma would catch a glimpse of it as it jumped over a fallen log or wove around a cluster of ferns. Occasionally, she'd see its eyes glow green in the darkness before winking out again, and she realized the cat was checking over its shoulder, making sure they were still following. She felt her chest swell with something that might be hope.

A cat leading them to Witch City made a strange kind of sense.

Eliza had hinted that, for witches, there was more to cats than met the eye, and Emma thought she might have been talking about familiars. She only knew about familiars from what she'd read in the books—ominous warnings about black cats and sewer rats that served as witches' companions and had a direct link to their masters' minds. It seemed they were often sent to spy on upstanding citizens. But if this cat was a familiar, it was only helping them.

Finally, the trees came to an end, and they came out of the forest onto a steep, grassy bank that dipped down to a large expanse of dark water. After climbing over a thick-trunked tree that had fallen across the path, they found the cat sitting at the top of the slope, just before the knee-high grass began.

The feeling of hope swelling in Emma's chest expanded as she looked out over the lake. She knew where they were now. This was the Serpentine, the famous boating spot enjoyed by London's elite. She and her mother had walked this very bank, though of course the grass hadn't been nearly as tall.

When she looked around for their guide, Emma saw that the spot at the edge of the slope was empty. The cat had vanished.

Not knowing quite what to do next, the group decided to take a brief rest on the shore of the lake below. Edgar sat down on a fallen log and began rifling through his bag, while Maddie and Eliza argued in low tones about where walking around the edge of the lake would lead them. Emma's stomach gave a great growl, which served to remind her that she had a handful of very squashed almond scones in her dress sash from their time in the palace earlier.

The four of them devoured the flattened pastries with gusto.

"There's a teahouse along here, I tell you," Maddie said between mouthfuls. "I've been here before. We should stop in. I've heard the Earl Grey is to die for."

"There won't be any tea left, dummy. It'll all have gone off by now," Eliza said.

Emma edged closer to Edgar. He'd pulled his leather notebook out of his bag and was writing furiously, his face scrunched in concentration.

"Are you . . . writing your poetry?"

He nodded once and continued scribbling, and Emma leaned over to peer into his pack. There were a couple more leather-bound books—volumes of poetry, his nursemaid had said—and a flat leather pocketbook with brass corners, about the size of a wallet.

"What's this thing?"

Edgar glanced up briefly and shrugged. "Whatever Georgie put in there. Take it out if you like."

Emma pulled the pocketbook out and placed it carefully on her knee. A monogrammed *Black* decorated the front. When she opened it, she had the unpleasant shock of finding the queen's face staring out at her. "Oh, ugh. Georgie's given you a poster of your mother."

Edgar lowered his book and glanced over, frowning. "What? Why would she do that?"

Eliza and Maddie had stopped their own conversation to listen, and Maddie cleared her throat and said, "Maybe Georgie didn't know about the room under the castle and the . . . well, you know."

Edgar grimaced down at the picture. "Throw it away."

Emma hesitated. The poster was unpleasant, of course, but it was the picture on the other side that drew her attention. It was Alexandria and Isolde, both of them much younger. In the black-and-white photo, they were standing side by side, wearing modest walking dresses. She'd never seen her mother looking so . . . plain before. Isolde was smiling at the camera, and for once she looked almost happy. She wore her hair loose, in ringlets around her shoulders, instead of the elaborate updo she usually preferred. Emma stared down at the photo, annoyed to find herself suddenly blinking back tears.

She still remembered it so clearly, the day Edgar had told on her: Isolde launching herself at the witch hunters, pushing them away from nine-year-old Emma. Even yelling at her beloved sister, protecting her daughter from the queen, of all people.

Isolde had defended her so fiercely that day.

They hadn't loved one another, exactly, but they were still family.

"I don't think she wants to throw it away."

It was Eliza who had spoken, and when Emma looked up, she found her staring, dark brows raised. "Emma, I know you don't want to admit that your mother knew, but . . . I think they both did. Keeping the photo, well . . . I don't think it's a good idea."

A surge of irritation hit her, and Emma bit back a reply. Of course Eliza would think that. Eliza hated the Black family. But her mother? Well, her mother was prissy and foolish and in need of constant attention, and she idolized her sister far more than was healthy, but she wasn't a *monster*, not like the queen was.

She couldn't have known.

Emma didn't want to argue, so she just shrugged and shoved the pocketbook back into the bag. "It's fine. I just . . . we won't look at it."

Eliza looked like she wanted to say something else, but she pressed her lips together tightly instead. Maddie cleared her throat, and opened her mouth as if to speak, but before she could get a word out, there was a rustling from somewhere behind them, and Emma jumped, turning back to scan the forest, heart hammering in her chest.

Had the witch hunter snuck up on them? She hadn't heard his heart this time.

The space between the tree trunks was clear; nothing moved. But when she glanced up toward the treetops, she could make out several black shapes fluttering in the trees.

More ravens.

She glanced sideways at Edgar, wondering if he realized that more and more were arriving. He couldn't just ignore the power. That wasn't the way things worked. At least, she assumed it wasn't.

Normally, she would have told herself it wasn't any of her business, but the fluttering shadows overhead made her nervous. She folded her legs beneath her and tried to shift on the bank to get more comfortable. Should she point it out? Or would that just make his anxiety worse, and end up attracting more? It really was a lose-lose situation.

"If we could just find the cat again," Maddie was saying now, "we could get out of this place."

Eliza sat up a little straighter. "Emma, use your power. Can you hear it right now? Is it close by?"

Both Emma and Edgar gaped at her, and Eliza shrugged. "What?"

"She's not going to just *use* her power," Edgar said scornfully, though Emma thought she could detect an undercurrent of fear in his tone, and it made her stomach turn. "Not on purpose."

Eliza frowned at him. "Your power is there for a reason: to help you."

She said this so matter-of-factly that it sent a flash of annoyance through Emma. "Want to know what my power does?" she asked, a bite in her tone. "It *stops people's hearts*. If that isn't evil magic, I don't know what is." As soon as the words came out, she snapped her mouth shut, wishing she hadn't said anything. Edgar visibly blanched, and even Maddie winced a little. Eliza shook her head.

"Growing up, I was taught that magic is never inherently evil. It's not good or bad, any more than a carpenter's hammer is. It's a tool designed to help you. *You* specifically."

"Of course you were taught it's not evil," Edgar shot back. "You were raised by witches."

"And you were raised by *her*," Eliza said, though this time, her voice didn't hold as much heat, and Edgar sagged a little, his face uncertain.

There was no arguing with that. If anyone was evil, it was the queen.

Emma glanced over at Edgar, who met her eyes and shrugged.

She stared out at the lake, her mind working furiously. What Eliza was saying might be true for *her*, but Emma's power was undeniably destructive. She'd stopped Edgar's heart back at court, the night of the hearings. And before that? Well, her mother had never put two and two together. She hadn't realized her heart had nearly given out during one of their screaming matches because of *Emma*. She'd blamed it on getting too worked up, on not eating enough that day, but Emma had felt it. She'd heard the erratic pulse stutter to a stop, seen her mother's face go pale and shocked, and Emma had known it was her doing.

And for one horrible moment, she'd almost been glad. She'd hoped this would be the end. That her mother would never scream at her again.

But then she'd stumbled back, horrified at herself, slamming the door on her power, forcing it into that still, small space at the back of her mind, where it couldn't hurt anyone.

Maybe her power wasn't evil, but in that moment, Emma almost had been.

"Do you think *I'm* evil?" Eliza tilted her head, smiling at her, and Emma shook her head, a little astonished at the question.

"Of course not!"

"Well then, maybe it's time you accept that you were lied to about a lot of things. You're a witch, Emma. That doesn't make you bad."

Emma pursed her lips and stared at Eliza, her mind frantically trying to keep up. It was going to take more than one day to shake off years of learning, of course, but much of what she'd been taught had already been proven a lie. That all witches were wicked and murderous, that Lenore Black was dead, that Witch City was a lie . . .

None of it was true.

When Eliza spoke again, her voice was sympathetic. "I know it's hard. You know what my coven told me whenever I'd struggle? *Trust your magic.* Yours has helped you, hasn't it?"

It had. The power had led Emma to Maddie when she'd first arrived in this strange place, and it had warned her about the monster coming too. Reluctantly, she nodded.

"Trust your magic, Emma."

That made it seem so easy, like her power was only good. Like it didn't come with the very real possibility of hurting someone. Of killing them.

She sighed. "I guess we should keep going."

Thankfully, Eliza didn't push the subject.

They made their way slowly back up the slope, heading for the edge of the forest. Emma was in the lead with Maddie, with Edgar and Eliza just behind. She furiously chewed the inside of her cheek, thoughts whirring around her head. It wasn't so hard to *believe* that magic wasn't evil, but behaving that way was another thing altogether. A fear of witches—and of magic, in turn—had been drilled into her since birth. It was hard to shake that off, even though she'd started to see the truth.

She turned to Eliza to say as much, but when her eyes locked on Eliza's face, she saw something change. Eliza's expression shifted. A split second before it happened, her eyes went wide and dreamy and her gaze changed focus, as if she were looking at something beyond Emma. A smile began to curl one corner of her mouth.

The words shriveled on Emma's tongue. She knew, suddenly, that something was about to happen. Something big. Something that would change everything.

There was no noise, nothing to warn them. Eliza was simply there one second, and the next she was gone. There was nothing in the space where she'd been standing but the tall grass waving in the breeze.

Chapter Twenty-Five

Emma stumbled mid-step, nearly pitching forward in her shock, and Maddie turned to her, frowning. "Emma, what—?"

"Where is she?" Emma stared at the empty space where Eliza had been, her confusion slowly leaking away, only to be replaced by horror.

Edgar spluttered and pointed at the grass, his hand trembling wildly. "She was here . . . she was just—"

"Eliza!" Emma turned on the spot. Her voice sounded high and thin, caught by the wind and carried away. There was no reply, only the rustle of grass and the distant call of birds in the trees overhead. "Eliza?"

"Eliza? Eliza!" Maddie had caught on now, and her expression was twisted in fear. "She was right here. I just *saw* her."

All three of them jumped at the sharp cry of a bird overhead, and Emma glanced up, panic making her breaths shallow and sharp. There were more ravens circling above them now. There had to be nearly twenty.

When Emma turned back to her friends, Edgar was hunched over and breathing hard. He clutched at the front of his shirt, white-knuckled, as if he could somehow anchor himself to keep from dissolving into nothing.

"Where did she go?" Maddie kept whispering. "Where is she?"

Emma didn't have an answer, but before she could even begin to think about what to say, she was distracted by the sudden sound of rustling, loud and persistent, in the treetops above her. She glanced up again, and then promptly wished she hadn't.

In the dim light, she could make out more black shapes winging their way overhead, settling into the branches above them. They were collecting impossibly fast now, forming rows and rows of hunched silhouettes along every branch.

The trees above them were filling with ravens.

There were so many that in minutes the tallest trees had begun to droop under their weight. And they were stirring restlessly, as if they were growing impatient.

Beside Emma, Maddie must have noticed the same thing. She'd tipped her head back to stare up at the trees and now said, her voice shaky, "Edgar, make them go."

"She was there, and then . . . gone." Edgar's voice was muffled—no surprise, given that he was hunched over, staring at his shoes. His entire body seemed to be shaking, and Emma realized with a pang of horror that the ravens seemed to be reacting to his emotions. The fluttering and croaking above them continued, rising in volume.

Maddie grimaced. "Why are they doing that? Are they going to attack us? Edgar, make them stop."

"I think he's panicking." Emma could hear the noise of the birds growing louder above them, but her gaze was fixed on Edgar. She crouched down to peer into his face, alarmed to see he was sheet white and swaying slightly on the spot. "Uh, I think he's going to pass out."

It was odd to see Edgar this way. He was usually blustering or stammering orders; even when the monster had grabbed his coat, he'd yelled at it. Up until this point, fear had seemed to increase the bossy prince act. This, though, was new, and Emma wasn't sure how to help him. A lump rose in her throat, and she felt a stab of panic herself.

"Ed?"

He didn't answer. He just breathed faster, swaying forward again. Emma braced herself in case she had to catch him. "Edgar, calm down. It's alright."

"Make . . . them . . . go." He was panting and shuddering, his face buried in his hands, as if he couldn't bear to look up and see the birds.

Above them, the ravens whipped upward in an angry black tornado—a surging, swirling tower of wicked beaks and razor-sharp talons. A few dropped down, swooping over their heads, and Emma ducked and raised her hands over her head, fear juddering through her bones.

"Edgar. They're just birds. You can send them away." She tried to keep the fear out of her voice, but she couldn't help flinching when she glanced up.

Edgar didn't respond; he rocked back and forth in silence, his chest rising and falling quickly. Emma could guess what he was going through right now: first, the panic over Eliza disappearing, and then the birds appearing—a clear sign of his magic. It was all too much for him.

"This is ridiculous." Maddie's voice wobbled, but she clenched her fists and stomped forward. Seizing Edgar by the shoulders, she wrenched him upright.

Emma started. "Maddie, wait, I don't think that's a good id—"

"Edgar Black, *you are not afraid!*"

Edgar stiffened.

For a moment he stayed very still and continued to stare straight ahead, eyes fixed on Maddie's face. He said nothing for a full second, and then, abruptly, he snapped to attention.

"You know, I say we look for that witch hunter chap. He's got some nerve following us around."

Emma stood stock-still, mouth open, as Edgar began circling the nearest trees, as if he expected the witch hunter to be spying on them from behind one. For a minute or two, neither she nor Maddie said a word; they both just watched, stunned, as he hunted around the tree trunks.

At last, Maddie broke the silence. "Well, that solves *that*, doesn't it?" she said with a wide grin.

With a start, Emma realized what had happened. Edgar's transformation hadn't just *looked* like magic—it was exactly that. It was like The Testing all over again, only now instead of Maddie using her power of persuasion against the nurses she had used it on Edgar.

Maddie had already taken a step to follow Edgar, but Emma seized her arm and yanked her back, anger boiling in her gut.

"What are you *thinking*?" she hissed.

Maddie tugged her arm away, giving the treetops a pointed glance. "Look."

There was a great stirring in the branches above, one Emma hadn't noticed in her distraction. The ravens were leaving, flying up into the air in a steady stream of black. Emma stood still for a moment, watching them as they headed away from the forest, growing smaller and smaller in the distance. She couldn't help but feel a trickle of relief in spite of her anger.

"Whatever they were going to do, I just saved us from it." Maddie smiled. "And my magic worked perfectly for once."

Edgar was marching around a particularly wide oak tree now, grinning hugely; it was an expression that looked eerily out of place on him. "I miss Eliza. And Georgie. I even miss my birds. Where are they going?" He tipped his head back and yelled at the treetops, "Hello. Birds?"

"Put him *right*," Emma growled. "You've changed his entire personality!"

Maddie's smile slid. "I can't *un*lie—that's not how it works. It will wear off eventually. It always does."

"You shouldn't have done it in the first place." Emma glared at her. "That's like . . . taking away his free will."

"More like taking away our chance of getting attacked by birds." Maddie scowled.

Unbelievable. She was completely unrepentant. "You can't just go around putting spells on people!"

"He'll be fine." Maddie's voice was sullen.

"Clearly not." Emma turned to wave a hand at Edward. "He's—"

Gone.

Edgar had been standing beside the big oak, and now he wasn't. There was no one under the tree.

Emma whirled around, her pulse kicking into a gallop. There was no one else in the clearing with them. He was not standing at the edge of the forest, and his leather bag was sitting at the base of one of the trees, slumped over, the top hanging open. He'd left his poetry behind.

Edgar was gone.

Chapter Twenty-Six

"Edgar?"

Emma's breath caught in her throat as she looked around the empty space. Again. She couldn't believe this was happening again. She kept hoping that Edgar would step out from behind a tree. The afternoon sun streaming down through the leaves cast flickering shadows that stretched between the branches and the forest floor, painting Maddie's wide-eyed face in orange and black.

"He's gone."

Emma's hand flew to her mouth as she stared helplessly at the forest around them. Edgar had vanished when they were arguing. Had he gone the same way Eliza had, just disappearing into nothing?

"Oh." Maddie's face was pale, her hand pressed to her lips. "Did he . . . is he . . . ?"

She couldn't seem to say it.

And then Emma spotted it, a scuffed patch of dirt on the edge of the clearing. She crept closer, holding her breath. Sure enough, a couple of shallow imprints could be seen in the earth, footprints leading into the woods.

"He's not gone." The words left her in a rush of relief. "He's just wandered off."

"To find the witch hunter," Maddie said, her voice slightly shaky, and Emma realized just how much trouble they were in.

"We've got to find him."

They left the clearing, following the footprints.

She wanted to shout at Maddie that this was *her* fault, that *she* had made Edgar fearless, and now he was going to get himself captured. But when she glanced over, Maddie looked just as terrified as Emma was. She kept raising trembling hands to adjust the strap of Edgar's bag as she walked. For now, Emma decided, she would let it go. She faced forward, fixing her attention on the dark pine trees around them and trying not to trip over rocks and roots.

Her stomach was churning, and she could hear her heart beating in her ears. She had to find Edgar. The idea of something happening to him, well . . . it didn't bear thinking about. No more than a day ago, she'd thought she hated him. But now, after everything they'd been through together, it was different. Now, she realized, they were family. In a different way than before. In a real way.

Maddie's brow was furrowed, and she was staring straight ahead, as if she was concentrating fiercely on something.

They walked on for several minutes. Occasionally one of them would call for him, cupping their hands around their mouth and keeping their voices low. It would be hard to hear him over the racket they were making, the crunch of leaves and sticks on the forest floor. On top of that, Emma wasn't sure if he'd even respond. What did being completely unafraid make you do? Would he ignore them? Maybe he wasn't afraid of losing his friends. Maybe he wasn't afraid of being alone now. She wasn't sure how far the lack of fear went. Would it somehow erase everything he'd cared about?

The thought made her feel a little sick, and the anger in her belly surged again. She curled her fists at her sides, forcing herself not to turn on Maddie. There was no point; Maddie knew what she'd done, how serious it was.

After another moment, Maddie spoke. "Emma, you were right. I'm really sorry." She bit her lip, and when Emma met her eyes, her face was grave. "I shouldn't have done that. I use it too much, you know." She cleared her throat, eyes on the ground. "I used to do it for attention. I talk a lot, and mother was always ignoring me, so I started saying more and more outrageous things. That's all it was at first—until it started working half the time. People actually *believed* me." Maddie flushed, ducking her head. "And then, as I got used to it, I just did it whenever I wanted."

Emma nodded. Some of her anger was trickling away. The idea of having a mother who told you to hush up all the time, or to be "seen and not heard," was not a foreign one.

Maddie pressed on. "It got so bad that my parents started locking me in my bedroom." She cleared her throat, and in the dappled light filtering down through the trees Emma could see her face was flushed. "I'd still trick the maids sometimes, lie that my mother had said to let me out. So they shipped me off to the nearest hotel; that way, they wouldn't even have to be near me. The coach driver who escorted me to The Testing blocked his ears up with wax."

"I'm so sorry," Emma said, and discovered that she was. Maddie's parents had wanted to be rid of her, and they'd been far more obvious about it than even Emma's mother had been.

Maddie was still blushing brightly, and she stared at her feet as she walked. "Thanks. I-I still feel terrible about it all. I know why they locked me away—it was a horrible thing to do to family. And . . . that means I should have known better. I shouldn't have done that to Edgar, even though I was scared."

Emma cleared her throat, turning to face the forest again. "Look, we've all done things we wish we hadn't. Let's just find Edgar, alright?"

Maddie was smiling faintly, saying something back, but suddenly all Emma could hear was that faint, familiar *thump-thump, thump-thump*. Unmistakably human, but too slow, too steady to be Edgar's.

She whirled on the spot, glancing wildly all around. "Mads, he's here somewhere. The witch hunter is back."

"Where?" Maddie was pivoting on the spot. "Where is he? Is he close?"

A beat of silence followed as Emma tried to concentrate, to hone in on the heartbeat. Once again, the forest around them was empty and still. There was no sign of Tobias McCraw.

"It's from up ahead, I'm certain. That way."

She pointed, and as she did, something stirred in the distant treetops, off in the direction she was indicating: a flutter of black wings across the afternoon sky.

"The ravens!"

They looked at one another, the dread on Maddie's face echoing her own. If Edgar was up there—strange, fearless Edgar—and so was the witch hunter . . .

Without a word, they both pitched forward, running full tilt for the place where the birds were steadily forming a column above the trees. That had to be where Edgar was, and if the birds had begun to flock that suddenly, it must mean he was in trouble. They had to get to him—and fast.

Emma darted around trees, nearly tripping over roots and rocks. Maddie was close behind her, and Emma could hear the rhythm of her heart right after her own, beating hard in her ears. It was overwhelmingly loud, and it sent a pang of fear through her.

Not right now. Not when she was so close to finding Edgar.

She was about to attempt to cram the Noise back when a third, more frantic pulse suddenly filled her ears—a quick double beat fluttering furiously in the back of her mind. She recognized it immediately.

Edgar.

Judging by the strength of the sound, he was just up ahead somewhere. And he was very frightened.

As she listened, the volume of the heartbeat seemed to increase, growing louder and louder in her ears. It sent her own pulse racing, and she slammed the door shut on her magic a second later. It was too loud, too fast.

"How are we going to find him?" Maddie gasped the words out. "They've spread out."

Emma looked up, slowing down to avoid tripping over a root in the path. Maddie was right. The ravens had arrived in such great numbers that they were no longer forming a solid line. They'd stretched across the sky, and the area of the forest they were circling was so wide that Edgar could have been anywhere.

Maddie cupped her hands to her mouth and yelled, "Edgar!"

Emma winced. She wasn't sure if making themselves known was wise, but they both went still all the same, hoping to hear a reply. There was nothing—just the rustle of wings and the calls of ravens from above.

"Can you hear him? His heart, I mean?" Maddie was still scanning the sky, brows furrowed. "You could find him."

Use the magic deliberately, she meant. For however long it took to find Edgar.

Emma bit the inside of her cheek. "You know what my power does, Maddie. What it could do to Edgar."

"You won't hurt him, Em . . ." Maddie paused, brows furrowed, and then her face brightened suddenly. "Remember what Eliza said about trusting your magic? I trust you, and I know Edgar does too."

For a long moment Emma just stood there, feet rooted to the ground. Maddie trusted her. She just wasn't sure she trusted herself. But what other choice did they have? Edgar was in trouble, lost in the forest and being stalked by the witch hunter. She had to do *something*.

Maddie was right. What was it that Eliza had said? Magic wasn't good or bad. It was supposed to be useful; it was there for a reason. She could use her magic to find Edgar, to save him.

Trust your magic.

Emma shut her eyes and took a deep breath, turning her thoughts inward. Slowly, ever so slowly, she cracked open the door at the back of her mind, letting the magic out a bit at a time.

At first, she heard nothing, and so she unleashed a little more.

Still nothing.

Trust your magic.

At last, she flung the door open and felt the power rush out, moving rapidly through her, setting the tips of her fingers and toes tingling.

And there it was, the steady *thump, thump, thump*, followed by that unmistakable double beat.

Edgar.

She shot forward, hearing Maddie's yelp of surprise behind her. They ran, weaving through the trees. The sound was leading them toward the edge of the forest, she realized. She could see more tall grass through the trunks up ahead. And as the forest thinned, the sky above became visible, revealing the flocking ravens, a swirling mass darkening the sky.

They had entered a wide, grassy plain, almost clear of trees.

She ran, sprinting across the field, the sound of Edgar's heart growing louder in her ears. Maddie followed, huffing and puffing. They rounded an outcrop of several trees, leaves sparse on their branches, and found themselves on a twisting dirt path. Up ahead, the path climbed a gentle slope to a crumbling stone bridge over a trickling creek. Beyond the bridge was a house, two stories, with a thatched roof overgrown by ivy. It had wide rectangular windows, and the wraparound porch was decorated with wildflowers that provided a welcome burst of color. The sign nailed to the overhang read *The Teahouse*.

The heartbeat here was impossibly loud. It thundered in her ears, and—

There.

Edgar sat on the ground at the base of the bridge, knees pulled up to his chest. His hair, as always, was ruffled and standing on end, but his nails—usually so carefully kept—were bitten down and bloody. He must have heard their approach, because he slowly lifted his head and fixed huge, scared eyes on both of them.

"What just happened?"

Chapter Twenty-Seven

It was Maddie who moved first, dashing up the path and flinging herself onto him, pulling him into a crushing hug. Edgar jumped, but Maddie hardly seemed to notice his surprise. "I'm so sorry, Edgar. It was a really dreadful thing to do, and it's all my fault. Can you ever forgive me?"

When Maddie finally released him, Edgar's face was bright red. "Er, I'm just glad you're here. Honestly, I felt like I'd woken up from some horrible dream, and you were both gone, and I was somewhere completely different, and"—he gestured limply at the air above him—"they all showed up a moment later."

Emma, who'd been scanning the surroundings frantically for the witch hunter, glanced up. The flock of ravens had only grown thicker, and they'd begun to form a kind of swirling cyclone in the sky.

"Where is he, Edgar? The witch hunter?" Emma darted another look around the clearing, ready to tell the others to run at any moment. The faint heartbeat had faded now, but that didn't mean he wasn't lurking somewhere nearby.

"What?" Edgar was chewing his thumbnail again, head tilted back to the sky, clearly distracted.

"The witch hunter. I heard his heartbeat. He was here."

"Come on, let's take cover just for a bit. Maybe the birds will go away," Maddie said carefully, and she shot Emma a look.

Clearly, Maddie was nervous about getting Edgar worked up again.

"Maybe."

No one spoke as they moved up the garden path and mounted the rickety steps to the teahouse. Emma trailed behind the others, taking one last, suspicious look around the clearing. It was still empty.

But she'd *heard* him; she knew she had. Which meant he was still on their trail.

Edgar was the first to reach the teahouse door. He jiggled the handle, and the door swung open with a rusty shriek of hinges.

The room beyond was open and airy, its windows hung with heavy red curtains. A number of circular tables were set up throughout, with faded, cream-colored tablecloths and high-backed cushioned chairs draped with cobwebs. There was a thick layer of dust on the carpeted floor and the tops of the tables. They ventured farther in, their footsteps echoing in the silence.

Each table was laid with fine china—a teacup and saucer at each place with a teapot in the middle—along with a silver tiered tray. The latter was filled with lumps of shriveled, moldy cakes and finger sandwiches. Emma wrinkled her nose at the sight.

There was also swampy-looking liquid in some of the cups. She was struck by the idea that the patrons had been sitting down to take their tea and had vanished halfway through. The entire city was like this; it was as if everyone had simply dropped what they were doing and left.

Or disappeared.

The thought made her stomach plunge, and she clamped her lips together tightly. There was no sense in saying something like that out loud, in scaring the others.

"Do you think there's food in here somewhere? Edible food, I mean?" Edgar's face was eager as he glanced at her. "My stomach's eating itself."

Emma knew what he meant. Her stomach's gurgling protest had only increased in the last hour. It had to be nearly evening by now. "I doubt there's anything, but we should check the kitchen."

"It's like I said before." Maddie spoke from behind her. "There won't be any tea left, or at least no hot water to boil it with. Which is a shame, because I do enjoy a good cup of tea. My mother used to get this really lovely black tea, but I think strawberry has got to be my favorite. Or, no . . . peppermint."

"I can picture myself drinking tea and writing my poetry here." Edgar's voice was wistful. "Just there, by the window."

They wove their way through the tables, heading for an arched doorway in the back of the room, which Emma thought might lead to a kitchen. Maddie continued her narration, this time discussing the best types of biscuits to go with tea. Emma paused to peer through a window as they walked by, her gaze scanning the edge of the forest for movement or shadow.

Edgar also stopped to look outside, and Emma noticed him flinch when he saw that the sky was still full of ravens. It was no good. The ravens knew he was in here. And they didn't seem to be losing interest.

They were halfway across the room when Maddie abruptly went silent.

Emma turned. "What, have you run out of flavors to talk—"

She was speaking to empty space. There was no one behind her, only another table full of dusty teacups. "Maddie?"

This couldn't be happening. She had to be here somewhere. She'd just run outside for some reason, or she was playing a cruel trick by hiding under one of the tablecloths. Even as Emma thought this, though, she knew none of it was true. She would have heard something, but there'd been nothing. Maddie had been talking one minute, and had been cut off abruptly the next.

Edgar stared at the place Maddie had been, and then over at Emma, eyes wide. "She's gone too, hasn't she?"

Chapter Twenty-Eight

Five minutes later, Emma and Edgar sat at one of the dusty tables, both of them pale and deathly silent. Neither had bothered to call for Maddie the way they had for Eliza. They both knew she hadn't left the teahouse, nor was she playing a trick on them.

No, Maddie had just . . . vanished. Exactly the same way Eliza had. There one second and gone the next.

Edgar groaned and dropped his head into his hands, and Emma glanced out the window at the birds circling the rooftop. There were so many now that they had begun to block out the already muted light of the evening sun. She didn't tell Edgar to get himself together though, or to make the ravens stop. She knew how it felt when your power seemed to be completely out of your control. She was just beginning to get a tentative grasp on her own.

Emma glanced over at him. "Maybe . . . maybe this is what the ambassador was talking about."

Edgar lifted his head to stare at her, so she pressed on. "I mean, maybe they've made it to the other side, and that's why they're gone.

This place is magic, right? Maybe it lets you through one at a time or something."

"You think so?"

It was a wild guess, but Edgar looked so hopeful that she merely nodded.

"It would make sense, right? We were separated when we arrived here, so why wouldn't leaving work the same way?"

Slowly he nodded, straightening up. He seemed utterly relieved, and Emma felt a little guilty, but at least he wasn't slumped over in defeat anymore. "Yes, that must be it," he said. "They're probably waiting for us."

"Well then, let's keep moving." It seemed to be the only thing to do. Stay on the move, vanish back into the forest, and lose the witch hunter who was following them.

They left the teahouse behind, traveling around it and through the overgrown backyard, climbing over the ramshackle remains of a picket fence. Beyond that, there was more forest, though it was thinner here, the tree branches sparser and empty of their leaves.

They walked for several minutes, and although they moved very fast, and Emma insisted on weaving in and out of the trees in what she hoped was an evasive maneuver, she couldn't seem to shake the feeling of being followed. Of being watched. The hairs on her arms prickled, and she kept a careful eye on the shadowy spaces between the trees. She grew even jumpier when the sun began to sink below the horizon, and the shadows steadily deepened.

Slowly, the forest floor gave way to a wide dirt track. For riding, Emma guessed. As they came around an outcrop, Emma staggered to a halt. Behind her, Edgar almost ran into her back.

There was a tall, black-clad person up ahead through the trees, and Emma jumped back, fists raised, heart racing.

McCraw.

Edgar moved to stand beside her and clutched her arm very hard, letting out a shuddering breath.

Seconds passed. Emma and Edgar stayed very still. Through the trees, the figure didn't move. Emma frowned, creeping a few steps closer to get a better look. On closer inspection, it didn't look like a person at all. It was... gray. She released a long breath, feeling foolish.

Another statue.

Exactly how many times was she going to be scared to death by statues in this wretched place?

As she drew closer, she could see that this one portrayed a woman sitting on a throne, skirts billowing out around her. Emma had seen a similar statue of the queen near Hyde Park, in the real London. But this woman's crown was different—more delicate, with pointed, leaf-shaped sections that rose up at the front. Instead of the Thistle Queen's scepter, this woman held a long staff in one hand, topped with a white stone, and at her feet was a cauldron, unbroken and standing upright on stubby legs.

"A witch queen," she said, though it was certainly not the horrible one depicted in her history books.

Emma couldn't help herself. She moved toward the statue as if pulled by some magnetic force, getting closer and closer until she was within arm's length of the base. This was a different woman than the last statue they'd seen, younger, her hair flowing in curls around her shoulders. Emma could see the woman's face clearly, the way she was looking down, almost as if she were staring right at Emma, a faint smile on her lips. It was so lifelike that it should have been eerie, but Emma didn't feel scared. Instead, she stepped closer, placing one hand on the base of the statue. The woman looked ... kind. Her eyes were soft, warm even, though they were hewn from stone.

If only the woman were real. If only she could tell Emma what to do next. Where to go from here. How to find her friends.

Something prickled at the back of Emma's skull. The tiny hairs at the nape of her neck were rising, as if in response to an unspoken threat. A moment later, she realized what it was. Edgar had not made a noise. As she'd crept forward to investigate, he'd been utterly silent. He hadn't commented on the statue, or told her how creepy its face was, or suggested that its presence here must mean they really were in Witch City. He had not said anything for more than a minute at least.

She clenched her teeth, not wanting to turn around, tears already stinging her eyes. But she had to—she had to see for herself. Slowly, so very slowly, she turned on her heel.

There was no Edgar behind her, only the thin trunks of the trees and the spaces between them. Only the overgrown grass around her, and weeds bursting up through the dirt path. Emma turned back to the statue, blinking away tears.

She was the only one left.

Suddenly, it felt as if there was an enormous weight on her chest, and Emma struggled to draw in a breath. She couldn't do this alone. Couldn't walk through the rest of Hyde Park and back into the ruined, overgrown London. She couldn't get to the other side by herself. And so she sat down heavily, at the base of the statue, ignoring the fact that the ground beneath her was slightly damp. She curled her knees up to her chest and stayed there, squeezing her eyes shut tight. In that moment she wanted, desperately, to just give up.

A sudden rustle came from the statue, and the ferns growing wild at the base shook violently. Emma's heart jumped, but calmed again when a soft meow broke the silence. A fuzzy black-and-white face peaked out at her from the foliage.

Not the only one left, then, but what good was a house cat when she needed directions?

The wind had picked up now, twisting icy fingers through her hair, dragging strands into her face.

"All my friends have gone." Her voice came out in a cracked whisper. "All I've got left is you, cat. I don't know if they're safe somewhere, or if they're in trouble ... they just vanished." Her voice was growing louder now, strengthened by the anger slowly swelling inside her. "What kind of place is this? I thought there was supposed to be a city, one where we'd be safe, and instead this place has *taken* all my friends from me."

She was practically shouting now, fists clenched at her sides. To her surprise, the cat didn't stir from its spot. It simply watched her with wide black eyes, tail twitching slightly now and again, as if it were waiting for her to run out of steam. Eventually she did, breathing hard, still staring at the cat. Finally, it turned on its heel and slunk around the base of the statue.

She tipped her head back to glance up at the stony witch queen looming above her. The statue was still and gray against the dark sky, against the black rain clouds gathering in the distance.

There were no ravens left in the sky, not even one.

Chapter Twenty-Nine

A minute passed, and then another. Emma stayed where she was. She was cold now, the dampness of the forest floor leaching the heat from her bones. The edge of the statue's base was digging into her back, but she didn't move. From somewhere behind her, the cat gave a loud, insistent meow, and Emma glanced angrily over her shoulder.

"No! I'm not in the mood to follow a *cat* anymore. Unless you can take me directly to my friends, please just *go away.*"

Another meow, louder this time, with a slight yowl on the end. Emma had the distinct impression she was being loudly scolded in whatever language passed for feline.

"I mean it. Leave me alone!" All she wanted to do was sit down and have a good cry, and this stupid cat wouldn't stop yelling at her.

There was another yowling complaint, longer and louder this time, and Emma finally vaulted to her feet, sheer irritation propelling her forward and around the base of the statue, navigating clumps of ferns and wild overgrown hydrangeas.

"I've told you, I don't want—"

Emma froze.

The ground beyond the statue dipped down abruptly, so that she found herself standing at the top of a mountain. Several hundred feet below lay an open valley.

This was nothing like the dark, overgrown forest of Hyde Park. It was a canyon filled with green poplar trees and an ice-blue lake with a waterfall at one end. But the truly shocking part was the city of towering stone in the center of the valley; the peaks and rooftops that rose into the cloudless sky; the flaming orbs of blue light glittering over the roofs and gables. A city nestled in the mountains, decorated with blue fire.

Impossible. She'd just been standing in front of a statue in the middle of Hyde Park. She should have been able to see the valley drop off beyond the statue, not to mention an entire city looming in the distance. None of this had been there until just now.

Her mind took a moment to catch up with what she was seeing and comprehend what exactly it meant—that, indeed, she was correct. None of this *had* been there a mere second ago.

Somehow, she'd crossed over; she'd left the In-Between.

This had to be Witch City.

It made sense now, the look of awe she'd seen on Eliza's face right before she'd vanished. Emma knew she had the same expression on her face now, as she stared at the towering city. She took a deep breath, and then another, before inching forward.

The city looked distant enough that she almost wanted to run. To bolt toward it in case it, too, decided to disappear. She didn't look back over her shoulder at Hyde Park and its statue; she was too afraid to take her eyes off the city.

This was not how she'd pictured finding the place—alone, without Maddie and Eliza and Edgar—but she steeled herself and kept going, carefully moving down the slope of the mountain.

There were arbutus trees and poplars here, bright-trunked and new; they let the moonlight filter down through their slender bows and waving leaves. It was so different from the impenetrable thicket of Hyde Park that Emma almost wanted to slow down and enjoy it. But she made herself press forward, weaving her way between ferns and bursts of colorful, fragrant flowers. Soon enough, she removed her jacket and tucked it under her arm, enjoying the warm night breeze that ruffled her hair.

It was strange, to move from winter, to fall, to spring—all in a manner of hours. Emma had begun to realize that it wasn't Edgar who had disappeared in front of the statue back there. *She'd* crossed over somehow, exactly as she'd suggested back at the teahouse.

She moved on, pushing through bright green ferns and tall grass. As she came nearer to the city, she could make out the peaks of roofs and weather vanes, clock towers, and flags snapping in the wind, and white plumes of smoke that signaled bonfires and wood-burning fireplaces. Up closer, the spheres of blue light hanging over the rooftops and towers looked like flickering flames caught in glass globes, and Emma found her gaze drifting back to them repeatedly, a nervous buzz of excitement in her stomach.

That was magic. She was sure of it.

The stone walls grew taller the closer she got. They had a reddish tinge to them, as if the entire city had been hewn out of sandstone.

She kept walking, trying not to think about what the others would have said upon seeing the city. It was no use, though; she could picture it all too clearly. Eliza would be suspicious, unsure of the towering walls, and Maddie would be bursting with excitement, already picturing a hot bath and all the food she could eat. Edgar would, of course, be nervously reciting poetry, or trying to put on one of his princely airs.

Instead, there was only silence as she followed the cat down into the valley, weaving her way between the poplars. There was a wooden bridge over a rushing river. It was well-maintained—the first piece of architecture she'd encountered in this strange world that wasn't being consumed by weeds and underbrush—and Emma felt a pang of excitement at this sign of civilization. She followed the cat across, gripping the railing with one hand, eyes fixed on the city ahead.

A dirt path led from the bridge straight up to the towering walls, and as she approached, she scanned the broad stone, dismayed to find no visible entrance. She'd expected a gate somewhere, maybe a drawbridge like the one at the palace. But there was nothing, only more smooth stone walls. Had the cat led her to the back of the city?

The animal stopped at the base of the wall and blinked up, first at her and then at the wall.

"Well, what am I meant to do?" Emma felt a sudden wash of annoyance at the expectant look it was giving her. She was about to tell it that she couldn't exactly climb the wall, and she certainly didn't have a broom to fly on at this point . . . Did witches even fly on brooms? She knew virtually nothing about the subject, as her history books had never covered it.

She tilted her head to stare up at the city again, stomach churning suddenly. Really, she knew nothing about witches at all, did she? Nothing about the city or what she was getting into. Everything she'd been taught was lies.

For one horrible, ridiculous moment, she thought that maybe she was wrong. Maybe every terrible thing she'd been taught about witches was, in fact, true. After all, the witches really did rule London years ago. Perhaps all the rumors were based on facts. What if those missing pages in the history books were really just things that no one was allowed to read because they were simply *that* despicable?

But no. Emma squared her shoulders and shook her head. She'd come all this way, and she needed answers. She needed to meet Lenore Black and find out the truth.

She rocked back on her heels and looked up at the wall again. Maybe she was missing something—a secret lever, or a button she was supposed to push.

Now that she was closer, she could see what looked like a number of large crystals set into the top of the wall. They were various shades, with the nearest one, just above her head, a light pink. It glowed softly in the dusk.

Was she supposed to use that to open the gate? She felt a flutter of panic in her stomach. Maybe you had to be really good at magic to get in, in which case, she was in a lot of trouble.

A sudden scuffling sound came from overhead, and a black velvet hat appeared over the ramparts. It had a very wide brim, and it was pointed on top, though the point listed to one side, which made it look a little drunk. There was an annoyed huffing sound from the hat, and the point swiveled back and forth. "Where've they gone and put the step stool? Hah, here it is. Probably using magic to get a lift. *Lazy*, the lot of 'em."

Emma tipped her head back farther, blinking as a pale, round face in a pair of silver spectacles appeared beneath the hat, frowning down at her.

"Who is this now? You're not meant to come around the back entrance. *Highly* irregular."

Emma only gaped at her, and then a low, musical voice from beside her left foot said, "It's alright, Gerty. She's with me."

Emma glanced back down, mouth agape, completely distracted from Gerty and her crooked hat. The black cat at her feet met her stare with even green eyes, head tilted, as if it were waiting for her reaction.

"Did you just . . . speak?"

"I did." The cat tipped its head the other way, though its mouth didn't seem to move, and Emma wondered if it was communicating telepathically somehow.

She supposed it made a strange kind of sense, really, that a familiar could talk. But while it was one thing to think about, it was another to see it actually . . . well, talk.

"Why didn't you say something earlier?" Emma said. "We could have used the help!"

"Yes, I do apologize. I'm afraid I haven't been entirely forthcoming," the cat said, still without opening its mouth. "The way the protection spells on our city work, I wasn't allowed to do much more than show you the right path once you'd crossed over. But . . . allow me to explain."

The black cat turned once on the spot, and then again, like a dog preparing his bed. It did not stop though, but sped up, as if it were chasing its own tail. Eventually, it was moving so fast that Emma had to squint, struggling to see past the blur of movement. It was like a furry, miniature tornado, and as it spun it lengthened, growing up and up until it was as tall as Emma . . . and then taller.

Emma stumbled back, alarmed, and clapped a hand to her mouth as it stopped abruptly. Where the cat had been only seconds ago, a woman was standing. Emma blinked frantically, as if she could clear her vision and make the cat come back.

The woman smiled at her, a little hesitantly. She had long black hair, which hung in waves over her shoulders, and dark brown eyes with black brows. Around her neck she wore a heavy silver chain with a row of multicolored crystals.

Emma recognized her almost immediately.

The woman from the wanted poster.

Emma's heart seemed to expand in her chest, and a mixture of panic and relief washed over her, a tangle of emotions that made her eyes sting and caused her to her blink frantically.

"Good to finally meet you, Emmaline."

Her heart was beating hard in her ears now. This entire time she'd been searching for Lenore Black, and now . . .

"My name is Lenore Black. And if I'm not mistaken, you're my niece." The woman's smile broadened. "Welcome to Witch City, Emmaline."

Chapter Thirty

I f it had been left up to Emma, she probably would have remained there—outside the city walls, staring at Lenore Black in shock—for ages. As it was, she stared for what felt like an embarrassing length of time, thoughts racing. There was some resemblance to the queen, certainly, and more still to her own mother. But there was something about Lenore that was very different from her sisters. A moment later, Emma realized what it was: Lenore was actually *smiling* at her—and it was not a smug, superior smile like her mother's, or a cold, terrifying one like the queen's. No. It was warm, and a little playful, and Emma realized with a start that Lenore was waiting for her to be done staring.

"I'm—I'm sorry . . . it's a shock." Her mind was spinning. She had so many questions, but she couldn't seem to form words.

"Of course it is. No need to apologize." Lenore shook her head, her face rueful. As Emma watched, she reached up and unclipped one of the crystals from her necklace, slipping it into the pocket of her dress. "I rather imagine you've heard very little of me, if anything at all."

Emma hesitated, not sure how much she should say. "I-I'm afraid they told everyone you were dead. That you died in the Great War."

"Yes. They probably wish that were the truth." Lenore let out a sigh. "Well, I know you must have all sorts of questions about our family, but I'm afraid we'll have to talk later. Your friends are waiting quite impatiently on the other side of this wall."

Emma stood up straight. "They're really here? They made it?"

"They did. Follow me this way, please."

Lenore called up to the witch on the wall, "Gerty, the wall, if you please." In response, the woman grunted and leaned over to rap a knuckle on the light-pink crystal embedded in the stone.

Emma watched in astonishment as a great section of the wall before them seemed to vanish with a hiss and a soft rush of air. "Was that . . . magic?"

"It certainly was." Lenore swept an arm forward, gesturing for Emma to go ahead of her, through the gap in the wall. "Welcome to New Londinium, or as we fondly refer to it around here, Witch City."

Emma was still half staring at Lenore—and trying not to *look* like she was staring. She'd been about to ask where the name Londinium came from when they stepped inside the city walls, and she staggered to a halt, momentarily forgetting how to string words together.

The city beyond the wall was London, but it was also nothing like London at all. There was the clock tower, standing straight and tall over the city, the face lit up in flickering blue light. Beyond it, towers and rooftops were glowing, lit with the white light of a thousand delicate silver lanterns hanging in doorways and stairwells. Here and there, glowing spheres of blue light hung high above the rooftops, illuminating tiles and gutters, making the smoke spiraling up from brick chimneys look like clouds of cotton candy.

Most astonishing of all, there were people *in the air*, zipping around and over the buildings, cloaks and jackets rippling behind them. Emma looked up, riveted, as a woman streaked past several feet above. She was standing very straight, shoulders back, clutching a large carpetbag in both hands. It looked like she was floating on a cushion of air as she moved forward, her green velvet cloak flapping gently.

A million questions pressed at Emma's lips, most of them starting with *how . . . ?* But, of course, the answer had to be *magic*, didn't it?

This place was nothing like she'd been expecting. Then again, she wasn't sure what exactly she'd been expecting to begin with.

"What do you think?" Lenore sounded amused.

"It's *brilliant*," Emma breathed, and then she didn't get to say anything else. A great clatter of footsteps could be heard from somewhere off to her left, and then something slammed into her, nearly knocking her off her feet.

"Emma, I'm so glad you're here!"

"You made it! Isn't it lovely, isn't it perfect?"

Emma shrieked, and then laughed, realizing the tangle of limbs, lace, and petticoats that had tackled her was Eliza and Maddie. Both of the girls were beaming. Their faces were flushed and freshly scrubbed, and they each had on a new dress—a brown-and-pink one for Maddie, and a green one with brass buttons for Eliza.

They both seemed equally relieved to see her. Maddie's freckled face was flushed very red, and Eliza grinned when Emma kept hold of her sleeve for a few seconds after she'd released her from the crushing hug. She was a little nervous they might disappear all over again.

They were here and safe. They'd made it. Her knees felt weak from the sheer relief.

"Can you believe this place, Em?" Eliza beamed around at the city, and Maddie chimed in, nearly bursting with excitement: "Isn't it wicked? Lenore says we can learn how to fly!"

Some of Emma's relief faded as she looked them over. "Wait, where's Edgar? Didn't he make it?"

"He'll make it. He's just a little behind."

It was Lenore. She'd come up beside them, and she touched Emma's arm gently. "He should be along soon. The In-Between tests everyone differently, and some take longer than others to come through."

"This way." She beckoned for them to follow her. "We'll get you something to eat, and when Edgar gets here, I'll show you to your rooms. It's the Ostara festival tonight, so I must warn you there'll be lots of activity in the market."

Ostara. The celebration of spring. Emma looked around, noticing planter boxes along some of the windows, green shoots just beginning to bloom. She'd been right to suspect it, but it was still a lot to take in, this confirmation that she'd passed through three seasons in a day.

She closed her eyes and took in a deep breath, and felt Maddie loop an arm through hers.

It was all overwhelming, but as they followed Lenore down the cobblestone street, Emma couldn't help relaxing a little. She had the same, strange sensation of rightness as when she'd first decided to follow the cat. Her aunt . . . the cat was her aunt the entire time. It was still a bit hard to wrap her mind around.

And Lenore knew how to shapeshift. Did all witches know how? Could Emma learn someday? And flying! Maddie had said they would learn how to fly. Her thoughts were racing at such a great speed that she almost felt dizzy.

Witch City may have looked a lot like London, but the atmosphere was entirely different. As in Forest-London, the air was cool and fresh here. There was no fog, either; she could see every building perfectly. The major difference was that this city was full of noise: people chatting, both on the ground and above them as they sped past or glided leisurely by.

At first, Emma spent a good deal of time gawping at the witches zipping back and forth above their heads. It was as if they had simply shed the restrictions of gravity and floated upward, arms still full of shopping, pushing prams containing small children, moving from one store window to the next to look at dresses. Men in top hats loudly discussed the fluctuating markets while drifting comfortably along together, and a baker woman in a white apron floated in front of the top floor of her shop, offering sweet rolls to the children who zoomed up to her.

Everyone was floating along as if it were the most natural thing on earth.

Eliza and Maddie seemed amused at the look on her face, and thankfully Lenore let her have a few minutes to get used to things. Had she not, Emma probably would have spent the entire time walking into lamp posts and walls as she craned her neck to look up. Surprisingly, there was also a great deal of foot traffic on the road, and a few horses here and there, pulling carts of milk or fruit.

The peaks and rooftops of the buildings were lit by silver lanterns, some hanging from doorways and shopfronts, others glittering from lines that passed from one rooftop to the next. Emma noticed sparkling clouds of fireflies darting between the floating witches, casting flickering yellow light over the tops of the roofs.

Even with the glitter of lights all around her, she was aware of exactly how exhausted she was. Her body felt sore all over, her eyes gritty. But she had no desire to sleep. This was all too exciting.

They moved past a little green-and-brown shop with a hanging sign that read *Tuttle & Williams. Pawnbrokers. Charm Loans. Crystal for Goods of Value.* Around the corner from that was a tall,

Tudor-style building. Its sign read *The Cat's Meow Public House &* *Inn* and was illustrated with the silhouette of a black cat arching its back. The front doors were propped open, and rollicking fiddle music spilled out into the streets.

As they rounded a corner, Emma found herself suddenly in the center of a group of young men and women who were staggering arm in arm down the crooked cobblestone street. They were very loud, laughing and talking to one another. One of the boys in front had a glass in one hand, which slopped amber-colored liquid onto his shirt sleeve as he gestured at something, laughing. The strangest thing, though, was the tiny cat strutting in front of them, weaving its way between the crowd and occasionally pausing to glance back if the young men and women lagged too far behind.

"Jeremy!" Lenore's voice was sharp as she pulled Emma out of the way and, in the same move, snatched the glass out of the young man's hand with a stern glower. "I know it's festival time, but honestly."

"Sorry, Ms. Black." The young man gave her a shame-faced look, and the girl he was with giggled behind her hand.

"Straight home." Lenore gestured down at the tabby, who gave a loud *merp* of agreement and continued forward. The boy and his friends ducked their heads and hurried past Lenore, following the little cat down the street.

"What was that?" Eliza had caught up with them, with Maddie just behind her. "We saw more cats earlier. Are they witches too?"

Lenore smiled, shaking her head. "Ah, no. Those are familiars. We use them as a kind of . . . guide, if you will. The city does tend to move about quite a bit."

"Here too?" Emma looked up at the buildings around her, feeling suddenly nervous. She didn't miss the great grinding and shaking of the In-Between London, and she didn't fancy more of the same.

"Yes. But it's quite a bit different here. Just a moment." Lenore pulled up short, and then motioned to something behind them. "See what I mean?"

Emma turned. The shop they'd just passed, *Dill & Tuttle*, had been a one-story brown building, with green trim at the windows. In its place was now a two-story cream-colored building with a red-and-white striped awning and a collection of chairs and tables out front: *Charlie's Chocolaterie—Hot chocolate 2-for-1, today only!* Emma blinked. There'd been no earthquake, no great grinding and shaking. She hadn't even heard it happen.

"Much better than before," Emma said, relieved. "But why all the moving?"

Lenore smiled at them and then continued to walk, still speaking, and they stumbled after her. "New Londinium was created for witches, by witches. And witches have always been hunted."

"It's on purpose, then?" Emma darted a look around the street. "It moves to stay hidden?"

Lenore nodded, her expression slightly smug. "Exactly, Emma. That's why Her Majesty is having such trouble finding it. Witch City is never in the same place twice."

At the mention of the queen, Emma felt her excitement fizzle out a little. She cleared her throat, not sure how to ask the question that was on her mind. "Back in our London, the witch hunters were ... well, they were hunting you. They had a poster with your face on it."

"Yes, they are determined, even after all these years."

They were passing a little blue shop with a giant golden telescope painted onto the window—*Mr. Galaxy's Shoppe & Observatory*, according to the sign. A selection of delicate-looking silver instruments seemed to be whirring and vibrating away, all by themselves. As Emma watched, a blue-and-gold planet rotated into view, followed by a spinning display of twelve little moons circling around it.

"My sisters never gave up the hunt. They have too much malice in their hearts to let me go." Lenore pressed her hand to the glass, tracing the golden etchings in the window. Her eyes were distant, her brows creased. She appeared to be remembering something painful, and Emma felt a bit guilty. Still, she had a right to know about her family, didn't she?

"What happened?" she asked. "Why did they lie and say you were dead?"

Lenore drew back from the glass, glancing down at Emma, a strained smile on her face. "I promise I'll tell you everything soon, Emma. But it will be a long process, and today we will just concentrate on reuniting you with your friends and getting you settled."

Emma wanted to protest. She wanted to know more. But Lenore was already turning away, clearing her throat.

She gestured up at the city walls in the distance, and said, in a louder voice, "As well as changing locations, the city shifts internally, too—as you've seen. The only way to navigate is with magic. Unless you have witch blood, you will wander these ever-changing streets completely lost."

Emma could tell her aunt was changing the subject. "That's really clever."

"Isn't it brilliant?" Maddie's eyes shone. "Even if someone did manage to find it and made it in, they'd just end up going in circles."

Emma glanced over at a young couple passing by, holding hands and whispering to one another. They were following a tawny-furred little cat whose bell jingled merrily as it trotted ahead of them. "How do the cats . . . ?"

"Familiars sense magic, which is woven through the fabric of the city." Lenore moved on, passing another cluster of shops lit by silver lanterns. "For the most part, they can get you anywhere you want go." She grinned. "Though they do tend to get distracted by mice."

As Lenore led them down the next street, a whoop of excitement came from overhead, and Emma looked up to see a pair of little boys zipping after one another. Just behind them came their mother, curly hair flying out around her as she leaned forward, sleeves flapping furiously in the wind. She reached out and snatched at the younger one's coat. "Slow down! No horseplay above the streets, you two!"

Emma watched with interest as they zoomed back and forth overhead; she made herself quite dizzy trying to keep track.

"It's a surprisingly simple spell." Lenore tapped one of the crystals in her necklace, clearly amused at the look of awe on Emma's face. "This way, ladies."

Emma looked back down at the street, feeling a little unsteady on her feet. It would be very easy to just wander around forever, craning her neck, staring up at the witches speeding by, at the blue orbs and the tops of the buildings. But now that she'd effectively come back down to earth, she could see they were making their way down the middle of what looked like Oxford Street.

They were heading for a tiny thatch-roofed inn at the corner of the crossroads. The double doors at the front were rounded with ornate brass handles, and a sign over the entrance read *The Push Broom Teahouse & Inn*. On the sign was the silhouette of a witch in black robes and a pointed hat riding a stout-handled push broom, a cup of tea in one hand.

"Brooms are terribly out of fashion. Nobody rides them anymore, but Gerty refuses to rename it," Lenore said fondly. "She's a traditionalist, through and through." She pushed the doors open, and they swung inward with a faint squeak.

Emma and the others trailed in after her. Just inside the door was a large throw rug, and a rack hung with cloaks and coats. Several wicker brooms leaned against the wall under the hooks. As Lenore showed them in to the next room, Emma was struck by the scent of flowers. The low wooden beams of the roof were woven with cheerful yellow ribbon and clusters of dried lavender, and moonlight streamed in through the oval-shaped windows.

Lenore led them up a set of creaky wooden stairs to the second floor, a wide hallway with doors all down either side. There were gold number plaques on each one, and Lenore handed them the key marked #1.

"There are bunk beds. You'll have to fight it out for who gets the top." She grinned. "I'll come get you tomorrow for breakfast, and I promise to answer the hundred and one questions you will inevitably have. But right now, I think it's best you get some sleep. Gerty's brought up a plate of bread and cheese, if you need something before bed."

Emma glanced at the number on the door. She hesitated, even as she felt a rush of longing at the thought of the bed behind it. She was ready to sleep on the floor, at this point. "But Edgar . . . ?"

"I'm going to get him now." Lenore smiled down at her. "I'll make sure he passes through alright. And don't worry—it's been mere seconds in the In-Between since you got here." When Emma blinked at her, startled, Lenore smiled. "Time works very differently there. A single night here will be no more than an hour there. You need not worry about him wandering for long."

Make that one hundred and *two* questions.

Emma just shook her head, at a loss for words.

"Go on in," Lenore said. "These two will show you where the water closet is. Goodnight, girls."

She patted Emma on the shoulder and then swept away before Emma could ask anything else of her.

"Come on." Maddie was already elbowing the door open. The room beyond was done in dark wood with green accents. There was an ornate, moss-colored rug spread over the floorboards, a cushiony green armchair by a fireplace, and two sets of wide bunk beds tucked away into the corners. There was even a low bookshelf just under the window, filled with colorful volumes. It was beautiful, but all Emma could see was the nearest bunk. The velvety-looking quilt on top of the squishy pillow. Everything seemed to hit her all at once, and the sheer exhaustion made her sway on her feet.

"Bed," Eliza said firmly, perhaps noticing that Emma was about to topple over. "Come on, there are nightshirts in the drawer and then it's straight to sleep." She gave Maddie a pointed look. "No talking until morning. She needs to rest."

Maddie and Eliza showed her the night clothes, and then the water closet, where Emma splashed her face with cold water from a crystal wash basin. She practically inhaled a slice of bread and a large chunk of the cheese from the platter that Gerty had laid out on the dresser, and then she fell into bed, scarcely able to believe how comfortable the mattress was, how luxurious the velvety green blankets felt on her bare arms and legs.

She had worried earlier that it would be hard to sleep. She was too excited, and there were so many questions to ask Lenore. There were too many things to learn about Witch City, and besides, she was still a bit nervous about Edgar, even if Lenore was with him right now. And yet, the moment her face touched the pillow her eyes drifted shut, and even with the soft whispers and shuffling of Eliza and Maddie getting ready for bed, and the gentle glow of the candle burning on the dresser, she was asleep within seconds.

Chapter Thirty-One

In the morning it was not Lenore who came to fetch them for breakfast but the crooked-hatted Gerty. She led them to the dining room downstairs before rushing away to the kitchen.

The dining room was filled with long wooden tables and benches, and there were witches packed in at every seat, laughing and talking. At the back of the room there was a long bar with a low glass partition, and hanging signs over the top said things like *Earl Grey Cream* and *Jasmine Black Tea* and *Aunt Margery's Cherished Memories Potion*.

It was still dim outside. The sun was just rising, and lights flickered in hurricane lamps along the length of the tabletops, surrounded by squat clay teapots and mugs of steaming tea. Emma watched an older witch lean down and let the steam from her mug bathe her face, eyes shut as she inhaled deeply. When she opened her eyes, her gaze was distant, her pupils a deep yellow.

Maddie looked delighted to be able to explain. "Memory potion. Lenore says the teahouse serves magical brews. Herbal mixtures to make you relive your best memories, or to relax you." She waved a hand toward the bar at the back. "She said no one does potions anymore because it's too much work."

"Come on." Eliza moved farther into the room, and Emma trailed after her. "Our table is this way."

Emma stared closely at the teapots on each table as they walked past, wondering which contained a memory potion and which was filled with plain old Earl Grey. The shop smelled like a tantalizing mixture of mulled wine, cider, and bergamot, and her mouth had begun to water.

Eliza led them to a set of tables at the very back of the room that had been pushed together to create one long dining table with benches down both sides. A number of people were already seated, each with a plate piled high with food. At first, all Emma could see was the feast set out before them: heaping baskets of fresh-baked bread, pots of strawberry jam, and trays of scrambled eggs. Her mouth instantly began to water, and then Maddie gasped and seized her arm, pulling her up short.

The witch hunter was sitting in the center of the bench.

Tobias McCraw had a plate stacked high with toast and eggs, but he didn't appear to have touched any of it. Instead, his gaze was fixed on Emma. When he started to get up from the table she jumped back, one shaking hand held up, as if to ward him off somehow.

"I knew you followed us here! I could *hear* you."

McCraw tilted his head to one side and frowned. "Actually, Ms. Black, I got here before you did."

Emma opened her mouth and then shut it again, at a loss. That wasn't what she'd expected him to say. Beside her, neither Maddie nor Eliza said anything, but they looked just as alarmed as she was, and Maddie still had a death grip on Emma's arm.

She wasn't going to let him hurt her friends.

She was opening her mouth to say as much when he spoke. "I'm very sorry I misled you, ladies. But it was necessary, as I wasn't sure if Her Majesty might be listening, even in the In-Between."

No one spoke for a moment, and Emma found herself reeling. It wasn't even so much his apology that shocked her, but the way he said "Her Majesty," all loaded with scorn, as if they were the most repulsive words imaginable. No witch hunter or soldier would dare speak about the queen in that tone.

McCraw turned to the person seated next to him, an older woman who'd been mostly ignoring the exchange up until now, and seemed to be in the midst of pouring him tea. She had blond hair, shot through with white, and dark, serious eyes. Emma realized with a start that the woman looked just like McCraw.

"Meet my mother," McCraw said, "the reason I was so desperate to find this city. She was driven from London years ago, when the hunts were still going on. I suspected she'd ended up here. That's why I joined the hunters in the first place, why I was so driven to rise up in the ranks. I knew they were actually looking for the city, and that they might have leads I could use. And it worked."

Beside her, Eliza and Maddie looked stunned, but they had both relaxed a little.

Emma shook her head vehemently, first at them and then at him. "No, he's lying. You're *lying*." She jabbed a finger at him. "After you disappeared, you came back. You followed us through Hyde Park, and in the woods. I *heard* you."

McCraw frowned. "I'm sorry, but you're mistaken. I arrived two days ago. I showed up here just after I . . . er, left. I'm sorry I left you in the room to face that monster, if that's what you're angry about." His expression grew very sober. "Trust me, I thought about that a lot after I arrived here, but Lenore assured me you'd escaped. Said she'd been keeping an eye on you lot."

He was lying. *Why?*

"You shouldn't be here."

"Well, at least your friend has some common sense, Eliza." The person who'd said this, a wizened old woman with a cloud of curly white hair, sat at the opposite end of the table glaring at the witch hunter. "I almost hexed him when he showed up this morning, bold as can be!"

The woman had to be ancient, Emma suspected, but she sat up straight on the bench, and her gaze was sharp as she glanced around at them.

Eliza laughed, and then slid onto the bench beside the old woman, taking one of her weathered hands in her own. "Gran, this is Emma." She glanced up, smiling. "Em, this is my gran."

Chapter Thirty-Two

Emma's awe over meeting the leader of the last London coven distracted her from glaring at McCraw. At least temporarily.

"It's nice to meet you, Ms. . . . "

"Call me Granny El." The old woman waved a hand at her, dark eyes twinkling. Now that the woman was smiling, Emma could see where the laugh lines came from. "You girls helped my granddaughter, and the way I see it, you need all the family you can get. I'm much obliged to you all for helping her get through."

"She helped us." Emma shot Eliza a look, and Eliza ducked her head, clearly embarrassed. "She's the one who helped me to finally start accepting my power."

The old woman grinned and patted Eliza's hand. "That doesn't surprise me at all. I knew my girl would get by. The ambassador said there was a plan afoot to get you all out. I wasn't worried one bit."

"The ambassador?" Maddie repeated. "You know her as well?"

"Who do you think helped the coven escape?" The old woman's smile tightened. "Irvingland has been helping us for years. There's an entire underground rebellion the queen knows nothing about. Why do you think they built that iron monstrosity, the *Witch Express*? We keep stealing our people out from under their noses."

Good for oranges and not much else. The insulting rhyme seemed rather ironic now.

"That's what she gets for underestimating an entire country, the little fool," Granny El muttered.

There was a loud, echoing pop, and Lenore appeared abruptly, right behind Maddie, who squawked and dropped the piece of toast she was holding.

"Look who it is," Lenore said, and stepped aside.

It was Edgar. He was red in the face, and his hair was rumpled, but he also had a sparkle in his eye Emma hadn't seen before. When he saw them, he grinned widely. "Last of all, of course. But still, I'm here."

Emma returned his grin, and then surprised herself by flinging her arms around him, hugging him fiercely. "I'm so glad you made it!"

Eliza and Maddie followed, and Edgar blushed furiously as they piled onto him, hugging him all at once. He gave an indignant yelp when Maddie said tearfully, "I thought for sure you would die!"

"Thanks for *that* vote of confidence."

"How did it go?" Eliza finally broke away, and they all slowly separated, leaving Edgar looking even more rumpled than before.

Edgar looked around at them, suddenly beaming. "I remembered what you said, Em."

Emma blinked, surprised. "What, me?"

"You asked me what the birds wanted." He shrugged, biting at his lip. "I never really thought about that until you said it. And then, when I was alone, I remembered that and I just sort of . . . asked." He flushed, rubbing the back of his neck. "Well, to be honest, I sort of shouted it at them."

"And what happened?" Maddie's eyes were shining.

"They all went really quiet. It was incredible. And then one of them flew down and got really close, and I actually let him sit on my arm." He grinned at their shocked expressions. "I know, I know, I was terrified, but . . . it talked to me!"

"It did not!" Maddie pressed a hand to her mouth. "Ed, that's brilliant."

"It was." Edgar's smile grew even wider. "I can talk to birds—well, just ravens as far as I know. And all they wanted was to help. They led me straight back to the path after that, and all the way to Lenore. It was incredible."

"You've never tried that before then?" Maddie asked, clearly amused.

"Well, no." Edgar looked indignant. He sat down at the table as the others returned to their seats on the bench. "They scared me. I kept ignoring them, hoping they'd go away."

"You'll find magic works in mysterious ways." Lenore smiled at them. "It sounds like you managed to find the key to unlocking your power."

Emma thought about how she'd finally trusted her magic in the In-Between. How she'd reached out for it instead of letting it overwhelm her. And it had worked.

"Lenore, er, Ms. Black," Maddie started hesitantly. "We all made it through the In-Between, but are there witches who don't? I think we may have met one."

Emma glanced over at her and they exchanged a look. She shivered, thinking about the horrible, face-shifting monster back in Forest-London.

"Ah, I think I know who you mean." Lenore nodded, expression grave. "Just as not all of us are bad, as Alexandria would have you believe, not all of us are good either. Sadly, there are some we've had to banish from the city."

Emma's mouth went dry. "Its face kept changing . . . into us. It chased us."

Lenore sighed. "You met the Witch of a Thousand Faces." She shook her head at Emma's wide-eyed expression. "Just a silly name the newcomers have given her. She was banished to the In-Between years ago. She can't come back to Witch City, but I think she believes if she can . . . get rid of someone, and change into them, she can take their place."

Emma shivered, suddenly eager to change the subject. "What is the In-Between, anyway? What's it for?"

"Well, it was the original Witch City," Lenore explained. "The issue was, it sits parallel to London." A rueful smile played across her lips. "Hundreds of years ago, the founder of New Londinium was betrayed by one of her own. Someone revealed the location. There was an army coming for the witches, and so they had to leave. They set up the new city here, and this time they were more careful. The abandoned city was set up with protection spells to keep those without witch blood out."

An army coming for them. The thought was enough to make Emma shiver. No wonder everything in Forest-London had seemed so perfectly preserved, as if people had simply dropped everything and left. Because they had.

"And the dratted thing is always moving." The low voice of Tobias McCraw startled Emma out of her memories, and she turned and glared at the man.

"Probably to keep away people like you."

The older witch beside McCraw, his mother, shook a finger at Emma. "You leave my son be. He has a good heart. And he's on our side."

Emma clamped her lips shut on her impulse to shout out that he was a liar. She knew what she'd heard in the forest. He'd been following them.

"Eat up, Edgar," Lenore said, breaking the tense silence. "After you're finished, I'll give you all a tour of the city." She grasped one of the crystals on her necklace, grinning at them. "Though maybe we'll walk this time. I don't think Edgar enjoyed the transportation spell."

"I didn't," Edgar said mournfully, when Emma glanced sideways at him. "I was nearly sick on her shoes."

"I think it's fun," Maddie said brightly. "You just go *poof!* And you're there."

Edgar looked dismal at this. "I'd be happy not poofing ever again, honestly."

Granny El seemed unimpressed with the conversation. She stabbed with more force than necessary at the baked potato on her plate. "These newfangled witches and their crystal spells. In my day, we did all the hard work ourselves."

"Granny, crystals make it easier to access powerful spells." Eliza leaned sideways, bumping her shoulder gently. "Not just those with high percentages. That way, magic is available to everyone. No one is better than anyone else."

Granny El paused, fork hovering over the potato, and then a wide smile split her face. "Child, how did I manage to raise you this well?"

"It's a mystery, Granny."

Emma dropped her gaze to her plate, smiling. She couldn't help feeling a pang of jealousy. The way Eliza and her gran talked to one another was so easy, so loaded with casual affection. It made her chest ache a little to think about home, and the way she and her mother spoke to each other—or screamed, more accurately. It was so different.

Emma banished the thought and turned her attention back to her breakfast. There was no point thinking about her mother now, or what might have been different had she stayed at the palace.

She wasn't there anymore; she was here, in Witch City, surrounded by others just like her, and she was going to enjoy the food on her plate and think about all of the no-doubt-miraculous things she would see on the tour.

She finished her toast and eggs, and once the others had finished too, Lenore led them out of the dining room, through the lobby, and onto the steps of the inn.

Even in the daylight, the winding, cobblestone street was lined on either side by small silver flames set inside globes of glass. It took several minutes to get down the first short stretch of road, because Emma kept slowing to look at them. They had no wick or oil that she could see, so they had to be magic. She had to force herself to keep moving and not stand and stare at them all day. From somewhere up ahead came the faint sound of music.

The shops on either side of the lane were all very pretty, with striped awnings and hanging lanterns at each of the oval-shaped doors. They passed the window of a knitting shop, hung with the most colorful, wild-patterned blankets Emma had ever seen. There was also a clothesline full of white-and-purple socks, with a tag that read *20 crystals off—today only!*

A sweetshop was next, with candied butterflies made out of spun sugar, enchanted to flutter their wings open and closed. Emma paused for a moment, enraptured. It was almost funny now to think about the horrible rumors that had circulated about Witch City. Here it was—all magical, with glittering streets and spun sugar— and people back in London were frightening one another with tales of murderous fountains and streets that led straight to hell.

It was all so ridiculous.

She paused, startled, when a sphere of blue light zipped overhead and then stopped, hovering over the awning above her. It blinked twice, short flashes of light, and then set to flickering like a candle.

Lenore laughed. "It's called a Find-Me-Here. They're faster than familiars for navigating the streets, though they take more magic. A lot of the higher percenters use them."

Emma stared up at it, riveted. "Higher percenters." She paused. "I'm . . . uh, forty. At least, that's what The Testing said. Could I use one?"

"I'm sure you could." Lenore lifted an eyebrow, looking mildly surprised, before turning away again to stare up at the Find-Me-Here. "We've got lots of fifteens and twenties—those are the most common—and even a few single digits who still find a way to get around. Your witch hunter is the first zero percenter we've had here." She grinned. "That will take some getting used to."

"About that." Emma's stomach flipped, and she cleared her throat, determined to say what was on her mind. "I don't trust him."

As they walked, she told Lenore about hearing his heart in the In-Between, and how she'd confronted him about it over breakfast, how the witch hunter denied it.

"You're sure it was his heart?" Lenore's brow furrowed. "There are plenty of animals in the In-Between, and even other people— witches trying to get to the other side."

Now Emma did hesitate. It seemed like too much of a coincidence, but she also didn't have any absolute proof that it had been him, did she? He'd never actually shown up at the exact moment she was hearing the heartbeat.

Before she could reply, Lenore reached out and put a hand on her shoulder. "You're right to be wary, Emma," she said gently. "I don't blame you. Many people who come from the In-Between are jumpy for days afterward. It's only natural, after all you've been through. But I hope you'll find it in your heart to give Tobias the same second chance Queen Alexandria should have given all of us witches. He's come a very long way to reunite with his mother. He's risking everything just by being here."

Emma wasn't sure what else she could say. It seemed so reasonable when Lenore put it like that, so she only nodded. But as she trailed after the others, and the streets grew busier, she couldn't help glancing around at the crowds of people walking by, unease tightening her chest. Even with Lenore's talk of second chances, something didn't feel quite right.

They continued on, and the faint music Emma had heard earlier grew louder now. It sounded like a flute, and maybe a fiddle. They passed a few more stores—a clock shop full of ticking and chiming, and a *Spirits* store that sold beer and wine, but also claimed on a sign out front to have "canned ghosts"—*Spirit in a jar! Good for arranged hauntings, driving out late renters, or Samhein Celebrations!* Edgar stumbled back from this, muttering that it sounded very dodgy.

After this, the street intersected with several others, opening up into a large square with a fountain in the center. Next to the fountain was a stage filled with musicians playing pipes and flutes— the source of the music they'd been hearing ever since they left the inn. A dancer stood at center stage, hands lifted to the sky, a pair of heavy-looking horns branching out above his head. The woman across from him had a crown of flowers adorning her dark curls and a white half-moon painted on her brow. They moved in tandem, spinning and swaying, white robes flowing around them.

It was beautiful, and Emma and the others stood and watched until Lenore said, "The dance is to welcome spring. It's tradition during the festival. Come this way."

They headed deeper into the square, into the thick of the celebration. There were witches everywhere. Many were decked head to toe in flowing dresses and veils, flowers of all colors strewn through their hair. Some had also accessorized with feathers and coins, while others had run a streak of color through their tresses, a sight that had all of them gaping again.

The fashions here were far more daring than in London, and the rich purples and velvety greens more vibrant than the dresses in her own closet. It was, Emma thought, like a new dimension of color. She was almost sure it had been achieved by magic.

There were stalls scattered seemingly at random through the square, and as they got closer to the center, she could see the statue in the middle of the fountain was a witch carved of jade-colored stone, a cauldron perched on one shoulder and a hand stretched up to the sky. Emma recognized her face, strangely enough. She was one of the same women from the statues in the In-Between. This time, though, she was depicted with her chin tilted up defiantly, a cat curling around her skirts. The stream of water trickling from her cauldron fed back into the shallow base at the bottom of the fountain, and the sound of the water mixed with the band's music.

Lenore must have noticed her staring, because she stopped to explain. "Abigail Hopper—one of the original founders of this version of New Londinium. She was the one who created the spell to keep the streets moving."

Emma gaped up at the statue until she realized the others had continued walking. They were heading eagerly toward the food stands in the center of the market. The stalls were a little bit of everything, it seemed. There were piles of fruit—apples, mangoes, and oranges, plus some brightly colored red fruit Emma had never seen in London—and tables full of a rainbow of fabrics.

Here in the square she saw more familiars, cats of every color walking alongside witches as if it were the most natural thing in the world, and here and there, a raven or a crow perched on someone's shoulder. One witch, a tall, skinny man in a dark blue dinner jacket, walked past with a white rat clinging to his sleeve. Edgar shuddered.

"Will we get a familiar too?" Maddie said, looking around at them eagerly. "Oh, I'd love to get a cat."

"You will eventually, if you'd like one." Lenore paused in the center of the market, just in front of the fountain. "Usually the connection comes when you've just begun to master your power. Familiars can be of assistance with that."

They made their way around the fountain. On the other side, Emma could see a large building at the edge of the square—a sprawling white mansion with pillars along the front. The metal plaque said it was the parliament, although in the London she was used to, there were usually a few flags on display. Here, she saw instead a stone column with a glittering quartz crystal attached to the top.

She tipped her head to one side, squinting up at the building. It was a museum back in Original London, she was fairly certain. Boring and full of dusty artifacts. "I recognize this, but . . . it's a bit different."

There was something decidedly *off* about it.

Something was going on under all the noise of the festival, she realized. A deep, slow pulsing had begun to fill her head, a pattern that sounded only remotely like a human heart. Emma paused, frowning, fixated on the steps leading up to the white building, listening to the Noise. What on earth made that kind of sound? It was much too deep for a human heart, too slow, and the rhythm wasn't quite right. It didn't feel like the monster back in Forest-London, either—the Witch of a Thousand Faces. That had had a sense of wrongness about it, but this . . . this just felt slightly alien.

"Lenore, there you are! Thank God!"

Emma started, turning to see a short, round man in a purple robe hurrying up to her aunt. His face was flushed, and he was very sweaty. "Allistar is at it again. Just look!"

They all stared in the direction he was pointing, at a small, rickety-looking wooden stall wedged between a fruit stand and a booth full of silver jewelry. The stall held an assortment of glass jars and vials, all full of suspicious-looking liquids. Some of the liquids were merely an odd color—Emma spotted a snot-green one that made her stomach churn on sight—but others appeared to be actually moving in their jars. One even seemed to be boiling, emitting a loud and constant hissing from under its cork.

"Allistar!" Lenore threw her hands up in irritation and then turned back to Emma and the others. "Sorry, one second. Have a look around the market and I'll be right back." She turned, raising her voice above the crowd. "Allistar Ripley, I *know* nobody gave you a permit for that stall . . ."

Edgar, Eliza, and Maddie were looking around the market eagerly, but Emma was listening hard, trying to pick out another of the low, pulsing lines of sound she'd heard a moment before. It had faded once she'd been distracted, but if she could just find it again . . .

It was faint at first. So faint she mistook it for the deep noise she'd heard before the interruption. But then it began to grow louder, and Emma stiffened.

There. She could hear it now: the low, steady *thump-thump, thump-thump.*

It was the same heartbeat she'd heard back in the hotel room. Back in the forest.

The witch hunter.

Tobias McCraw was here; she was sure of it.

Maddie was standing next to her, and Emma whirled around and grabbed her arm.

"Emma, what—"

"I hear him." Her voice was low, urgent. "McCraw, he's here somewhere."

Maddie stood up straighter, but she only frowned at Emma. "Wha . . . I mean, so what? He's here, isn't he? In the city? It's not so surprising that he'd come to the festival, same as us."

Emma scowled as she looked wildly around at the crowd. Maddie didn't get it. It wasn't that simple. He had to be up to something, because he was *definitely* following them.

There. She spotted a tall figure across the square, his face partly obscured by a round-brimmed black hat. He was walking next to his mother, moving quickly through the crowd toward them.

"Ow, Emma! You're going to break my arm."

"It's him, right there."

Edgar and Eliza were hovering behind them now, watching over Emma's shoulder, and Edgar said hesitantly, "Uh, that's not him, Em. That's not even the same hat he wears."

Emma blinked, releasing her grip on Maddie's arm. Maddie sighed with relief and rubbed at the red spot on her skin.

As Emma stared, the man pushed up his hat, laughing at something his companion had said. She saw that he was a sallow-skinned, narrow-faced man, nothing like McCraw at all. And his companion was not McCraw's mother, but a young man.

Emma bit her lip, blushing furiously. Maybe Lenore was right. Maybe she *was* simply jumpy after the In-Between.

"Sorry, I thought it was him for a moment. That hat . . ."

Maddie shuddered. "I absolutely don't blame you. It's hideously similar, and he should be kicked out of the festival for his garish taste in headgear."

That actually made Emma smile, and she had just begun to relax when the pulsing sound came again. Not the witch hunter's heart this time, but the impossibly low rhythm she'd heard earlier—the one she'd never heard before. This time, she was sure she wasn't imagining it. This was real. This was something strange and new.

And this time, she could tell exactly where it was coming from.

Before she could really consider what she was doing, she was on the move, heading straight for the steps of the huge white building.

Chapter Thirty-Three

" Emma, what—where are you going?"

Emma didn't answer at first, didn't even realize she was being asked the question until Maddie caught up with her, grabbing her sleeve so the crowd couldn't separate them. "Emma?"

"I'm . . . there's the sound. The Noise." She was still fixated on the steps, on the round pillars at the entrance of the building. This version of the Noise was so different. Lower and deeper, more compelling. It seemed to take over every thought in her head.

Maddie seemed to understand what she was talking about, because she turned around and beckoned for Eliza and Edgar. A moment later, Emma found all three of them following her up the steps. She glanced back once, to see if Lenore or anyone else was watching, but there was so much going on in the square below that no one seemed to take notice. And besides, there were plenty of people on the stairs, laughing and talking or eating sugared cakes from paper napkins. Anyone paying attention would just think they were searching for the best vantage point to watch the performance on stage.

"What does it mean?" Maddie asked. "What are you hearing?"

Emma had no idea what it meant. She just knew she hadn't heard this particular Noise before—and that there was a strange kind of pull to it. She *had* to know what it was.

She said as much as they ascended the last of the many stairs and arrived at the top of a long stone platform. Before them waited a set of arched double doors inlaid with brass bands and scrolled designs. Directly in front of the doors were two very tall people in black jackets. Each had a large red crystal hung from a heavy chain around their neck, and their expressions were very serious as they stared at Emma, who suddenly found all the words she possessed had flown straight out her left ear and vanished into the ether. For a moment they all stood there staring at one another, and Emma thought about turning to flee down the stairs.

It was Maddie who finally broke the silence. "Erm," she said. "This is Emmaline Black, and Edgar Black. You know, Lenore's family? We're supposed to be getting a tour."

For one dismaying moment, Emma thought Maddie was trying to use her power on the guard. And then he bent down slightly, to make eye contact with Maddie, and cocked his head to one side.

"Are you now?"

Maddie only nodded. Her eyes were very wide, and she looked, Emma thought, like she was very much regretting her lie.

Thankfully, the guard straightened up and grinned at his partner, a woman with a tight blond bun and a sun-weathered face. She rolled her eyes toward the ceiling, and then backed up to press her shoulder against the door, leaning into the entrance to call out, "Newcomers coming in, Janie. Give them the tour, would you?"

After a second of hesitation, they passed through the entrance. Emma flushed at the amused look both guards were giving them, but she put it out of her head. She didn't care what they thought; she just wanted to know what she was hearing.

They passed through a short, sparsely decorated hallway, and through another pair of doors after that. The room beyond was massive. There was a door set in each wall, with red-cushioned benches beside each, and hanging ferns in silver pots brightened the corners. The floor was tiled in jade and black, and their footsteps echoed as they moved inside, the door thumping shut behind them. There was a balcony that ran around the inside perimeter of the space, and at the very back of the room was a platform with a set of four velvet-cushioned chairs.

Not a Throne Room, Emma realized, as they stood in the center. Not exactly. But somehow she knew that this was a place where the witches came to decide things. Where they held discussions, and figured out what they were going to do together, instead of ordering people about from a great big dais towering above everyone else.

She moved farther into the room. Hundreds of feet overhead, windows were set into a domed ceiling, and the hall was airy and bright in spite of the dark decor. All at once, the pulsing sound in the back of her head grew louder, until it was all she could hear. Somehow, it was drawing her toward a spot in the floor just ahead.

Exactly in the center of a wide circle of chairs was an oddly shaped well, made of what looked like cloudy white crystal. It was roughly waist-high and it glittered in the sunlight streaming through the windows above. It wasn't round exactly, since the walls ended at strange angles on each side, but set into a shelf that ran around the outside was a series of stone cat statues with glittering green gems for eyes. And it was definitely, strangely, the source of the Noise pounding in Emma's head.

What was a *well* doing in the middle of the parliament building, and why was it emitting the Noise?

Emma stepped closer and noticed for the first time the guard leaning up against the wall beside the platform with the velvet chairs. Unlike the guards outside the building, this one was dressed in charcoal gray, though she had the same heavy chain and red crystal hanging from her neck. She was whip-thin but muscular, and her slate-colored hair was woven into a thick braid that trailed down her back.

The others jumped as they noticed her, and the woman's thin face brightened.

"I thought I heard Pat hollering up there. New witches, are you? Come on in."

This, Emma realized, must be the Janie the guard outside had shouted at. Her heart was hammering in her chest, though she wasn't sure if it was due to Janie's sudden appearance or the fact that the Noise was still so loud in her ears. The others trailed behind her, staring at the guard, who smiled widely back at them.

As she got closer to the well the Noise increased. This time, though, she noticed a strange undercurrent to it, one she hadn't heard before. Under the steady *thud, thud* was a gentle hum.

"What . . . what is this?"

The Noise seemed to grow louder with each step, until at last she was at the edge of the well, her chest tight as she peered down into it. The pulse was like thunder now, shaking her bones. The hum was there too, though it was lower.

"The heart of the city." Janie's eyes glittered. "Have a look, but don't get too close."

Cautiously, Emma stared down into the well. Blue light flickered in the depths, pulsing and crackling, and sparks ran through the surface. It reminded Emma of the strange fire she'd seen in the Find-Me-Here, but there was far more of it, and it appeared to be in some sort of liquid form.

"But . . . I can hear it. I don't understand."

"It's magic."

All four of them jumped as Lenore's voice echoed behind them. Janie cackled. "Good afternoon, Lenore. Come to collect your niece and nephew?"

"Yes, thank you, Janie." Lenore looked quietly amused as she looked around at all of them. "I was told you might be here."

Emma ducked her head, face burning. "Sorry, I couldn't help myself. I-I heard it from out in the square."

Thankfully, Lenore looked more intrigued than angry. "Very interesting." She swept closer, skirts whispering over the marble floor, and placed a hand on the smooth stone wall of the well, leaning over to peer down into the fire. "I'd thought your magic was merely sensing the heart—the life of a person, so to speak. But I may have been wrong."

"What do you mean?" Emma took a step back from the well, still feeling a little guilty. She was almost sure she wasn't supposed to be in here—and certainly they weren't supposed to have wandered away by themselves.

"This is magic: pure, raw, and unfiltered. In its original form." Lenore gestured at the fire. "You appear to have the ability to sense it. I'm not sure what that might mean. You could have incredible power, Emma." She tilted her head to one side, eyes shining. "Tell me, do you hear almost everyone's heartbeat, or just those with stronger powers?"

Emma bit her lip, thinking hard. She heard her friends' hearts all the time, and occasionally unspecified hearts, people she couldn't pin down. "Well, I don't hear it *all the time*, if that's what you're asking. I hear my friends' a lot though." She darted a look over at the others. "Which was alarming at first."

"Probably over a certain percent," Lenore mused. "Fascinating."

Eliza's brow was furrowed as she stared at the well. "I thought magic was inside us."

"It is." Lenore straightened up, patting her chest. "In your heart, to be exact, which is probably what Emma is sensing. But magic also exists in nature. We've used a good amount of it to create the city core, which is how Witch City stays hidden."

Lenore grasped the chain around her neck, touching one of the crystals at her throat. "Mostly we work with charmed crystals. They're a stable conduit for small amounts of magic, which we can set with intentions to get specific results."

Emma frowned at her, and Lenore laughed.

"I'm sorry. Let's try that again. The crystals are magic. They let us do almost anything—like fly. But for something like keeping the city running, keeping us hidden, we need a far bigger amount." She gestured at the well. "Like that."

Magic. Magic that was keeping this entire city hidden.

Emma stared down into the well, a little awestruck. All along, she'd been hearing magic, the pulse of power in others' hearts. It made a strange kind of sense. That was why everyone's rhythm sounded a little different. Everyone's magic was different.

It felt like the puzzle pieces were finally fitting together.

"The statues." She gestured at the stone cats circling the edge of the well. "Are they magic too?"

"They are. They're imbibed with strong enchantments, a kind of key to allow us to pass freely in and out of the In-Between without getting lost. Much like the Find-Me-Here, but more powerful, since the In-Between is particularly challenging." She paused. "But there is too much to learn about magic and the heart of the city all in one day. I promise I'll tell you all there is to know . . . eventually. I'll even take you to the library. The full history of Witch City is there."

Edgar perked up, brows raised. "You have a library here?"

Lenore laughed. "Of course. And you're more than welcome to check out whatever you'd like. We have poets you've probably never heard of—poets that had to flee persecution for witchcraft. There are a surprising number of them."

Edgar looked shocked and delighted by this revelation, and Emma felt excitement spark in her chest. The Witch City library.

Books *without* missing pages. The true and real history of the war. Of the royal family. It was certainly a place they'd have to visit.

Lenore turned on her heel, nodding at the guard. "Good afternoon, Janie. Thank you for making sure my niece and nephew didn't blow themselves to smithereens."

Edgar stumbled and nearly fell over. "Smithereens?"

"Yes. You see, as all of us learn in school, the way witchcraft works is that you attach your own natural magic to the magic in a vessel, say . . . a crystal."

Lenore was making her way toward the front door as she spoke, and they all hurried to follow her. "And that vessel allows you to access magic, and activate a spell. If you access too much magic in a vessel—say, a *well* of magic—you get an overload." She smiled brightly down at Emma, who swallowed hard. "It's like a wineskin. It only holds a certain amount of wine, and when you overfill it . . . it explodes. Sometimes, if it's greatly overfilled, it will take out some of the surroundings as well. So if any of you had reached into the well . . ."

"Smithereens," Emma said weakly. The thought made her feel a little ill. It was a good thing Janie had been there to keep an eye on them.

"Yes, smithereens," Lenore agreed. She walked back through the front doors of the building and down the steps, smiling at the guards as she went past.

Chapter Thirty-Four

L enore walked them across the square again, weaving through the crowds and activity. They paused briefly to watch a fire-breathing witch entertaining a crowd of awestruck children, and on the walk back to the inn, Edgar insisted on stopping in front of the library. It was only a street away from where they were staying, and though none of the others were nearly as excited about the library as Edgar was, Emma still found the place quite enchanting. It was a tiny, thatched-roof cottage with rust-red bricks, and a hanging *Library* sign done in scrolling gold writing.

They then returned to the Push Broom Inn, and Lenore led them up to their room on the second floor.

"Alright, I've got to get some of the other newcomers settled in, so you lot might as well sit and have some tea. I've had Gerty send it up to your rooms already, and you can have a lie down if you like." She smiled at Edgar. "I dare say you'll need one by now. Then I'll come get you later this afternoon and we'll head over to the Candlewick School for Magic for a tour."

Emma's mouth fell open, and Maddie piped up from beside her, "There's a school for witches? Does that mean we'll learn magic? And how to fly?"

Lenore's eyes sparkled. "Yes, of course, though you'll be learning math and spelling too. But your studies will mainly be in magic."

A school for magic.

Even Emma, who'd had a series of terribly boring tutors and had always hated lessons, thought it sounded rather exciting.

Lenore began to turn away, and Emma hesitated for just a moment before clearing her throat pointedly. They'd been promised answers at some point today, and so far they hadn't had any.

Lenore turned back, brows raised expectantly.

"Um, sorry." Emma shifted from one foot to the other, feeling her face begin to heat up. "But I have questions. I know you and my mother probably didn't have the best relationship, and neither did we, if I'm being honest." She paused, feeling a nervous flutter in her stomach. "She's . . . she's hard to live with." She glanced over at Edgar, who nodded in agreement. "Both of our mothers are . . . well . . ."

"Bad people," Edgar finished, his voice hoarse.

Lenore nodded and then sighed, her expression softening. "My sisters—your mothers—they weren't always like that. We had . . . a difficult childhood." When Emma and Edgar continued to stare at her expectantly, she smiled faintly and nodded. "Well, you can imagine a little how we grew up in the shadow of a fallen kingdom. The witches had taken over and wiped out our family. We were rescued and taken in by a distant cousin." Lenore's voice was soft, and a little strained. "We were raised to loathe magic, to believe it was evil. And so we learned we had to stamp out our own."

For a moment there was only silence, and then the words clicked somewhere inside Emma's brain. "Our own?" she blurted out, at the same time as Edgar said, "What?"

Lenore nodded slowly. "We all had some level of magic, though Isolde and Alexandria would never admit it. But it was there. We each suppressed a major piece of ourselves, and it affected us all differently. I was full of self-loathing, and Alexandria went terribly cold, became hardened. I think it was something Isolde admired."

Emma's pulse was pounding hard in her ears now. She recalled how the queen drank thistle wine every morning, and how her own mother had panicked and made her drink the juice. Isolde had *known* they had witch blood. She'd simply been continuing her habit of attempting to stamp it out. She'd been scared.

The thought made her feel a strange rush of sympathy, though it was tinged with anger.

Lenore drew in a breath and shook her head, as if shaking off thoughts of her past. "I'd better go. Rest up a little."

She began to turn away, her smile forced. Emma gripped the doorframe, heart still pounding furiously against her ribcage. It was just beginning to dawn on her that this was it. This was their new home.

She wasn't ever going to see Isolde again.

The idea left her feeling breathless, and a little ill. But not sad. Not exactly.

"My mother, she couldn't have known about the nooses under the castle, all the children who were taken there every year—" Her voice broke, and she cut herself off, shaking her head. "She couldn't have known, could she?"

No one said anything. Beside her, Edgar shifted, eyes fixed on Lenore's face as she turned back to them.

Lenore blinked, and Emma was dismayed to see the glitter of tears in her eyes. "Oh, Emma, I'm sorry, but I can't tell you that one way or another. You know your mother better than I do." Lenore reached out and squeezed Emma's shoulder. "We clearly have a lot to discuss, we three. And we will, soon. But for now, get some rest, all of you. I'm heading into the In-Between to help someone along, and I'll be back to collect you in a few hours."

They said goodbye to one another, and then Lenore left.

For a moment Emma stood there in the doorway, thinking hard. There'd been something horribly sad in her aunt's face. Something that made Emma's chest ache, and her stomach feel leaden. Whatever had happened between the sisters must have been truly horrendous—and Lenore was still clearly hurt about it all these years later.

Emma turned to follow the others into the room and then hesitated, listening to the sound of Lenore's footsteps retreating down the hall. Yes, there was definitely something she still wasn't saying. Something she didn't feel comfortable sharing, or that she felt wasn't the type of thing a child should know. And as much as Emma wasn't impolite enough to pry it out of her, she did think she and Edgar deserved to know—especially after everything they'd been through, after all the time she'd waited for answers. They were part of the Black family, after all. They should be allowed to know their own history.

Lenore was hiding something, and Emma was going to find out what it was.

Chapter Thirty-Five

Emma slipped into the room, closing the door gently behind her. When she turned, Maddie and Eliza were perched on one of the bottom bunks. Edgar was sitting on the floor, his back to the bedpost, a plate of sandwiches from the tea tray already balanced on one knee. They all stared at her expectantly.

Emma blinked at them. "What?"

"We know that expression," Eliza said.

"You're not satisfied." Maddie folded her arms across her chest. "You want answers."

"It's just," Emma said slowly, "I feel like she's holding something back."

She glanced over at Edgar, who nodded. "I think so too. Like there's something really horrible she doesn't want to tell us."

They were quiet for a moment. Emma stepped over to the window, which had a good view of the streets below. After a moment Eliza joined her, and then Maddie, and Edgar. It was the second day of the Ostara festival, and they watched witches zip past, cloaks flying behind them. A faint sound of bells could be heard, mingling with the fiddle music, as a horse pulling a white carriage full of witches decked out in flowers and ribbons passed beneath their window.

For a moment, Emma let herself relax.

It felt both strange and wonderful to have a moment to breathe, to simply sit and reflect on the fact that they had made it. Even if Lenore was hiding something from them, they were in Witch City, and they were together. They were all okay.

They were silent for another few minutes, watching a crowd of children with wooden wands decorated with colorful crystals play a game of chase, shrieking with laughter as they blasted one another with what looked like bits of confetti.

"Well, what do we want to do?" Maddie said after a moment. "How do we begin to look if we don't have a clue what she might be hiding?"

"I imagine everything we'd want to know is quite nearby." Eliza leaned forward, resting her chin on her hand, elbow on the sill. She peered out the corner of the window, nearly mashing her cheek to it. "In the library."

"But we're not allowed to just go out on our *own*," Edgar protested.

"Nobody said that, actually," Eliza pointed out.

"But it's implied." Edgar crossed his arms over his chest. "No one expects a bunch of children to go out wandering by themselves."

"We're not just children—we're *witches*," Maddie said firmly. "Witches who want answers." She glanced sideways at Emma, who frowned, thinking hard. She was determined to learn more, but she hadn't actually thought about sneaking out right this minute. It seemed rather daring.

"It's just a library," Eliza said, "and it's on the next street over. It's not like we're going down to the pub to try out the local ale."

That was true. Of all the things they might get in trouble for, going to the library seemed the least likely.

"I suppose," she said slowly, "that no one told us to stay put, not exactly. If anyone asks, we could just say we're out to find a good read to pass the time. Or we want to find something by the witch poets Lenore told us about."

Edgar didn't look entirely satisfied, but he also didn't protest when Emma shrugged into her coat and slipped out the door. In fact, he followed her so quickly he nearly stepped on her heels, and Emma was fairly certain he was thinking about new poets.

The hallway floor was creaky under their shoes, and at first, Emma winced with each step. After a minute, however, when nobody came out of a room to check on them, they began to grow bolder.

Once downstairs, they made their way through the empty, lavender-scented landing, and into the vestibule.

Thankfully, no one was there. Emma reminded herself that it wasn't that they were doing anything wrong, technically, but they probably weren't supposed to be out on their own.

Not to mention that the moment they left the building, Emma remembered that the city was *constantly shifting*. If they got lost, they had no familiar to help them, and no Find-Me-Here.

Outside, the sun was bright, and it had warmed up slightly since the morning. There was a clear blue sky, and the faint breeze that ruffled her hair smelled like campfires and fir trees. Emma breathed in deeply before moving down the steps.

The library was only one street over, and they soon found themselves climbing up the stairs to its tiny front porch. As they walked they could hear the noise and music of the festival, but thankfully the street between the Push Broom Inn and the library seemed empty, aside from a chubby orange tabby on the top of a fence, who paused in its washing long enough to squint at them.

Once they were on the porch, Emma let out a sigh of relief. When she glanced back over her shoulder, the Push Broom Inn was still there. Hopefully, it would stay put.

She tilted her head back to look up at the library sign, and was surprised to see that it contained more words than she'd initially noted—in smaller script at the top and bottom. It read *The Edwin A. York Library of Charms, Enchantments & Witchery.*

"Oh, what does that mean?" She turned to look at the others, who were all staring up at the sign as well. Maddie's eyes were wide and excited.

"Charms, as in magic. That's brilliant. Quick, let's go in!"

Maddie bolted forward, pushing open the door, which gave a cheerful jingle to announce their entry. Emma and the others followed close on her heels. What could a charms library possibly look like?

Inside it was tiny, and the warm, wooden interior reminded Emma more of a holiday cottage in the English countryside than an actual library. But it was the floor-to-ceiling shelves that drew her attention. The entire place seemed to be made of shelves, in fact, and there were sliding ladders along all the walls. Instead of books, the shelves held a series of silver boxes. Each bookcase was labeled at the top—with *10 percent*, *15 percent*, *20 percent*, and so on, with a little arrow pointing up next to the number. In the corner a narrow shelf was marked *1–10 percent.*

Additionally, each shelf on the case was clearly a subsection of sorts. The first shelf on Emma's left held a sign that said *15 percent: Flying—Bouncing, Floating, Dancing, Swimming, Jumping, Wishing.*

"What on earth does that mean?" Eliza stopped in front of the shelf, staring up at it in awe.

"Different types of flying!" Maddie's eyes were shining. "You know, like how the way you fly in dreams is always different? It's like that."

Emma moved closer, heart thumping in her chest. The thought of flying was so enchanting that she momentarily forgot why they were there. "Are these the crystals she was talking about?" She gestured at the first box on the shelf. It had a glass top that revealed a series of cloudy pink crystals inside, resting on beds of blue velvet.

"Enchanted stones, like in Lenore's necklace." Maddie reached for the box, and Edgar smacked her hand.

"Don't touch anything! You'll get us in trouble."

"These look really valuable." Eliza drew back a little. "Maybe he's right. Just . . . don't touch anything."

They moved deeper into the room. The library was bigger than Emma had first thought, with a little section in the back corner with a cast-iron fireplace and several worn-out, cushiony armchairs. Emma flitted from one shelf to the next, feeling a little dizzy with excitement. She passed *Artistic Talent*, with subsections like *Cooking, Drawing, Dancing, Sewing, Singing, Painting*, and *Morphing: Subsection B—Animal, Plant, Mineral, Man.*

Deeper into the library she found an enormous section labeled *Lecture Notes*, and paused there, scanning the shelves. How were there charms for lecture notes? The sections here were labeled *Math, Geography, English, Science,* and also *Divination, Necromancy, Mediumship, Animagery.* She paused at *History* when she saw a box of crystals with the words *Great War* etched across the front.

No more blanked-out pages. No more omissions. No more lies.

Slowly, with shaking hands, she flipped the latch on the lid. Behind her, Edgar sucked in a breath, but he didn't say anything. In fact, he pressed forward, peering over her shoulder. There were six crystals laid out on black velvet, all of them various shades of cloudy blue. Holding her breath, Emma reached in and took one carefully between finger and thumb.

The crystal was cool to the touch, the outside smooth and glassy. She thought she felt something when her skin made contact, like a tingle in her fingertips. And then . . . nothing.

Frowning, she turned to the others. "What's meant to happen?"

"You've got to activate it."

They jumped, and Emma fumbled the crystal, nearly dropping it. There was a woman in the doorway. She was tall and thin, and she wore a pale-gray walking dress and silver-framed spectacles. Her hair was a riot of black curls, and Emma spotted a pencil poking out from above her ear.

"The silver holders to the right of the shelf."

Emma blinked at the woman—a librarian, she supposed. She was pointing at something over Emma's left shoulder, which turned out to be a hook on the wall that held a number of silver chains with claw-shaped pendants.

"You fit the crystal in the cage to get started." The woman's voice held a faint note of amusement. "You're the new ones, aren't you? Lenore's niece and nephew. I can see the resemblance." She tapped her own necklace with one long fingernail. "You're restricted to non-active spells. Unsupervised, of course. Lecture notes and prophecy records and the like, until you pass Year Ten exams."

The woman glided over and plucked one of the silver necklaces off the hook, eyeing Emma with a dark, quizzical gaze. When she held it out, Emma took it carefully. "Thank you. Are you the . . . the charms librarian?"

"I'm Sophia." The woman smiled, watching as Emma slid the necklace over her head. "I didn't expect anyone, since the festival is in full swing. Does Lenore know you're here?"

"Uh . . ."

"Of course she does." Maddie stepped up beside Emma, her smile wide and sincere.

Sophia made a noncommittal humming noise, and then reached down to pluck the crystal from Emma's hand. "Here, like this."

Emma looked down. Sophia's fingers were slender, her nails long and pink. She took the pendant between her thumb and index finger and flipped it upside down, so that the prongs were facing upward. Then she snapped the crystal into place before stepping back and letting the pendant fall onto Emma's chest. "You'll have to be over ten percent for it to work, I'm afraid."

"I am." The crystal was warm, and slightly heavy against her skin, and Emma frowned at it, brows creased. "When does it start working?"

"Give it a few seconds. And you may want to sit down."

"Why—"

The lights flickered. Emma blinked, glancing around at her friends, who were still staring at her expectantly. "Did you see—"

They flickered again, rapidly, on and off, and then her friends' faces were strangely blurry, and Emma's breath caught. Finally the lights went out altogether, plunging her into darkness.

With her sight gone, she suddenly became aware of a gentle humming coming from the crystal, low and soft, much quieter than the well of fire, but clear all the same. When the lights came back on, she was not in the library anymore.

Chapter Thirty-Six

Emma was standing in the center of a narrow dirt lane. One side was filled with blocky brick houses, the other with an assortment of mismatched, shambling wooden huts. There was garbage strewn across the street and littered in the gutters, and flies buzzed over heaps of refuse.

The air was hot and putrid, and Emma put her hand over her nose, eyes watering.

The only way she could be certain she was in London was because the clock tower was visible in the distance. She had a moment of confusion when she realized it was standing upright, unblemished.

Did this mean she was in the past?

She glanced around, frowning. The dirt lane was mostly empty, though there were a few children sitting on the steps in front of one of the wooden shacks, and a pair of women walking toward her, speaking quietly to one another.

Nobody seemed to notice Emma.

She was just thinking she might ask the two approaching women what part of town this was when a voice abruptly boomed from overhead.

"1807: The first whispers of an uprising begin in London, as a young Alexandria Blackwell and her sisters, rescued from the palace by a royal cousin while their family was being slaughtered, begin to work on a plan to reclaim the family's stolen throne."

Emma jumped, looking around wildly. There was nobody around, save for the women and the children on the steps, and none of them even glanced up. No one else seemed to have heard the voice. She glanced both ways down the street, then up at the roof-tops and down at the dirt pathway. When she happened to catch sight of her own feet, she drew a sharp breath in surprise.

Her feet were *see-through*. She could see the dirt road right through them.

Abruptly, she felt the weight and warmth of the crystal around her neck. Yes, that was right. She wasn't actually here. She was in someone's lecture notes. *That* had been the voice from overhead. She let out a breath of relief, and it slowly began to dawn on her what the booming voice had said.

Blackwell?

A voice just in front of her caught her attention, and Emma turned as the two women finally passed, apparently blind to her presence.

"I've packed the entire room with it," one woman was saying. "We'll see soon enough if she was telling the truth."

Emma went still, shock spiking through her, pinning her feet to the spot. That voice was horribly familiar.

When she turned to look at the women more closely, her heart dropped into her stomach.

The speaker's hair was down in loose waves, and her light-gray cloak was frayed at the edges and worn at the elbows and wrists, but it was unmistakably Queen Alexandria. Worse still, her companion was even more familiar, though her cloak was a dull-brown color that Emma couldn't imagine her mother being caught dead in. It was, however, undeniably Isolde. Like her sister, her face was younger and less lined, and her hair was long and curly.

The sight was enough to suck the air out of her lungs, and her heart beat hard in her ears. Her instinct to bolt tried to take over, but she drew in a deep breath and told herself firmly that this *wasn't real*, or at least . . . it wasn't real in the current moment.

Her mother didn't look her way.

"This is dangerous, Lex," Isolde was hissing, and she darted a look over her shoulder. "You know the witches have ears everywhere. What if she has a way of communicating with them?"

"By the time they can get themselves in gear to do anything it will be too late." Alexandria's voice was fierce, her dark brows drawn down. "We strike *now*. The rebels are there. Our troops are just waiting for my word." She brandished a fist at Isolde, and Emma saw it was full of purple thistle flowers. "We have this." Her face grew suddenly ugly, and full of triumph. "Lenore gave us their weakness. She betrayed the witches. That's not something they saw coming. *Six years* I've waited, hidden away, and now, the tide turns in our favor."

Emma felt a jolt of shock. Alexandria had to mean the rebel witches—which meant that Lenore had been part of the group that had overthrown the Black family. She'd betrayed them.

Was this what Lenore had been hiding? She certainly hadn't mentioned that earlier.

Isolde's dark eyes grew wide as she stared at the thistle in her sister's hand. "We don't know if she was lying—"

"We will."

Alexandria turned sharply on her heel. Pausing in front of one of the wooden shacks, she pulled a ring of keys from her cloak.

There was a jingle and a click as she fitted the key into the lock and yanked the door open.

Without thinking, Emma hurried forward, following closely behind her aunt and her mother. The shack they stepped into was tiny, only about half the size of Emma's room in the palace, and it smelled of the familiar, weedy stench of thistle and smoke. As Alexandria had hinted at, it was packed with green and purple thistle. There were fresh buds in vases, and dried thistle vines hanging upside down from the rafters. Thistle was strewn across the dirty floor, and there were even clumps of the weed stuffed into the cracks in the walls.

The smoky interior was lit only by a single candle, and in the dim light it took Emma a moment to figure out exactly what she was looking at.

In the middle of all of this was a narrow, dirty mattress, straw spilling out of the gaps in the sides, and on the mattress lay a woman, her curly hair spread out around her. There was a drop of blood on her pale throat, and dark circles beneath her eyes.

Emma pressed a hand to her mouth, something squeezing her heart painfully in her chest.

Lenore Black was clearly unconscious. She was breathing shallowly, and her face was pale and beaded with sweat. Alexandria made a noise of triumph. Striding into the room, she bent down and shook her sister roughly by the shoulder. Lenore didn't stir.

"She did this before when we tested the tea. What if she's faking again?" Isolde hovered over them, one hand fluttering to touch Lenore's cheek before she drew back, her face twisted with disgust. "Ugh, she's covered in sweat."

Emma tried to swallow past the sour taste in her mouth. She'd never wanted to slap her mother this badly before, which was saying something.

Without a word, Alexandria picked up Lenore's hand and held it over her face, letting it drop. Lenore's arm was like rubber, and it fell hard across her lips and nose. Isolde grimaced.

"She's not faking." Alexandria looked satisfied. "She's half dead. The thistle dart worked."

The thistle dart. Emma squirmed a little in the doorway, feeling her skin crawl. Her history books had mentioned those. They had turned the tide of the Great War, following the discovery that a dart to the neck could inject thistle directly into the bloodstream and completely incapacitate a witch.

Emma balked when Alexandria whirled around, moving swiftly toward her—for the door, she realized a second later. She backed away hastily as Alexandria moved past her, followed quickly by Isolde.

"Let's go tell the men what we found. The reign of the witches ends today!"

They swept away down the street, faces grim. Isolde was slightly slower than her sister, a step behind, and she looked back once, brow furrowed. Her expression made Emma's stomach twist; for a moment, just a bare half-second, it looked as if her mother was hesitating. And then her sister snapped something at her, and she turned to hurry after her and didn't look back again.

Emma stood in the center of the street, staring at the wooden shack, where Lenore lay unconscious and surrounded by thistle. A wave of horror crept over her, now that the scene had time to sink in. Isolde and Alexandria hadn't just kept Lenore trapped in that hut. They'd been *testing* things on her, trying to figure out what form of thistle would make her the weakest.

This was how the dart had been discovered.

They'd tortured Lenore. No wonder she'd shut down when Emma asked what happened.

Emma's stomach twisted, and for a moment she thought she was about to bend over and be sick, right there in the middle of the garbage-strewn street.

Her mother had left her own sister. She'd walked away with the full knowledge and belief that Lenore was going to die.

Of course, Emma knew it didn't end like this. Lenore had not died in this hovel, poisoned by her sisters. She was safe in Witch City, but still . . . it felt awful to leave her here, even if it wasn't technically real. Stranger still, she'd just learned that Lenore had been the one to tell her sisters about the thistle. She'd betrayed the witches and given her family the information about their weakness. Lenore's weakness. Emma's weakness.

She was the reason for the thistle nooses.

Emma jerked up straight at another noise from the street, a voice calling for Lenore. She felt a burst of optimism and turned, hoping to see her mother hurrying back. But the woman running down the crooked dirt path was tall, with narrow, dark features and a cloud of black curls. She was wearing a plain black cloak, but Emma recognized her all the same.

The ambassador.

The woman stumbled to a halt in front of the house and then ran inside with a cry of dismay. She kicked clumps of thistle aside and hauled Lenore off the mattress with more strength than Emma had thought her capable of. When the ambassador emerged onto the street, she had Lenore's still form draped over her arms, and was looking into her face with such tenderness and concern that Emma found she had to turn away.

It felt private.

As Emma turned away from the scene in the street, there came a mighty *swoosh* from overhead, and the dirt road beneath her blurred as the low voice boomed:

"After the uprising, the Great Hunt began. Every witch in the countryside was hunted down and hung with a thistle noose. Houses were burned and the countryside was ransacked, all in the name of the hunt."

There was a flash in front of her, and suddenly Emma could see the city laid out before her, the towers and turrets outlined in great plumes of black smoke. There was a distant grinding of stone on stone, and faint screams, and when Emma whipped around she saw the clock tower in flames, one side crumbling as it listed sideways.

She flinched, and then the city was a blur, fading away like smoke. A field now, full of tall stalks of purple thistle. She had time for a startled realization—that it was the *queen's men* who had burned the city, not the witches—and then the booming voice continued with its tale.

"In the year that followed, thistle was in such high demand that supplies ran low. Alexandria Black, the new queen, paid an enormous fee to farmers who would agree to turn their fields into grounds for new crops."

Emma's surroundings blurred and morphed around her once again. She was in the palace now; she recognized the great stone walls and the massive iron chandelier hanging above her, though she didn't immediately recognize the room. There were a number of green armchairs with ugly, jewel-encrusted pillows set around the space, and a great oak table in the center. She turned, finding herself facing a set of large wooden doors, and realized she was in the Throne Room, or to be more precise, *behind* the Throne Room. This was the Battle Suite, the space just behind the throne. It was empty, though there was still a scattering of maps and pins on the table, and someone had left a piece of parchment spread out with notes scribbled across it, and a quill and pen in the center of the map. A fire was currently burning in the huge stone fireplace, filling the room with the scent of cedar.

When Emma moved to peer out the narrow window, she felt her chest tighten.

The clock tower was crooked, the same way it always was, but the side was far blacker than Emma remembered, and it was visibly crumbling here and there. There were also blast marks in some of the roads, and several of the buildings had been entirely obliterated, leaving huge gaps in the streets.

She'd heard of the Great War of course. Everyone had. But it was one thing to see it in textbooks and another to have it actually laid out before you.

She straightened, startled, as the door slammed, and she turned to see Queen Alexandria sweeping into the room, Isolde close on her heels. Seeing her mother like this was somehow worse than the earlier vision. She looked much closer to the version Emma had always known. Her hair was gathered in a curly updo on the top of her head, and she wore a choker of pearls around her throat. Her dress was a glittering silver satin that complemented her sister's gold.

Emma swallowed hard as she watched the two women sink down into armchairs by the fireplace.

"Ambassador Jaqueline is such a bore," Isolde complained. "If Irvingland is so concerned, they should take all the witch children themselves. I notice they're not offering."

"They're not children," the queen replied sharply. "They just look it. They're witches. Tiny monsters." She narrowed her eyes at the door. "And if they can't see that, well then, we'll just have to do things more subtly."

Isolde raised a pale brow. "What are you thinking, sister?"

Queen Alexandria swept forward, clasping one of Isolde's hands. Her sister's face brightened. "You know as well as I do, Iz, our noble husbands are out fighting a second war. The hunts are vital to our cause."

Isolde nodded enthusiastically, and Emma's lip curled in disgust.

"But they are not enough." The queen pulled back. "Every child must be tested, not just the adults. We can't let anyone slip through the cracks. If they're witch enough to do magic, they're witch enough to hang. We must begin to draft The Testing Laws, and arrange, as I said, for methods more on the subtle side. Paint a nice picture for the public, just so nobody panics. For the good of society."

"For the good of society," Isolde repeatedly quietly. Her gaze combed across her sister's face, and Emma had a surprising realization. Her mother really did idolize her older sister. It was evident something had shifted between them since the Great War. Alexandria had become more than just the older sister and leader. She had become a queen in the eyes of her own sister—a kind of avenging goddess who had rained down retribution on the witches who'd murdered her family.

The hero worship on Isolde's face was painfully obvious.

Isolde hesitated. "And what . . . what of our own children some-day? We know our family—I mean, Lenore . . ." She let her words trail off, and she wilted slightly under the stern look her sister gave her.

"Isolde, after everything, don't you trust I know what is best for us?"

Slowly Isolde nodded.

"You know what our mother was. She was the one who started all of this when she let those devils into the palace." Alexandria clasped her hand to her chest, brow furrowed. "So you know why we must cut out the rot in this family. Why we are remaking our-selves as *Blacks*."

Emma felt her breath catch, and she had to clutch the window-sill to keep from staggering backward, as the room suddenly seemed to be swimming around her.

But Isolde was nodding again, and now Alexandria leaned for-ward in her chair. She spoke in low, challenging tones. "And are you prepared to do what we must, Isolde, even if our own children fail The Testing someday?"

Isolde cleared her throat, looked her sister straight in the eye, and nodded once again. "I'm prepared, Alexandria."

Emma knew this wasn't real—at least not in the moment—and yet, she could feel the cool stone windowsill as she clutched it so hard her fingertips went white. It was difficult to breathe, and this time she was sure of it: the room *was* spinning violently, the corners of the stone roof melting inward.

She thought she might throw up.

Her mother had known. Not only that, but she'd been part of the planning, had been there when the queen suggested The Testing, when they'd decided to set up the underground hanging platforms, when they'd agreed to fool the public.

Isolde Black, her mother, had agreed to hang Emma even before she was born.

Chapter Thirty-Seven

The Battle Suite blurred and stretched around her, and then abruptly snapped back into place. Emma blinked, and when she opened her eyes, she was shocked to find herself back inside the tiny charm library. She'd been standing in front of the fireplace staring into the flames, and her fingers ached from clutching the edge of the armchair beside her. Her stomach was still churning.

"Emma? What did you see?"

Maddie, Eliza, and Edgar were crowded around her, faces concerned. The librarian was no longer standing by the shelf.

"Where is she?"

"What?" Eliza glanced over her shoulder, shaking her head. "Oh, she . . . she slipped out as soon as you went under."

"She's probably gone to get Lenore. We're not supposed to be here." Emma snatched up the box of crystals, grimacing at Edgar's noise of protest. "It's a library. I'm going to borrow them."

"What was it? What did you see?" Edgar demanded. "You've gone sheet white."

Emma paused in the midst of turning for the door, fingers pressing hard into the silver and glass box. Who knew what else the crystals would tell her? What other horrible secrets they might reveal? She wished she'd never gone looking for answers. "My mother knew. She knew about everything."

The anger hit her without warning—a sudden, vicious rage that wanted to lash out, to tear something to shreds. Hot tears burned the backs of her eyes, and she whirled on Edgar. "The picture. Where is it?"

Edgar only blinked at her for a moment. Then, wordlessly, he fumbled in his pocket and brought out the flat leather pocketbook that Georgie had tucked into his bag back at the palace, the one with the picture of Isolde and Alexandria. He held it out between them.

Slowly, Emma reached out and took it. She opened it and let it sit in the palm of her hand. Ignoring the queen's poster, she focused instead on the portrait of the sisters, on their arrogant, stupid faces.

She couldn't stop remembering the way Lenore had looked lying on the mattress, pale and unconscious, surrounded by this-tle. Or the look on her mother's face, the blind devotion, as she had pledged to do whatever it took to defeat the witches, including hanging her own children.

She knew she should snatch the picture up and tear it to pieces, but instead, Emma was irritated to find tears crowding her eyes, blurring the picture in and out of her vision. She blinked furiously, determined to look at her mother's face one last time before she destroyed the image. Never again would Isolde make her feel guilty or ashamed of what she was, afraid of what her power did. She had nearly stopped her mother's heart all those years ago, but that had been an accident, and she'd been living with that fear ever since. But no more . . .

For a moment, Emma's thoughts seemed to stall, and she stared down at the picture, still blinking furiously, brow furrowed. The memories were flying in fast now: Isolde's shaky hands the day that they'd argued, her pale face, the way she'd clutched at her chest. A slow, horrifying realization was dawning on Emma.

She heard magic in people's hearts.

Real magic, *full* magic. She didn't hear the heartbeats of just anyone—not those without witch blood, or even those with a slight percentage, but actual, full-blown witches.

Lenore had said she didn't think her sisters had enough witch blood to do magic, but that couldn't be true. Her own mother—Emma's grandmother—had been a witch. Apparently, the Black family had been full of witches, which was rather ironic.

As if in response to this realization, the low, faint thumping of a pulse interrupted Emma's thoughts. She straightened her shoulders, taking a sharp breath. That pulse was so familiar now. It seemed to follow them everywhere they went, and as it beat on, growing steadily louder, the *thump-thump, thump-thump* filled her with a strange kind of clarity and slowly unfolding dread.

If Tobias McCraw was zero percent, as Lenore had said earlier, then Emma most certainly wasn't hearing the witch hunter's heart.

Then who . . . ?

She glanced down at the picture, at her mother's face, at the queen's. The Noise seemed to grow impossibly loud in her ears.

Thump-thump. Thump-thump.

The poster on the other side of the picture caught Emma's eye, and she froze.

The picture was different.

Instead of sitting up straight on her throne, the photo version of Alexandria was leaning forward slightly. Her smile had changed too, her lips now parted to bare her teeth in a snarl. And her eyes . . . that's what really froze Emma's blood. The queen's black-eyed gaze was now focused.

The Noise seemed to echo around the room, filling Emma's ears, taking over her thoughts. She couldn't seem to tear her eyes away from the poster.

The queen was staring right out of the picture, directly at Emma.

"Emma? What is it?" Maddie was saying. "You look—"

The queen in the picture *blinked*.

Emma shrieked, reacting instinctively by chucking the picture away from her. The pocketbook hit the ground with a thump and lay spread open, picture facing the ceiling. A stream of black smoke snaked up from the queen's photo, and Emma stumbled back.

The smoke didn't evaporate. Instead it grew, so rapidly the children barely had time to move. They scrambled away as the shadowy column shot up, towering over them.

Maddie shrieked, and Edgar's strangled cry of "It's her!" sent a stab of paralyzing fear through Emma. She opened her mouth to scream, and a hand shot out of the cloud, long, pale fingers covered in silver rings. The hand seized her throat and dragged her into the heavy smoke. She coughed, lungs burning, her throat stinging. She could hear Edgar's voice from somewhere in front of her, high and panicked, and Eliza and Maddie's screams.

Her head was spinning. The smoke and the hand around her throat were choking the life out of her, and darkness crowded in, thick and impenetrable, until it was all she could see.

Chapter Thirty-Eight

"Emma! Emma!"

Someone grabbed her elbow, yanking her out of the black cloud, though she couldn't see who it was through her streaming eyes. Her throat felt tight and coated with dust, and she doubled over, coughing hard, light bursting in front of her eyes.

"Emma, are you alright?"

"It was her," Eliza said. "You fell, and when Maddie and I went to help you, the queen took him!"

"What?" Emma stood up straight, so fast the room swayed alarmingly, and she coughed again, bracing a hand on the back of the armchair. She blinked rapidly, trying desperately to clear her head. "I don't... I don't understand. How...?" She didn't seem to be able to string words together properly. Her heart was beating so fast, in her throat and her wrists, her blood rushing in her ears. The room kept spinning in circles.

"Are you okay? I think you inhaled a lot of smoke." Maddie edged forward, grabbing her arm, and then hesitated, waiting for her. "We've got to tell Lenore, okay? Can you walk?"

"What happened?" Emma looked around. One of the shelves had been knocked over, and crystals sparkled between chunks of shattered glass spread across the floorboards.

The picture frame lay in the center of everything. The poster had shriveled into ashes, and there were scorch marks on the floor.

"She came through that." Eliza's voice shook. "It was magic. Emma, she took Edgar."

Emma looked around the room, heart sinking. Eliza was right; there was no Edgar. Only more shelves full of boxes and crystals, aisles of charms.

Heart in her throat, she crept forward, unsure if it was safe to touch the picture frame. She wrapped the end of her sleeve around her hand, using it to press the frame flat onto the ground. There was only a blackened, empty silhouette where the queen had been.

"You say she came through this." Her voice was hollow in her own ears, and very shaky. "How did she do that, unless . . ."

The words seemed to die on her tongue as it occurred to her— the posters in London, mandatory, hanging on every doorway, in every shop window.

Semper Vigilo.

She's always watching.

Horror twisted in Emma's stomach, and she looked down at the burnt poster. *This* is why she'd felt watched every step of the journey. *This* is why she kept hearing the heartbeat. "I thought it was McCraw, but it was her this whole time. She's been using the posters, and she was with us the entire way. She used us to get here . . ."

"That dratted nursemaid," Eliza said, her voice tight with anger. "Edgar's *Georgie*—she slipped him the poster."

"I can't believe the queen's a witch." Maddie shook her head. "She's been hunting us down, and she's *actively* a witch. What an absolute hypocrite."

"We have to take this to Lenore," Emma said. "Lenore will know what to do, how to get Edgar back."

There was another beat of silence, and Emma realized they were both waiting for her. She shook herself and took a breath, turning for the exit. Her hands were shaking, but she clenched her teeth and marched for the door.

They had to get Edgar back.

They moved out onto the porch and were immediately met by the distant, brassy clanging of bells and a great thumping of footsteps as Gerty charged up the stairs toward them, her face red.

"Good . . . yes," she gasped, clearly winded. "Your aunt sent me to get you. The queen . . . she just showed up in the center of the square, as open as you please!"

"We know!" Emma barreled past her, and Gerty straightened up with a surprised squawk.

"Wait, where are you going?"

Emma was halfway down the stairs already, with Maddie and Eliza following close on her heels. "I've got to tell Lenore. She's got Edgar."

"Wait, *what*?" Gerty stumbled down the stairs after them, still red-faced and puffing. Her hat had been knocked back off her forehead and was barely hanging on. "Wait! You can't! Lenore's already gone."

Emma halted at the bottom of the stairs, whirling on Gerty, who flinched. "Gone where?"

"The queen's vanished, so Lenore went into the In-Between to find her."

"They don't know where she is?" Maddie demanded.

"No." Gerty's round face was pale now, and Emma noticed her hands were trembling as she wound her fingers into the fabric of her dress. "But the queen . . . she stole one of the keys from the fountain. And now she's sure to go back through the In-Between, she's bringing it back to London ..." Her voice trailed off, and she flinched, as if she couldn't quite manage to spit out what came next.

"So ...," Emma said slowly, "if she brings it back to London ..."

She realized, with a slowly dawning horror, what came next. "She'll have access," she said. And when Eliza and Maddie turned to look at her, she shook her head, dread building in the pit of her stomach. "If she goes back, she'll expose all of us. Witch City isn't hidden anymore."

Chapter Thirty-Nine

"If she's leaving the city, then why take Edgar?"

Emma was pacing back and forth over the creaking floorboards of the library. It felt like her insides were itching, like they were too big for her skin. She couldn't stop moving. She wanted to *do* something, but Gerty had stationed herself by the front door, after telling them in no uncertain terms that Lenore had requested they stay put and wait for her here.

"Well, Edgar *is* her son," Maddie said slowly.

Emma whirled on her, and Maddie blinked, alarmed. "Did she say anything before she took him? Tell me exactly how it happened."

Maddie hesitated, exchanging a look with Eliza, who shook her head, looking just as worried. "I-I'm not sure exactly. It all happened so fast, and I was running for you because you'd just been dragged into the smoke and you were coughing and choking. I thought you might be really hurt and . . . I didn't even look up until she was already dragging him out the door." She shuddered. "She doesn't look that strong—she's so pale and skinny—but she took him."

Emma resumed her pacing. "I don't understand. She obviously got what she wanted. She's free in Witch City, so why take him with her?"

She was in the midst of turning back to Maddie and Eliza when a flash of black from outside the window caught her eye. She skidded to a halt, boots sliding on the floorboards.

"What was that?"

"What was what?" Gerty poked her head in the doorway, looking nervous as Emma headed for the window. "Where are you going? Your aunt will have my head—"

"There!" Emma leaned forward, nearly pressing her cheek to the windowpane. There was another flurry of movement against the darkening sky, high above the city.

Ravens.

"It's them." She whirled around, excitement coursing through her. "It's his birds!"

Maddie and Eliza both rushed for the window, and Gerty followed. For a moment they stood there gaping as the sky slowly filled with ravens.

"Mercy!" Gerty sounded impressed, and a little frightened. "That Edgar's a powerful witch."

"Yes," Emma said grimly, glancing over at Maddie and Eliza. She could see the realization on their faces too. This wasn't good. "And you know what this means, don't you?"

Maddie nodded slowly, still staring out at the birds, eyes wide. "He's out there."

"He's still in the city," Eliza said in a low voice.

Emma bit her lip. "And so is she."

"We have to rescue him," Maddie said urgently, looking over at Gerty. "She's close. She's probably in this neighborhood, even."

"You don't know that." Gerty's eye twitched, and she shook her head wildly, her gaze darting out over the street. "In any case, we're to stay here, safe in the library. I'm sure Lenore will take care of it."

"She's got our friend." Eliza took a step forward, frowning when Gerty stepped in front of her, hands on her hips.

"I'm afraid Lenore was very clear about you lot staying here."

"She doesn't know how close he is though," Emma protested, frustration making her tone sharp. "He could be right down the street!"

"You honestly think you children are the only people who can see those birds out there? This is a city full of highly trained witches!"

Emma sighed. She knew Gerty was right—if there was ever a city that could take care of itself, it would be a city full of witches, but still . . . there was simply no way she was going to sit here waiting while Edgar was out there with that horrible woman.

They needed a plan.

Gerty moved back to her position on the porch, in front of the door, hands on her hips, and Emma exchanged a pointed look with Eliza and Maddie. In return, Eliza raised a brow, and Maddie gave a subtle nod. Both were such tiny movements that no one else would have picked up on them, but Emma knew they had all come to the same conclusion. They were simply going to have to go around the obstacle.

"You three just . . . go back and sit by the fire or something." Gerty frowned at them. "Don't think you can slip past me." Arms folded, she set her back to the door.

Emma made her way toward the back of library, glancing once more out the window in the door to make sure Gerty wasn't suspicious. The older witch was now staring up at the flocking ravens, her hat tipped back on her head.

"Quick, this way." Emma slipped into the shelves, heading past the 5 percent category, 10 and then 15, before stopping at the 20 percent section, and finding the Flying category.

Emma opened the box, nodding at the others. "Pick one."

Eliza's eyes widened and she quickly snatched up the *Jumping* crystal. Maddie only hesitated a moment before picking *Bouncing* and Emma hovered between *Wishing* and *Floating* for a bare second, before opening the box and selecting the *Floating* crystal.

She still had a chain on from earlier, but she pulled another two off the hook for Eliza and Maddie, who both snapped their crystals into place, faces expectant.

As with the lecture notes, the magic took a moment to kick in.

Maddie was the first. After a minute her brows shot up. "Oh! Oh, I can feel it! I think I just have to . . ." Her forehead crinkled, and she bent her knees and jumped. Instead of coming back down, Maddie shot up toward the ceiling with a shriek of delight.

"Hush, Mads." Emma glanced toward the door, nervous. Thankfully, the flock of ravens overhead had only grown larger, and Gerty was still staring up into the sky.

Eliza had jumped up and down several times on the spot, experimentally, and was now frowning down at her crystal. "I can feel something, but why isn't it working?"

"Yours is jumping, right?" Emma glanced around. "Maybe you have to jump *off* something?"

"Oh, right. Hold on."

While Eliza made her way up one of the sliding ladders, Emma clicked her own charm into place. At first nothing happened, which she'd been expecting, but after a few seconds a feeling of warmth washed over her, and the crystal warmed against her skin. And then she felt it, a feeling of lightness. It was almost like buoyancy, like she was in water, still standing, but able to float if she needed to.

She rose up onto her toes ever so carefully, pushing off a little.

Instantly, she floated a few inches into the air, her feet dangling above the ground. She gave an involuntary cry of delight. Kicking her feet propelled her upward, and when she tipped her torso forward the magic seemed to respond with another wave of warmth before sending her gliding smoothly ahead.

Just behind her, Maddie was slowly floating back to the ground, her face delighted.

"Alright," Eliza said, and Emma turned just in time to see her leap from the center rung of the ladder, arms outstretched. Emma winced, but Eliza didn't hit the ground. Just like Maddie when she'd pushed off, Eliza continued on a straight path through the air, one fist thrust out.

She glided forward, moving smoothly between the shelves, her face breaking into a delighted smile.

"I'm doing it! Oh!" Eliza's other arm shot out as she approached the door, fingers splayed. "Oh. Um, I'm not sure how to stop!"

Thankfully, the door was slightly ajar, so instead of running into it, Eliza went *through* it. Not so lucky for Gerty, as she was standing very close, and when the door crashed open it struck the back of the poor woman and knocked her forward and off the stoop.

"I'm sorry!" Eliza cried as she shot past.

"Eliza!" Maddie's eyes were wide, and she hit the ground and lifted off once more, this time angling for the door. "Eliza, wait for us."

"At least she's heading the right way." Emma pushed off again, moving for the open door right behind Maddie. Outside, she breathed in the evening air and the scent of bonfires.

It was the perfect night for flying, and even better for rescuing a friend.

She zipped right overtop of Gerty, several feet above her in the air, just as Gerty was scrambling to her feet, cursing, and snatching her hat off the ground.

"We're sorry!" she shouted down. "We're going to find our friend!"

Chapter Forty

The flight down the street was nerve-wracking, not just because all three of them were still learning to control the path of their flight—though that was certainly a factor—but also because the sky was full of ravens, who often swooped down around them as they went by. Whenever Emma looked up, it was to see black birds arrowing past above her. The sky was full of more ravens than she'd ever seen before.

"This is far more than in the In-Between." Maddie, currently floating down from another jump, had to raise her voice above the noise in order to be heard.

"Yes, and now we have to follow them." Eliza didn't look happy about it, but she at least seemed to be getting the hang of her flying power, steering herself in the right direction.

"We don't have a choice," Emma said.

The streets were crowded, which turned out to be rather good cover, as the girls blended in with the other witches in the air. Emma was just thinking that they might get away with this when she heard a sharp cry of outrage, and they turned to see Gerty barreling after them, waving her hat in the air. "You lot get back here! And give those crystals back. You don't even have a library card!" She ducked with a frightened screech as one of the ravens plummeted toward her, nearly flying into the side of her head.

A moment later, Emma and the others were also forced to undertake a mid-air dodge, as another raven swooped down. There was a sharp *crack* on the stones just to Emma's left, and several witches still in the air above her shrieked, dodging more ravens as they flew by.

Hands over her head, she glanced up to see one of the large black birds winging away over the buildings. There were still ravens zipping by overhead, but none of them looked as if they were about to dive again, and Emma let out a breath and dipped down carefully, trying to see what had fallen out of the sky and hit the stones. It took a few minutes of experimentation, but eventually she figured out that if she put her legs together and pointed her toes, she could lower her feet to the cobblestones.

There was a statue lying on the ground, and Emma clapped her hand over her mouth, recognizing the smooth stone shape of a cat.

A key. One of the ravens had dropped a key at their feet.

"Oh." She looked up again, squinting into the dark sky, where she could make out the shadowy shapes of birds flying far overhead. Sure enough, many of them seemed to have something clutched in their talons.

"The keys," she gasped out. "They're taking the keys."

Gerty was staring up into the sky too, her face full of horror. "The keys! Oh my lord, they've got the keys." The next second, Gerty was in motion. Shoving her hat down firmly over her ears, she dashed forward, seizing Emma by the shoulders. "You stay here, do you understand me? I have to go warn the council that they've got all the keys."

"I—yes," Emma stammered, but Gerty was already gone, running full tilt down the narrow road leading to the square, her billowing sleeves flapping behind her.

"She's forcing him to control the ravens." Emma turned back to the others. "That's why she took him."

"What happens when she gets all of the keys?" Eliza's voice was strained. "What happens when she doesn't need him anymore?"

Maddie blanched. "We've got to save him."

"Let's go." Emma shoved the cat statue into her bag before kicking off the ground once again. They were going to get Edgar.

Chapter Forty-One

The three girls were halfway down the next street when a flare of orange fire appeared over the rooftops in the distance. Several streets away, a pillar of white smoke began to rise against the sky.

"What was that?" Emma asked.

"I don't know. Look!" Eliza jabbed a finger toward the smoke. It wasn't just smoke that was billowing into the sky. The flock of ravens had shifted, turning into a giant funnel as they rode the hot air from the flames.

The girls exchanged a glance. Where Edgar was, his birds went.

The streets were chaos now, filled with witches all staring up at the smoke. More witches in flight shot past overhead. They were all heading in the same direction, and a moment later the bells began to toll again, an alarm sounding out over the city.

"Edgar," Eliza mouthed, and Emma nodded, feeling her skin go hot and cold.

Before any of them could move, there was a squawk and a flash of black, and a raven came barreling between them. Emma squeaked and leaned back instinctively, which sent her zipping back several feet.

The large, glossy bird had landed in the middle of the road beneath them. It shook its wings out and tucked them away before fixing them with a piercing, black-eyed stare. Emma watched in astonishment as the raven hopped closer, ducking its head and bobbing up and down at them.

"I think . . . I think it's trying to say something." She had to raise her voice over the noise of the bells.

"Maybe Edgar sent it," Maddie said eagerly. "Maybe he's trying to tell us where he is!"

They paused to watch the bird for a moment, and it watched them back, head cocked to one side. Then it crowed impatiently and took another series of sideways hops toward them.

Emma was suddenly sure Maddie was right: the raven had been sent to find them. As she watched, the bird suddenly fluttered into motion, launching itself into the air and winging away down the street.

"Quick, follow that raven!"

It was very odd, attempting to follow a bird down the street. Emma and the others raced after it, down twisting side roads and bumpy alleyways, between rows of shops and stands. It was rather touch-and-go, and Emma worried they would lose the black bird among the rooftops. Several times she had a near miss, so fixated on keeping an eye on the bird that she almost ran into the side of a building. Making things even more difficult, the city itself seemed to sense a threat, and the streets had begun to shift very rapidly. One moment Emma was looking at a wide-open lane, and the next she found herself heading straight toward a very tall, crooked building that hadn't been there a moment ago.

The raven gave a throaty cry and banked sharply, and Emma gasped, doing her best to follow before she slammed straight into a sign hanging on the front, which was shaped like a giant boot. It was frustrating, but Emma and the others forced themselves to slow down and carefully navigate the bends and forks in the roads that appeared and disappeared.

Thankfully, it didn't take them long to figure out where the bird was heading. Over the tops of the buildings, they could see the stage where the dancers had been only a few hours ago.

"The parliament!" Maddie cried, as they made a beeline through a strangely empty square and straight for the steps of the building. "How is she hiding there? Isn't it swarming with witches?"

"They're all going for the smoke, the explosion," Eliza said, and then turned to look at Emma with wide eyes.

Cold dropped down Emma's back as she met Eliza's stare; she knew they'd realized the same thing at the same moment. "She's distracted them."

Eliza nodded. "It's a decoy."

The parliament. The well of fire. The city's core. Emma's mouth tasted sour, and her throat felt thick and tight. Whatever the queen was planning, it couldn't be good.

The raven flew straight to the statue at the front of the parliament building and settled on the upraised hand of the witch. When Emma landed at the base and looked up at it, the bird cocked its head and made a hollow clicking noise.

Emma kicked off and flew past the statue, straight up the length of the stairs, before settling down at the top near the entrance. The others followed, stopping at the wide double doors. Emma looked around, confused.

The guards were nowhere in sight.

It didn't seem like a good sign, but there was nothing for it but to push on.

She took a breath and pressed on the right door. It swung open easily. Emma marched through, her own pulse thrumming in her ears, and then stopped just inside the short hallway beyond, pulling up so quickly she nearly spun backward. There, standing in the front hall, his face miserable, was the witch hunter, Tobias McCraw.

He was already shaking his head frantically. "Sh-she found me. I'm supposed to guard the door."

Emma narrowed her eyes at him, half triumphant. "I *knew* you couldn't be trusted!"

McCraw's brow was creased as he looked first at Emma and then at Eliza and Maddie. "I can't let you past." His voice broke strangely on the last note. "Sh-she has my mother. If I cooperate, she says she won't hurt her."

"She has Edgar too." Emma edged toward the inner door, dismayed when Tobias stepped solidly in front of her, shaking his head.

"I'm so sorry, but I can't let you—"

"You're happy to let us past, in fact, you were just about to go."

Maddie's voice, from behind her. Emma watched as Tobias McCraw blinked, looking suddenly dazed, and then nodded slowly. "Uh, yes. I'd be happy to let you through. Go ahead, children."

He stepped aside, holding the door open for them.

Emma darted a look at Maddie, who shrugged apologetically and hissed, "What other choice do we have?"

She was right.

Emma stole through last, making sure the others got past. She felt a wave of guilt as she did so, and whispered as they slipped by, "I'm sorry about this." She'd have to apologize to him again later on, for accusing him of lying when she'd first arrived in the city. She really had been wrong about him.

Tobias McCraw only nodded at her and then gave her a lopsided, slightly baffled smile before closing the door behind them.

They paused at the second set of doors. The right side had been left open a crack, and Emma inched forward and peered through.

The room beyond was lit by gas lamps along the walls. The flutter of wings drew Emma's attention upward, and she saw ravens circling just below the wide-domed windows, the flickering lantern light flashing across their black wings.

Two people stood in the center of the room within the circle of chairs, facing one another across the expanse of the crystal well. Edgar was on one side, standing very straight, his face pale but determined. And on the other side was Queen Alexandria.

Emma felt the back of her neck prickle as the queen stepped around the well and closer to her son—and by chance, to her. Now she could hear it, the faint *thud-thud, thud-thud*—the Noise that had followed them in the In-Between, that she'd sensed in the forest, that she'd heard in the square.

The same pulse she'd attributed to the witch hunter, all that time.

Speaking of the witch hunter, Emma didn't see any sign of Tobias McCraw's mother. She chewed her lower lip, thoughts racing. That might mean the man was lying, and that he was simply helping the queen because he was on her side. If that was the case, they'd have to account for how fast Maddie's lie would wear off.

"Can't you make your birds get here any faster? Do remember that lives are at stake, young prince." The queen held up what looked like a sheaf of papers—posters, Emma realized—and shook them at Edgar with a poisonous smile.

"Don't threaten me." Edgar drew himself up. His face was fierce, his chin in the air. He spoke as if he'd loaded every ounce of princely contempt into his voice. "You're a murderer. You have the blood of *children* on your hands."

Emma couldn't help but admire his firm tone.

The queen gave him an icy stare. "Witches, not children. They're monsters, Edgar."

"Remember who you're talking to. I'm one of those monsters." Edgar shook his head, his expression full of disgust. "And you are too, I finally realize. The difference is that you're too much of a coward and a hypocrite to accept it. I'm ashamed I ever called you my mother."

Queen Alexandria drew back, her face pale. Two spots of color were visible high on her cheeks, and she looked suddenly furious. Then slowly, her expression hardened. Emma's blood ran cold as the queen's mouth twisted into a sharp, vicious smile.

"You think I came after you because I wanted you back? You're a means to an end, Edgar. You can get me the keys, and I can take them back with me. And then I will wipe my sister's little town off the map."

"You can't," Edgar snapped at her. "They're bound to know what your plan is. They'll stop you going through the In-Between."

The queen laughed—a short, contemptuous sound. "Lenore is an idiot. She thinks I'm restricted to her pathetic In-Between, as if I'm not more powerful than all of you put together."

Emma felt a stab of alarm, and beside her Eliza shifted, like she was about to leap forward. Maddie kept glancing over at her with wide eyes, but Emma put one hand out to stop her, her mind working furiously.

They had no plan, not really. They'd been in such a hurry to find Edgar that they hadn't stopped to think what they'd do once they found him.

Silently, she mouthed at Maddie, *Lie to her?* And then, pointing to herself and Eliza, *We'll go for Ed.*

Thankfully, Maddie seemed to understand. She looked very nervous, but she nodded and crept forward a little.

After what seemed like forever, the queen turned away from Edgar, staring down into the crystal basin. She was facing away from the door now. Emma nudged the others and nodded, kicking off the floor again, into the air. She bellowed at the top of her lungs, "Maddie, now!"

This had the effect she wanted, as the queen whirled around to face her, her face slack with shock. It gave Maddie time to step forward, and say loudly, "Y-you have to get to the In-Between. The keys are waiting for you there."

There was a second of silence as the queen stared at Maddie, brow creased. Emma held her breath, blood rushing in her ears. It had to work.

If it didn't . . .

Queen Alexandria's brow suddenly softened. The posters she'd been holding slipped out of her grip, hitting the floor at her feet with a soft *thwack*. "Ah, yes. I've got . . . to get there."

Emma almost laughed in relief as the queen turned for the door and took a staggering step toward the exit. Out of the corner of her eye, Emma could see that Eliza had crept sideways and was now beckoning wildly to Edgar.

Edgar nodded, eyes wide, and began to edge slowly sideways, away from the well.

Emma relaxed ever so slightly as Edgar put more space between him and his mother, but she froze when the queen stopped abruptly. Alexandria shuddered and shook her head, her face twitching. And then her expression shifted from blankness to sheer fury. She began to whirl around, hands raised. Panicked, Emma launched herself into the air.

A moment later, Emma's shoulder struck the queen across her cheek and temple. She felt something slam into her stomach, something that knocked the wind out of her and sent her plummeting downward. Together they hit the marble floor, and a scream of pain and outrage sounded deafeningly close to Emma's left ear.

The queen screamed again, scrambling to her feet. And then, to Emma's surprise, she swooped forward and grabbed a handful of posters from the floor.

Before any of them could move, the sound of pounding footsteps echoed through the room, and then Captain McCraw came hurtling through the door. The queen stood, frozen, as he charged toward her, his face screwed up in determination.

"Let go of my *mother*!"

Emma had a split second to wonder what on earth McCraw was talking about. Then he collided with the queen with an awful crash, knocking them both flat. The queen's eyes went wide as she hit the marble floor and she screamed in outrage, snatching at his cloak, clawing at his face. Then there was a loud *crack* and a puff of smoke, and Queen Alexandria and Captain McCraw were gone, papers floating gently to the ground in their wake.

Chapter Forty-Two

For a moment no one said anything, and then Edgar asked softly, "Is she . . . gone?"

Another *crack* rang out, and the queen reappeared directly behind Maddie, her face filled with vicious triumph. Emma had time for a wordless scream of warning, and Maddie turned just as the queen shoved her violently into the marble wall. There was an audible *thwack* as Maddie's skull made contact, and she crashed to the floor. Her face was white as she curled her knees up to her chest.

"Maddie!" Edgar launched himself forward, and there was a shrieking cry from overhead as several of the ravens plummeted out of the air, hurtling toward the queen.

Queen Alexandria screamed, throwing a hand up to protect herself. She disappeared, and the ravens plunged through the empty air with disappointed cries. Edgar gave a shout of outrage, which cut off abruptly as Queen Alexandria materialized behind him, snaking an arm around his throat.

"No!" Flames sprang from Eliza's fingers and raced up her arms, and Emma scrambled up from the floor, rage crashing through her. They stood across from the queen, flames lighting up the space between them. Emma looked down at the posters scattered across the floor, blood rushing in her ears. The queen, the way she was vanishing and reappearing . . .

"Eliza, the posters! You've got to burn them!" Emma glanced down at the nearest one, shocked to see the face of Captain McCraw, his eyes wide in terror, his arms thrown up in front of him. Her gaze whipped to the other papers, and a horrified shudder went through her.

There. On the nearest sheet of paper, a detailed painting of a woman in a black robe with golden buttons, her blond hair pulled back in a tight bun, a look of shock on her sun-lined face. And there. Another poster: her fellow guard, one hand thrown up, his mouth frozen open in surprise. And the poster beside them—an older woman with salt-and-pepper hair. Tobias McCraw's mother.

They were all there, frozen in the papers. Trapped.

Emma leapt forward and snatched the posters, heart beating furiously. This was far worse than she'd thought. "She's using these." She raised her voice above the sound of the ravens, thrusting one of the posters up for Eliza and Edgar to see. "Look."

Edgar stopped struggling against the queen's grip to stare at the image of Tobias McCraw's face, a look of horror spreading across his features as he realized what the queen had done. Eliza, too, figured it out. Her flames flared higher, and she cast an arm down at one of the posters, sending a ball of flame across to curl and blacken the paper.

There was a pulse pounding in Emma's ears now, so familiar—though faster than usual—and she knew if she opened the door all the way, if she let the power crash through her in a rush, she could stop the queen's heart in her chest. Instead, she cracked it open a sliver, and then a tiny bit more, clenching her teeth in concentration.

Queen Alexandria released Edgar abruptly, shoving him so that he stumbled and hit the ground on his hands and knees with a grunt. She started to turn for Eliza, eyes on the burning poster, when she froze. Her face went white, and she pressed a hand to her chest.

Sweat broke out on Emma's brow. "If you move, I'll stop your heart. Eliza, the posters."

Eliza rushed forward, casting flames onto the papers strewn across the floor, which began to shrivel and blacken rapidly.

Alexandria was still clutching at her chest, gasping. Her eyes snapped up and met Emma's, and Emma felt a cold chill drop down her spine.

Before anyone could move, a voice rang out across the room.

"Everyone please stay *exactly* where you are."

Chapter Forty-Three

L enore Black stood in the doorway. Perched on one shoulder was a large black raven, and when Emma glanced over at Edgar, he'd hauled himself up into a sitting position, and was now staring at his mother with a cold smile.

When the raven on Lenore's arm spotted him, it gave a satisfied croak and launched itself into the air; it flew across the room and landed on Edgar's arm. The prince reached up to place one hand on the bird's feathered back.

"You're finished, Your Majesty," Lenore said firmly. "Time to give up."

As Lenore spoke, Emma saw them. Council witches stood silhouetted in every doorway, blocking each exit and entrance to the stone room. When she glanced up, she could see more overhead, hovering over the domed windows.

The queen was surrounded on all sides.

Relief swept through her.

"Emma, you and the others behind me, please." Lenore's voice was firm but steady, and Emma turned to obey. Before she'd taken a step though, the queen began to laugh.

It was a high, unpleasant sound, and it sent shivers down Emma's back.

"Something amuses you, Your Majesty?" Lenore's voice was cool, but Emma was sure she detected tension beneath it.

"Only this," the queen said, still smiling. "I have hunted you and your filthy kind all my life, and I don't intend to stop now."

"Alexandria, you *are* my kind." Lenore's face grew sad. "You're my sister, and you're a witch. Our mother—"

"Don't you *dare* speak of her!" Queen Alexandria's face twisted with disgust and rage. "She is dead to me, and to Isolde. She betrayed her *real* family for that filthy witch scum and she got what she deserved when they double-crossed her." She took a step forward, fists clenched. "She let them into the palace that night! How could you have joined them after what they did, Lenore? How can you *still* be on their side? What's the matter with you?"

"Our mother made a mistake. As did I." Lenore's eyes were filling with tears. "But I have paid for that mistake many times over now."

Emma pressed her lips together, struggling to stay silent. She'd seen it all in the vision from the crystal, of course, but to hear Lenore admit to being one of the rebel witches was still shocking.

Lenore continued, her voice soft. "How I wish you could see that there are no *sides* anymore. There are just witches and non-witches. The witches who destroyed our family don't exist now, Lexa—"

"Shut up!" Queen Alexandria cried. Her eyes were huge and glittering in her pale face. "You don't get to call me that. You're just as bad as she was. You let yourself become a monster. A filthy, unnatural magic user." She was practically spitting the words now, her face growing more and more red.

"Please." Lenore had to raise her voice to be heard over the queen's shouting. "Alexandria, I don't know how many times I can apologize for what I did. I was young and foolish—"

The queen didn't seem to hear her. "You have no *idea* what I'm capable of. What I'm willing to do in order to destroy *all* of you."

Emma tensed, frowning, as the queen turned to stare at her once again, black eyes glittering. Instinctively, Emma took a step back. Her heels bumped the base of the well.

The queen smiled, a thin, horrible expression, and her gaze dropped down to the posters clutched in Emma's hand. Emma knew she should *do something*. Throw herself forward, cast the posters away from her, tear them up, maybe. But before she could even begin to move, a loud *crack* echoed through the room, and Emma's fingers began to burn. She dropped the posters with a cry of terror, stumbling backward as the queen materialized directly beside her.

Alexandria didn't even look at her. Instead, she spun around and plunged a hand directly into the depths of the well. There were shrieks from around the room, and more than one witch started forward and then stopped, pulled up short by Lenore's warning cry.

The moment the queen's hand hit the blue fire her body went stiff, her face white and slack. She trembled all over, so violently that Emma thought she could hear the woman's teeth clacking in her jaws. For a moment, it looked as though she were merely having some sort of fit, and then the blue flame in the basin began to flicker lower and lower, and the queen shook harder. Her entire body convulsed in wild spasms, and sparks began to zip along the surface of her skin. Little zaps of electricity, like miniature streaks of lightning.

Beside her now, Lenore reached out and grabbed Emma's arm. "I need you to run—" she began to say, and then the queen *screamed*, the sound so high-pitched and raw that Emma's hands flew to her ears automatically. The noise drowned out everything, filling the room with shrill, keening echoes, bouncing off the walls and ceiling until the entire, massive hall was filled with the horrible chorus.

The queen's eyes fluttered open, and Emma saw with horror that her pupils and irises had been fully taken over by glowing blue light, as if she were burning from the inside out.

"Run!" Lenore cried. "Everyone, get out *now*."

Her aunt seized her arm, tugging her backward, but Emma was frozen to the spot. Not just because of the horrifying sight, but because of what she was *hearing*.

Even over the bloodcurdling screams it was there—the familiar low, thrumming *thud, thud, thud*—and it was simultaneously the same as any regular heartbeat and also radically different. It started out normal, perhaps a bit fast due to fear and excitement, but as the blue fire filled the queen's eyes, her heartbeat sped up, faster and louder, until it was like the frantic banging of drums in Emma's ears.

Not only that, but she could hear the beating of the city's heart again, that low, deep rumble. Slowly, it was speeding up to keep pace with the queen's heart—faster and higher, almost frenetic.

There was something horribly wrong about the sound. Something that felt dangerous. It sent prickles of dread over Emma's skin.

It wasn't supposed to sound like that.

She forced the feeling of dread aside, trying to concentrate on the queen's pulse, on the nearness of her heartbeat. The Noise felt different somehow, it was more . . . present. Now it felt like she could reach out and touch it. The idea scared her more than anything else had so far. It made her bones feel as if they were made out of ice. But what if she, Emma, could stop this?

If the queen's heartbeat continued on like this, she was going to die. And from the sounds of it, she was going to take all of them with her.

Emma wasn't exactly sure what she could do, but she knew she had to try *something*.

Lenore cried out as Emma wrenched her arm away and sprinted forward, straight toward the queen. Alexandria was still trembling all over; her eyes had rolled back in her head, and her body was stiffening in multiple spasms per second. Something was happening to her skin. The sparkling electricity was branching out, lighting underneath her flesh, until the queen's entire body seemed to glow.

Emma dashed forward, breathing hard, terrified but sure of what she had to do. It felt like noise exploded all around her then—screams from Eliza and Lenore, commands to stop, her own boots pounding on the tiles and the sound of people running for her. And then she was no more than a foot away from the well, from the twitching form of the queen, and she reached out and seized the woman's arms.

Touching her felt like being struck by lightning, and Emma gasped as searing heat blazed through her. She ground her teeth and held on, closing her eyes, forcing herself to ease the door open wider, to let more of her power out.

There it was: the frantic drumming heartbeat, growing louder and louder, until it felt like something was pounding on the inside of her skull. She just wanted it to stop. It had to stop.

She reached out with her senses, grasping at the connection, tentatively at first, and then more firmly, until at last she had it. Somehow she could *feel* the queen's heart in her chest, the organ squeezing and contracting, on the edge of bursting, and beyond that, she could feel the magic flooding through it, the ebb and flow of the fire, the power that surged through the queen's heart.

Just as Lenore had said: a witch's magic was all in her heart.

Now what? She could sense the heart, sense the magic. But she'd simply acted on impulse, with only the vaguest idea of what to do next. It only made sense that the next logical step would be to fully unleash her power, like she'd done in the In-Between in order to find Edgar.

But this was different. This was bigger. More dangerous.

What would happen if she used her magic now? She could picture all sorts of horrible outcomes, both for her and the queen. Or . . . what if she simply made it worse? Made the queen's heart explode faster?

She couldn't think like this, couldn't doubt herself, not after everything she'd gone through in the In-Between, not when she and her friends had come all this way.

It was just like in the In-Between. Eliza had taught her to trust herself, Maddie had helped her learn to unleash her power, and in Edgar, she'd finally found her true family. Family that had been willing to stand up to his awful mother.

Emma could do it too. She just needed to trust her magic.

Trust herself.

She took a deep breath and pictured herself opening the door fully, letting the Noise out . . . first a trickle, and then a flood as she released her magic fully. It took a few long seconds for it to happen, but finally she felt it. The queen's heart stuttered in her ears—not the heart, she realized suddenly, but the magic *inside* the heart. Alexandria sucked in a shuddering breath, though she continued to shake and twitch, and her eyes were still shut tightly.

Emma frowned, concentrating hard. She could feel her own magic *inside* the queen now, drifting like a thin cobweb between them, creating a connection. At first she was frozen, knowing what she needed to do but not sure how to do it.

She pictured the door—the grain of the wood, the brass handle, the squeaky hinges—now flung open wide to let her power out. Then she pictured the queen's heart, thrumming with power, and the magic pulsing inside it. Finally, she pictured her own magic like a hand reaching out for that heart, fingers closing around it.

A second later, the queen's eyes fluttered open. Emma nearly drew back, but then the queen went limp again, and she gritted her teeth and made herself hold on. She had to force the magic out somehow, to drain it back into the air around them.

For a few seconds she was at a loss, not sure what to picture, what to visualize in order to make it work. Then she remembered what Lenore had said about the crystals, about how they were a conduit for magic. She tried her best to picture the wineskin Lenore had mentioned, tried to imagine tipping it over and emptying the contents back out.

There was a murmur of excitement in the room as soon as she started, and Emma heard the shuffling of feet on the stone floor. She could feel the magic being collected, and she realized that the other witches had gone to work right away, returning the raw magic back to the well. She wanted so badly to open her eyes and watch what they were doing—to learn—but she was afraid to lose her hold on the queen's heart, and on the power steadily draining out of it.

The queen's skin was hot under Emma's fingers. At first Alexandria didn't seem to realize what was happening. Her body relaxed and went limp as she leaned against the edge of the well. But after a minute, her eyes snapped open and she pulled herself back, trying to tug her arms out of Emma's grip, even as the tremors still shook her body. But Emma held on, wrapping her fingers more tightly around the queen's arms.

She felt the others hovering nearby, ready to knock the queen back if she managed to escape. But she couldn't let that happen. Somehow, she knew that if anyone but her touched the queen right now they would be just as overcome by magic, and equally at risk of combusting right on the spot.

The more magic Emma drained out of the queen, the more the woman seemed to realize what was happening. As her struggling grew more desperate, Emma's hands slid a few inches down her arms. Emma ground her teeth and gripped the queen's wrists tightly. They were so close now that she was looking up into the woman's face. She could see how lined Alexandria's skin was, how pale she'd become from the years of drinking thistle wine. It was the same thing that had made her mother sick. An entire kingdom was slowly poisoning itself, driven by fear and hatred.

She found herself suddenly, fiercely angry, and she tightened her grip all the more, growling up at Queen Alexandria as the woman struggled against her. "I know you left your own sister to die. She made a mistake when she joined the rebels, but she's family. You and my mother are both monsters. If people knew what was beneath your palace, they would know what a wicked, vile creature you are. If you see my mother, tell her I said the same goes for her."

Slowly, painfully, and after what seemed like an eternity—in which Emma's hands began to shake and she could feel her own power begin to weaken—the tides shifted. Queen Alexandria's heartbeat leveled out, growing quieter as each pulse of magic was released into the air around her. At last, the queen gave a wail of dismay, and as Emma felt the last electric spark of magic drain away, she let her grip on the heart relax.

She spent a full moment searching for more, her fingers aching with the effort of clinging so hard to the queen.

Then came a warm draft of air and the scent of vanilla, and someone said softly from overhead, "Emma? It's alright now. It's done."

Slowly, she let her eyes flutter open. She and the queen had both sunk down onto the floor beside the well, and she found herself on her knees beside a prone Alexandria, still holding tight to the queen's wrists.

Lenore was standing over her, brow creased with concern. When Emma made eye contact, she smiled, clearly relieved. "Alright?"

"I . . . yes, I think so." Emma released the queen's wrists and climbed unsteadily to her feet, glancing down. Alexandria was lying on her back on the floor, staring blankly up at the ceiling. She was breathing hard—long, ragged breaths.

It took a long moment for Emma to gather herself. She glanced around the room, feeling as though she were waking from some strange dream. Near one of the doors, she spotted the small, still form of Maddie, with Eliza and Edgar hovering over her.

Ignoring the surge of dizziness that came when she moved, she hurried over to her friends.

"Maddie?" she said softly, trying to keep the tremor out of her voice. "Can you hear me?"

Maddie's lashes flickered, and then her eyes fluttered open. A second later she groaned and squeezed them shut again. "It hurts."

"You've fetched up against the wall rather hard. Let me have a look at you."

Emma moved back as Lenore knelt down beside Maddie.

"Perhaps a minor concussion. I'll get you down to the infirmary and into a bed. Can you stand?"

Maddie climbed to her feet, very slowly, with the help of Lenore and the others, and Emma could have cried with relief. She reached out and took Maddie's arm, sliding it around her waist, before turning to look back at the scene by the well.

A few of the witches had gone to work on the posters, and the guards, Tobias McCraw, and his mother were now free. The ex-witch hunter clung to his mother's arm, looking angry and disheveled. Other witches had gathered around the prone form of the queen, who was still lying flat on her back, her face slack with shock. As they moved Maddie toward the exit, Lenore broke away for a moment and hurried over to the well. She leaned down to press a hand to the queen's shoulder and then straightened quickly and moved to rejoin the group. She gave Emma a startled look before masking her expression and waving at the other witches.

"Escort her to the cells. I suppose our jail will have its first permanent guest at last."

The witches moved to obey, but before they could reach her Tobias McCraw was there, hooking his arms beneath the queen's, hauling her to her feet.

"If you don't mind, I'll take her down myself." He glanced over at Lenore, his face serious. "And I'd be happy to volunteer my services as a guard, if you'll have me."

Lenore considered this for a moment, and then nodded slowly. "Welcome aboard, Tobias."

At this, something seemed to snap in the queen. She burst into motion, thrashing against Tobias, her face twisted in rage and fear. "No, no! It's gone! I can feel it! It's gone!" As he tried to drag her out of the room, she dug in her heels, much like a child having a tantrum would, and tried to beat Tobias off of her.

"It can't be gone!" She froze abruptly, and Emma felt a chill as the woman's dark eyes fixed on her. Then the queen lunged for her, screaming, nearly tearing herself away from the ex-captain. "*She* did this to me! She did it! I'll kill you!"

Emma watched, mouth hanging open, as Tobias McCraw dragged her away, Alexandria screaming and lunging at Emma the entire time. It took the ex-captain and several witches to haul her out of the room.

Lenore glanced down at Emma, voice low. "Don't worry. They have her well in hand. Let's get Maddie to the infirmary, shall we?"

Emma only nodded and turned her attention back to Maddie, who was currently being propped up by Edgar and Eliza.

"Emma?" Maddie blinked around the room, frowning deeply, as if she were trying hard to remember something. "Everything was a bit blurry and it all seemed to happen really fast, but . . . did we beat her? Did we win?"

She stared at Maddie, who looked decidedly dazed, and then at Eliza—tired but fiercely triumphant—and finally at Edgar. He was propping Maddie up on the other side, but the expression on his face was one of utter relief. She smiled.

"Yes, Mads, we won. Now let's get you to bed."

Chapter Forty-Four

The infirmary was a tiny wooden cabin down a side road just off the street that housed the Push Broom Inn. The place was decorated with tartan-patterned wallpaper, and someone had lit the hurricane lanterns that lined the walls, filling the room with flickering light.

Narrow wooden dressers stood between the beds, each with a glass mason jar on top, full of tiny blue lights that Emma found very interesting to watch as they buzzed back and forth and bumped into one another, casting a faint silvery-blue light over the surroundings.

There were three cots along each side of the room, all empty save for Maddie's. She'd picked the one nearest to the tall stone fireplace in the corner, and Emma, Edgar, and Eliza had made themselves a terrible nuisance by camping out overnight after Maddie had been admitted and nearly all of the next day. The nurse had given them strict instructions that they were only to stay until lights out, and that Maddie would need a proper sleep to recover from her concussion.

"I hope you don't have to stay in too many more days." Edgar settled himself on one arm of the squishy chair Eliza was sitting in, crossing his arms over his chest. "Why can't they just magic you better?"

"Apparently they are." Maddie leaned over to show them the chain she was wearing around her neck, which was set with a cloudy quartz crystal. "But it takes a few days."

"I think I have something to help while you wait."

They all turned to look at Lenore, who was standing in the doorway, laden down with a huge wicker basket of food. "The council put together a bit of a picnic for you lot. We figured you'd all stay here with her through dinner again. And I've brought you some school books. I thought you might like to explore the intermediate spell books, things you'll be learning at Candlewick later."

"*Would* we," Maddie sat up straight. "Edgar's been insisting on reading me poetry, and it's almost as painful as my head was at first."

"*Hey,*" Edgar protested.

"Now don't go doing anything too wild. You're still healing." Lenore sounded stern, but her eyes were sparkling, and she set the basket and books down on the end of the mattress.

"There you are. *101 Spells for Beginners* and *A Witch's Almanac* are particularly good. Of course, school isn't for a few weeks yet, and you'll be running wild through the streets of the city for the summer, I don't doubt."

The aroma of fresh-baked bread was coming from the basket, and they wasted no time digging in. While their mouths were full of cheese and bread, and the sweetest apples Emma had ever tasted, Lenore brought them up to date with everything going on in the city.

"The queen is in the cells now." She folded her hands in her lap, scanning their faces as she said this, and stopping a little longer on Edgar than on the others. "She'll remain there for a very long time, most likely. But perhaps not forever, because something very strange happened during the fight."

They all stared at her, waiting.

"Her magic is gone." Lenore looked straight at Emma. "Wiped out completely. She was quite powerful too, so that's no small feat."

There was silence for a moment, and then Edgar spoke, his voice full of bitterness. "Good. After she gets out, she can go into the In-Between and keep company with the Witch of a Thousand Faces, because I never want to see her again." He paused, and then shook his head, eyes fixed on the carpet. "Between her and Georgie, it seems like . . ."

He let his words trail off, but Emma could guess what he was thinking: that everyone who'd had a hand in raising him had ended up betraying him.

Beside him, Eliza reached up and wrapped an arm around him. "You've got us now, Ed."

"Yeah," Maddie said around a mouthful of apple. "You're stuck with us forever, whether you want us or not."

Emma smiled at the look of dismay Edgar gave her, along with his admonishment to "Chew with your mouth *closed*, Mads." She turned her attention back to Lenore as Eliza asked a question.

"What was it that drained her power? It wasn't the blue fire, was it?"

"No," Lenore said slowly, and her expression became very solemn. "The blue fire should have just continued filling her. She would have exploded and taken all of with us, but she didn't . . ."

Slowly, they began to catch on, and soon her friends were all staring at her. Emma felt her face begin to glow, and she admitted, "I drained the magic out of her heart. All of it." She hesitated, and Lenore nodded. "I'm sorry if that was wrong."

"No, Emma, it's a good thing you did," Lenore said. "I think we'd all be in a lot of trouble if you hadn't. But Emma, that's a lot of power for one person—the power to take away power. I hope you'll understand when I ask you to never do that again, unless you absolutely have to. A situation like the one you were in should be the only time."

Emma nodded slowly. "I understand."

She did. There was something unnerving about the way the queen had reacted when Emma had drained the last of the power out of her. She'd been in shock at first, and then there was all the screaming about how something was gone. It made Emma's stomach turn just to think about it. The magic was a part of you. To have someone drain that away . . .

No, it wasn't something to be taken lightly.

All the same, she hesitated, and Lenore seemed to guess that another question was coming, because she paused by the bed and looked at Emma, brows raised. "When you told her that you'd made a mistake . . . I mean, when I saw the vision at the library, the history lesson . . ." She stopped, afraid that Lenore would shut down again, or worse, that the haunted look would come back into her eyes.

But Lenore just smiled gently. "We all have mistakes we have to make up for, which is why I was hoping my sister might be reasoned with, that she might take a second chance if I offered one." She sighed. "My mistake was being too young and idealistic, believing I was on the right side of history when I was, in fact, decidedly not."

"But you turned on the rebel witches." Emma remembered what she'd heard in the lecture note visions, what Alexandria had said about Lenore betraying the witches. "You betrayed them to save your family." When Lenore nodded, Emma pressed on. "And then . . . they still did *that* to you. They almost killed you."

She tried not to think about Lenore lying helpless on the mattress, surrounded by toxic thistle. It made her angry all over again, that her mother could have walked away from something like that.

"They never did forgive me." Lenore smoothed a hand over the bedspread, over the bumps in the patchwork quilt, lashes flickering as she looked down. "But to be honest, I'm not sure I fault them for that. I was young and foolish, and the witches I fell in with weren't calling themselves rebels anymore. They spoke of banding together with the non-magical, of becoming one instead of making them our enemy. I convinced myself they were different, but their rhetoric was much the same, and it became more radical the deeper you were drawn in." She pressed her lips together hard, and then looked back up, gaze shifting from Emma's face to Edgar's. "We had grown up learning that everything about our magic was evil, and I was desperate to find a way not to hate myself. For the next six years we were in hiding, living in one village and then the next. At one point, I got a job at the palace, in disguise. When my sisters learned that, they kicked me out, which only served to fan the flames of my discontent."

Lenore gave a rueful laugh. "It was easy to fall in with the wrong sort of witches then. They were everywhere. I confess that I ended up getting in deep with them, deep enough to learn the secret of thistle. But when I learned that 'becoming one' with the non-magical would be achieved by any means, violence included, I got out. I told my sisters, hoping for forgiveness. But by then it was too late. To Isolde and Alexandria, I was the enemy."

It was a lot to take in, but Emma thought she understood. She knew all about being afraid of your magic. Or really, of yourself.

Edgar's eyes were distant, as if he'd been deep in thought this whole time. "My mother said she would never be a witch. That all witches are filthy and evil, but when her power was gone . . ."

Emma flinched, remembering the screaming, the threats. Her voice dropped to a whisper. "I thought she'd be happy."

Edgar nodded.

Lenore's face was grave. "It's strange, isn't it? You can be so opposed to something that you spend your entire life fighting it, only to realize it truly is a piece of you. My sister learned that only after losing it, when it was too late." She smiled at them. "But not all of us must learn that way, thankfully."

There was a moment of silence in which Emma looked over at her cousin. Edgar bit his lip, gaze drifting to the window, where a single glossy raven perched. His expression was a strange mix of anticipation and dread; Emma knew exactly how he felt.

Her power was something she was only just learning to accept. The thought of accepting it completely, of embracing it completely, was intimidating. But it was also exciting, because who knew what else she was capable of? What they were all capable of.

She leaned over, bumping her shoulder into his. When he looked up, startled, she grinned at him. It was slightly strained maybe, barely a half-smile, but he seemed to understand the spirit of it, because he smiled back.

They might have a lot to unravel together—learning their magic, unlearning the ever-present fear, adjusting to this newfound knowledge—but at least they would be doing it together.

Lenore plucked one of the dinner rolls from the basket. "I'll leave you lot to it." Her smile stretched wider. "And Maddie, if you get bored while you're laid up, there's a particularly wonderful spell for beginners on invisibility, on page thirty-three. When I was your age, I managed to vanish my left foot entirely. It was very amusing."

Maddie looked delighted at this, and she was already paging through one of the books as Lenore swept out of the room.

On the armchair, Edgar and Eliza had begun arguing almost the moment Lenore had gone, and were now going back and forth about who had eaten more candied almonds. Eliza was poking Edgar in the armpit to emphasize her points, much to his dismay.

Emma leaned back, watching her friends, and let herself relax for the first time in what felt like forever.

Out the window, she could see the faint firefly flicker of lanterns on the rooftops, and the silver-blue glitter of Find-Me-Heres floating above the peaks and chimneys of the shops and houses. A half-moon was hanging just over the red bricks of the walls, illuminating Witch City in a display of shadows and silver as witches skimmed over the cobblestone streets.

Emma could picture herself here over the summer, she and her friends roaming the city in search of carts of baked goods. Dreamy mornings spent on the porch of Charlie's Chocolaterie, cups of hot cocoa steaming in front of them; nights spent searching the midnight market for sparkling crystals, and colorful ribbons and chains. Learning to fly—properly this time—chasing one another through the air over the bustling streets.

Somewhere far out in the distance, through the velvet stretch of night, through the darkness punctuated by twinkling blue light, Emma could make out a familiar sound. It was deeper and slower now. A gentle, steady noise she found strangely soothing with its familiar rhythm. The pulse of the city's core.

It wasn't just *Noise* anymore, she realized, and it didn't scare her. It sounded . . . right.

It sounded like home.

Acknowledgments

Seven Years. That's how long it's taken to get Emmaline Black and her friends from my head, to the page, to the shelves. No doubt to many writers, this is a reasonable length of time. Time in which they craft beautiful literary work, full of meaning, and long passages of gorgeous prose that will leave a lasting impression on the world and go down in history. For me, it just meant the story was being stubborn.

It's been a long journey, and there are so many people over the past seven years who have helped with previous versions of this manuscript, that I have no doubt forgotten some of you. For that I apologize. Thank you, whoever you are, for being a part of this process, which has helped me grow so much as a writer. I'm sorry I cannot mention you all by name, partly because it would take up several pages, but mostly because I have the memory of a goldfish.

Now on to everyone that helped with this version. The final rebirth. The book that lived.

A big thank you to Silvia Molteni, my amazing agent. Not only for doggedly championing my work, but for always providing valuable creative notes along the way.

And to Lynne and Peter, my PRH superheroes. Thank you for believing in this book, even when I sometimes didn't. Thank you for tirelessly working with me to make this a better story.

Also, to my writer friends IRL, Rebecca, Tiffany, Kayla, and Whitney, for listening when I needed a good writing-related rant. And to Kayla for letting me come over and drink tea and panic about deadlines.

And last but not least, a huge thanks to the Word Nerds. This book is dedicated to you because it's been evolving and changing for the exact same length of time our vlog channel has been growing, and you guys have been with me through every step of the process. So thank you to all the Word Nerds, both past and present: Kellie, Meghan, Emma, Erica, Calyn, Rachel, Desiraye, Helen, and Kyra.

And thank you to my writer's group, also made up of Word Nerds (of course). You've helped me brainstorm so many plot problems and talked me through so many creative dilemmas that I can no longer count them.

Also, to Kellie, because *Escape to Witch City* would not be here in its final form without you. I still count that brainstorming session in the lobby of a Toronto hotel while it poured with rain outside as one of my favorite moments in the creative journey thus far. Thank you for rekindling my excitement in the story. It felt like we re-injected the magic that day.